FULL P[...]

Charles Spencer was born in 19[...] [edu]cated at Charterhouse and Balliol. After spells on the *Evening Standard*, *The Stage* and the *London Daily News*, he became theatre critic of the *Daily Telegraph* in 1991. *I Nearly Died*, his first novel featuring Will Benson, is also published by Gollancz.

Praise for *Full Personal Service*

'Charles Spencer's second novel is a success . . . he crams in some delightfully nasty stuff'
Gerald Kaufman, *Daily Telegraph*

'Will's distasteful job and unappealing colleagues give Charles Spencer plenty of scope for expressing disapproval, without restricting his talent for vivid description of filth of various kinds. *Full Personal Service* has some funny moments and some horrible ones. The mystery is well handled; the clues, fairly and neatly disguised'
Natasha Cooper, *Times Literary Supplement*

'A very pleasing mixture of the sexy, comic and suspenseful' *The Stage*

Also by Charles Spencer in paperback

I NEARLY DIED

CHARLES SPENCER

FULL PERSONAL SERVICE

VISTA

First published in Great Britain 1996
by Victor Gollancz

This Vista edition published 1997
Vista is an imprint of the Cassell Group
Wellington House, 125 Strand, London WC2R 0BB

A catalogue record for this book is
available from the British Library.

ISBN 0 575 60200 7

Printed and bound in Great Britain by
Caledonian International Book Manufacturing Ltd,
Glasgow

97 98 99   10 9 8 7 6 5 4 3 2 1

For Nicki and Edward,
Jerry and Syd

Monday 17 July 1995

Then we must rate the cost of the erection.
Henry IV Pt2

Lydia was such a tease. She was sitting on the sofa in her denim shorts and lacy black bra looking a picture of virginal innocence. Then she undid the bra, and fondled her breasts before tugging at the zip of the shorts to reveal a tuft of blonde pubic hair. I stared intently, concentrating, the sweat forming in oily beads on my forehead. Lydia herself looked wonderfully cool. She took off her shorts, but retained her white stiletto shoes and the black stockings. Her right hand moved down as she began to explore herself, and her back arched. Nothing was stirring down below. I felt as sexy as a bowl of porridge.

I tried Laura next, who was lying on a rumpled bed, and then Stacy, who was disporting herself by the side of a swimming pool. Nella was dressed as a cowgirl, Julianne was sponging herself in a bubble bath. I put down the magazines with despair. Perhaps a cigarette would help.

Needless to say, smoking was banned at the test-tube baby clinic, but I'd discovered on a previous visit that the window opened. I rolled an Old Disgusting with hands that still trembled from the previous night's assault on the bottle of Scotch, and leant out as far as was possible without falling on to the pavement two floors below. I lit up, and the first drag was like a rusty metal file being scraped across the back of my raw throat. I looked at my watch. It was 10 a.m. and I'd been trying to ejaculate for the past forty-five minutes. The traffic growled below me and there was a stench of diesel in the oppressively hot and humid air. I fought off a rising tide of nausea, flicked my half-smoked roll-up out on to the street, and shut the window.

The chaps' room at the embryo factory was got up to look like a four-star hotel – though oddly for a room devoted entirely to masturbation, it was devoid of both a bed and a lock on the door. There were expensive table lamps on the occasional tables, an oriental rug on the floor, blandly inoffensive modern art prints on the walls. And, of course, a little plastic pot and a neat pile of soft-porn magazines. The only trouble being that soft-porn magazines had ceased to be much of a turn-on since I started working on them myself.

They were obviously going to be completely useless on that morning of queasy, hung-over desperation, so I closed my eyes and forced myself to have sexual fantasies. Amazingly, an alarmingly sadistic saga involving my ex-girl-friend Cathy seemed to be doing the trick. I pumped grimly on, hating myself. And then someone knocked on the door.

'Hold on a minute,' I yelled, but the knock was repeated, louder this time, and I lost both the rhythm and the disturbingly effective reverie. I pulled up my pants and trousers and strode furiously to the door, flinging it open with a snarl on my face.

It was, embarrassingly, the most sympathetic of the clinic's nurses, who had always been especially kind to my wife Kim. The contrast between her fresh, wholesome face and my own vile fantasy brought a flush to my cheeks.

'I'm so sorry to disturb you,' she said, blushing herself, 'but Mrs Benson has already had her anaesthetic and Dr Lefevre is about to remove the eggs. Then we suddenly realized we hadn't yet had your sperm. Is there a problem at all?'

'Yes, there is a bit. I was just . . .' She peered at me with an expression of concern. 'I suppose the eggs can be kept for a while?' I asked.

'Oh yes, for a couple of hours. And we can always freeze them, and use them again next time if, um, you know, there's a real problem today.'

'Right,' I said with a grimace of a smile. 'I'd better get back to work, then.'

'Fine. I really am sorry to hassle you like this. Just bring your jar to the desk as soon as you can.'

She withdrew. I closed the door and slumped on the couch. The idea of coming now seemed about as likely as winning the jackpot on the National Lottery. Perhaps it would be best to call it quits. Kim's collected eggs could be frozen and used next month. But I knew in my heart of hearts that this was a terrible option. It was an acknowledged fact that frozen eggs were less likely to develop into fully viable embryos than fresh ones, and the idea of Kim waking from her deep slumber and discovering that her whisky-wrecked husband had been unable to fulfil his side of the bargain was too humiliating to contemplate. I decided to go for a walk. With any luck there might be a shop nearby offering stronger fare than the clinic. I opened the door gingerly and looked out. I didn't want any of the staff to see me leave the building and conclude that I'd done a runner – they'd probably freeze Kim's eggs immediately. The coast was clear. I legged it down the corridor, took the stairs two at a time, hurled myself into the clinic's revolving door, and shot out on to the streets of Victoria. I hadn't gone twenty yards before I saw the phone box. The interior was covered with lurid cards advertising the services of local prostitutes. A sordid eyesore, some might say, but at that moment it seemed like a glorious beacon of hope.

There was an amazing variety to choose from, and just reading the cards offered an anticipatory thrill. *Busty Indian: Hot as a Vindaloo* promised one. *18-year-old stunner from Oz* screamed another in retina-bruising Day-glo pink.

Luscious and Juicy, Fresh and Fruity announced a third. The tastes of masochists and those in need of a dominatrix seemed to be especially well catered for. *Strict disciplinarian requires grovelling maid* read one. *On your knees, dog, and lick my boots* commanded another. TV, rubber and leather fetishists could all look forward to a good time. So could devotees of watersports, and those who liked their girls with A levels.

I tried the busty Indian first, but the phone rang for ages without a reply. So too did the number of the stunner from Oz. *Naughty Schoolgirl for Spanking Fun* sounded rather jolly, and looked it too, with a cartoon of a St Trinian's type exhibiting a tingling bum, but unfortunately she was out too – at school, perhaps. Doreen *You've tried the rest, now savour the best* wasn't answering the phone either. At ten-thirty in the morning this wasn't altogether surprising.

I was on the point of taking a break, and killing time with a cup of coffee on Victoria station, when suddenly, alarmingly, the phone was answered.

'Can I help you?' said a surprisingly cultured voice.

'Um . . . yes, well, er . . . um.' I'd been failing to get through to anyone for so long that I'd forgotten which card I was dialling. No, there it was. *Mature (32) Buxom Brunette (44DD) offers slow unhurried massage in her cosy Pimlico flat.* But having discovered all this arousing information, I wasn't at all sure what to say. There was a bit more umming and aahing at my end before I stammered out: 'Is that the mature buxom brunette?'

'Well, yes and no,' replied the voice at the other end. 'Jenny's usually here, but she's off sick at the moment. We've got another girl on. The thing is, are you a big tits man? Are big tits absolutely essential?'

'Um, I'm certainly not averse to big tits,' I said, and muttered a silent prayer that Kim might forgive my intended trespasses. 'But I can cope without them. The main thing is I need someone who'll be kind and under-

10

standing. I've got a bit of a problem. I'm also in a bit of a hurry.'

'Well, Sophie's a lovely girl, but she's not into anything kinky. Not her scene at all. There's lots of other places for kinks.'

'No, I don't want anything kinky,' I said, though I must confess I was beginning to wonder. It would have been rather fun to have been spanked by a naughty schoolgirl. Stop it, I told myself firmly. This isn't supposed to be fun.

A voice at the other end of the phone cut into my reflections.

'So, shall I tell you where to find us, then?'

'Yes, yes of course. And there won't be too long a wait, will there?' Another thought struck me. Had I got any money? I checked my wallet. Fifty quid and some change in my pocket. I hadn't a clue what the going – I suppose that should be the coming – rates were. 'And, er, how much? I asked gauchely.

'We start at thirty-five pounds,' said the voice, with a sudden hint of ice. Perhaps it was a terrible solecism to start talking about money with a prostitute. Still fifty quid ought to cover me. I wasn't going to go all the way. Just into a little plastic pot. 'And we are in the Belgrave Road, about ten minutes walk from Victoria.' I jotted down the address on the back of the card which I'd removed from the kiosk wall. 'And what do we call you when you arrive?' The voice at the other end of the phone was beginning to sound more regal than ever, eerily like Princess Margaret asking the names of the dancers at the *Royal Variety Show*.

I toyed with the idea of giving a false name. But since this was a business trip rather than a joyride I gave my real one. Somehow this small act of honesty took some of the guilt out of the proceedings. 'Will,' I said, 'Will Benson.'

'Right. Thank you, Mr Benson. Or shall I call you Will? We look forward to seeing you soon.' I half expected her to ask, in true Royal mode, whether I'd had a long journey and visited prostitutes often.

I emerged from the phone box and rolled another fag. There was a real excitement to all this, like waiting to go on a terrifying but exhilarating roller-coaster.

I walked down Belgrave Road, past the Apollo Victoria, the bus station, and a distinctly promising-looking pub with tables outside, flower-filled hanging baskets and a blackboard announcing an impressive list of real ales including my particular favourite, Marston's Pedigree. If I was quick there might be time for a reviving, normality-inducing pint before going back to the hospital.

By the time I'd reached the address, not far short of Pimlico Tube station, I was in a muck sweat. The hangover had returned with a head-banging vengeance and once again the idea of producing a sperm sample seemed almost laughably fantastic. I made my way gingerly down the flight of steps to the basement and rang the bell. The door was answered by one of the ugliest women I'd ever seen. She wore a puce tracksuit which, baggy though it was, couldn't disguise a bulk that made the Michelin man seem svelte. Her complexion was yellowish and deeply pored and when she smiled she revealed a David Mellorish gap between her front teeth.

Please God, please God, don't let this be Sophie, I prayed to myself, and I was seriously contemplating a doorstep getaway when she spoke. 'Will Benson, I presume? I'm afraid Sophie is seeing someone else for a few more minutes but please do come in for a cup of coffee while you wait.' The maid, then, not the tart, thank Christ.

The word 'cosy' hardly did justice to the tiny basement flat. The front room was filled with a red velvet three-piece suite; one of the armchairs was occupied by a small army of teddy bears of varying sizes, colour and furriness. Horse brasses and garish reproductions of great masterpieces in gilt frames were dotted all over the curry-house wallpaper, and the mantelpiece was covered with kitsch glass ornaments of our feathered friends. Beneath, a gas fire with fake logs burnt brightly and insufferably hotly on this sweltering July day. The thick, ruby-coloured curtains were closed and the room was illuminated by half a dozen pink-shaded table lamps. The place was a nightmarish mix of womb and nursery but it clearly called for comment of some kind.

'Gosh, what a lovely room,' I said. 'Really . . . quaint.'

'Yes, we like it,' said the fat slag, with one of her horrible smiles. 'Do take the weight off your feet while I make the coffee. My name's Henrietta, by the way,' she added.

She went next door, and I looked at my watch. Well over an hour till the noon deadline.

'Is Sophie going to be long?' I asked through the service hatch.

'Her client does occasionally take his time about it, but he should be drawing to a conclusion about now. How did you hear about us incidentally?'

'One of those cards in a phone box at Victoria,' I said.

'I'm so glad you chose us,' said Henrietta. 'We like to give the impression that we are a little more refined, a little friendlier than the average establishment.'

A door on the far side of the room opened, and a woman in a white full-length towelling dressing gown came in.

'This is Mr Will Benson,' said Henrietta, sticking her head through the hatch. 'Mr Benson, may I introduce Sophie.' I wondered if I ought to go over and shake her hand but that, surely, was preposterous.

'Right, nice to meet yer, Will.' Just a touch of sarf London and very nice she looked too. Thirtyish, petite, with blonde hair in a pageboy cut, and a mischievous smile.

'I've gotta bit of a problem, Will. The only way out's through this room and my punter's a bit shy about meeting anyone else. Would you mind sitting in the bathroom for a couple of minutes? You can take your coffee in there and it looks as if you could do with a bit of a sponge-down anyway. I'll come and get you when he's gone. Sorry it's so flaming hot. Poor old Henrietta's got bad rheumatism and dodgy circulation and she has to keep warm.'

The bathroom was plain and functional, white tiles, clean towels, with a new-looking bath, bidet, basin and loo. I gratefully slapped cold water on my face, then made quick and refreshing use of the bidet. I could hear muffled voices from the bedroom, and curiosity got the better of me. Who was Sophie's punter? Was his reluctance to meet other punters a sign that he was recognizable, even famous? I crouched down and put my eye to a fairly capacious keyhole and waited.

Sophie came out, holding the man by the hand. He was on the far side of her, and taller than she was. I caught a quick glimpse of what looked suspiciously like loon pants, circa 1969, a leather cowboy hat and, more incredibly still in this heat, a shaggy afghan coat. He had his head bent down as he whispered into Sophie's ear and I caught a glimpse of a pale pudgy face and mirrored sunglasses. Within a second they were out of my range of vision, and I went and sat demurely on the edge of the bath, waiting to be summoned.

Sophie came in a few minutes later, still in her dressing gown. 'You look a bit cooler,' she said. 'If you want to go into the bedroom and take your clothes off I'll just have a quick shower and then come and see to you. Henrietta said there was a bit of a problem. Anything serious?'

'No, nothing serious,' I said with a grin. I realized I had the serious hots for Sophie. I picked up the Tesco carrier bag that held my plastic jar in its brown envelope, the *Telegraph* and my tobacco tin, and went into the brightly lit bedroom. It contained little more than a vast double bed, a couple of chests of drawers, a fridge and a TV mounted on a bracket on the wall. With a couple of fans blowing, it was mercifully cooler than the claustrophobic sitting room, and there was a sexy whiff of musk-oil in the air. I took off my clothes, folded them neatly on a chair and as I lay down on the bed the television flickered into life of its own accord.

It showed a man with an embarrassing Afro hair-cut and a Zapata moustache preparing to enter a woman who was moaning expectantly. The words 'hung', 'like' and 'horse' came to mind. It was turning into a vintage day for feeling inadequate.

At this moment, Sophie came in, wearing a black lace teddy, black suspenders and stockings and a pair of high-heeled shoes.

'Ah, Mr King-size again,' she grinned. 'I'm sure Henrietta only puts him on to wind up the punters. I've probably seen more cock than you've had hot dinners, and I've never seen one like that.' I began to cheer up. Sophie's unembarrassed frankness inspired real affection.

She came and knelt beside me on the bed, and told me to turn on to my stomach. Then she handed me what looked like a restaurant menu pretentiously bound in heavily embossed leather.

'I'll just start the basic massage and you can have a few minutes to choose what extras you'd like,' she said in a voice that had suddenly acquired a plausibly sexy breathiness. The husky voice was clearly a fake, but it was a good enough fake.

As she poured baby oil on my back, I opened the leather folder. *Sophie, Jenny and Henrietta bid you a warm welcome to their deluxe love-nest* it began in fancy italic script. Then, in larger bolder letters, came the à la carte menu.

Straight massage	*£35*
Topless massage	*£40*
Hand relief	*£45*
Breast or oral relief	*£50*
Reverse massage	*£60*
Full personal service	*£75*

Blimey, I thought. I'd only just get the job done for my fifty quid. Assuming, that was, that the hand relief wasn't on top of the straight massage fee. Sophie broke in on my panicky mental arithmetic.

'I get the idea you've never been to a place like this before,' she said.

'No, this is my first time. And I've got – '

'There's no hurry, sweetheart. Let me just explain the services and then you can tell me what's bothering you. Relax, enjoy it. You're paying for it, after all.'

'Right,' I said, more or less reassured.

'OK then,' she said, as her fingers worked the oil into my lower back. 'It's a rising scale. You don't pay the extra price for each thing you want. Say for instance you fancied a blow job and a reverse massage. The cost would be sixty pounds. And if you fancied the full personal service, you can have any of the other extras you like thrown in for free. The only other factor is there's a time limit of forty minutes. But if you want a full hour it's just another twenty quid if you choose the full personal service.'

She made all this sound like the kind of special offer you might pick up at Tesco's.

'There are a few technical terms – ' I began.

'Right, well you're having the straight massage now. If you want me to take my top off so you can have a feel of me tits, it's forty quid. Not that they're much to write home about.'

'I think they're very nice,' I said.

'Well, ain't you the gallant,' she replied. 'Anyway, to carry on. Hand relief speaks for itself. A quick Arthur Rank to you and me. Breast relief is really Jenny's speciality. I can just about manage it if you're desperate.'

'What about the reverse massage?' I asked.

'Well, that means we can muck about together on the bed in almost any way you like short of full sex.'

'Which presumably comes under the heading of full personal service?'

'Got it in one, darling,' she said. 'I insist on a condom, of course.'

'Of course.'

Sophie was doing delicious things with her fingers and the agonies at the clinic seemed to have taken place on a different planet.

'Right,' she said after several minutes, 'turn over and we'll talk about what's troubling you.'

I turned over as requested.

'Well, your problem isn't the usual one to judge by the state of that,' she said with a grin. 'What's causing all the grief?'

'I was having the usual problem a bit earlier. My wife and I are having great difficulty in conceiving – '

'Don't tell me. They want a sperm sample for testing and you couldn't come up with it at home?'

'It's even more desperate than that. We're having IVF treatment at the clinic up the road and my wife's under the anaesthetic and having her eggs removed as we speak.'

'Blimey. Pressure like that would put anyone off their stride. So let's get the urgent business over with first. Where's your little specimen jar?'

I leant across the bed and pulled it from my carrier bag.

'We'd better be a bit careful about this,' said Sophie. 'Can't have you shooting off and missing the pot. I think the safest thing would be if you stand up and I kneel in front of you. Just get the jar ready in time, OK?'

More than OK by me. She took her top off before she knelt down and went to work. Sophie was not a tart to short-change a customer, and though her breasts were small they seemed to me, flooded with relief and gratitude, to be quite perfect. With a few practised flicks of her wrist I got the entire contents safely into the jar. Jesus, what a relief.

I'd been in the room with Sophie for less than fifteen minutes and I now had all the time in the world to saunter back to the hospital and hand over my sample before Kim came round from the anaesthetic. I triumphantly screwed

17

the cap on the jar and put it inside the brown envelope. Sophie rewarded me with an ironic round of applause.

'I hope you're not in too much of a hurry,' she said, going over to the fridge and taking out a half-bottle of champagne. She eased off the cork, poured two flutes and passed one over to me.

'No, I've got half an hour,' I said.

'Cheers, then,' she said, clinking my glass. 'Do you want to talk? A lot of my customers want to talk.'

I found that I did, too. So I told her all about how Kim and I had met on the trade paper *Theatre World*, and how Kim had announced, to my surprise but also to my intense pleasure, that she'd like to have a child soon after we had started going out together.

'Nothing happened,' I told Sophie, 'and after a year we went to a doctor, and then all the tests began, and making love according to what the temperature charts said, then this test-tube baby business. This is our sixth attempt.'

'It's a bleeding shame,' Sophie said. That seemed to sum it up, really. To my embarrassment my eyes welled with tears, and Sophie silently handed me a tissue.

'Thanks.' I got myself under control.

'Have they discovered what the problem is?' she asked.

'They thought it was me at first. Low sperm count. Naturally they told me to cut right back on the booze and fags, and lose weight. And amazingly I managed it. Down to twenty-one units a week, just the occasional miserly roll-up rather than forty Camel a day, endless hours of boring swimming. But I do have occasional lapses with the booze. In fact I had one last night. Though the sperm count is just about respectable now. But then Kim finally got her appointment for a laparoscopy on the NHS and they discovered her tubes were damaged. IVF treatment was reckoned to be the only option. What about you? Do you have children?'

Sophie's sympathetic face became mask-like.

'I don't talk about me,' she said. 'I give away enough of myself in this job as it is.'

'Of course, sorry,' I said.

'You probably think this is a terrible way of life, don't you, deep down?'

'Not at all,' I replied, though I couldn't help wondering how an obviously intelligent and good-hearted woman could bring herself to have sex with whoever happened to ring the front-door bell.

'It's not nearly as bad as you think. My soul's my own. And it pays well.' I wondered if there was some pimp lurking in the background, creaming off a hefty cut of his own, but it seemed impertinent to enquire.

'But don't you find you're having to, er, attend to some really horrible men?' I asked. 'I mean for all you knew I might have been a psychopath.'

'You get an instinct for these things. If Henrietta doesn't like the look of someone, she just turns 'em away at the door. Says I've been called away. And if I can't stand the sight of 'em, I toss 'em off double quick and say I'm expecting a visit from the Vice Squad any moment. You should see them scuttle about then. They're on their way out before they've zipped their trousers up.'

A small cold hand started squeezing my guts.

'God, they don't still have police raids, do they? I thought this kind of set-up was more or less legal now.'

Sophie giggled at my all too evident panic.

'If we don't cause any trouble we don't get any trouble from them,' she said. 'Though the odd cop has been well known to pull rank for a free wank. But it's quite a settled business, this, and we mostly get our regulars.' She might have been a landlady complacently describing life at a country pub where the police turned a blind eye to the occasional lock-in. There was something about Sophie that inspired truth-telling, something about the whole anonymous yet intimate encounter that brought the confessional to mind.

'I'm afraid I looked through the keyhole at your last client. He looked like some kind of refugee from the flower power era.'

She grinned. 'Spot on.'

'Who is he?' I asked, fascinated.

'Would you like it if I told the next punter who you were?'

'I wouldn't mind. My name wouldn't mean anything to anyone else.'

'But what if you were famous, or had once been famous?'

'No, I wouldn't like that. There'd always be a risk of the tabloids getting hold of it.' I thought back to the comedian Joe Johnson, and the way the *News of the Screws* had tried to wreck his life and career after lurid revelations about rent boys.

'Exactly,' said Sophie. 'Girls on the game like me are a bit like priests, or should be,' she said, picking up on my own earlier but unspoken thought. 'The secrets of the massage parlour should be sacred. But what I will say about the guy you saw is that he's very kind and very sad. But then most people that come here are sad fucks in one way or another. It gets bleeding tiring feeling sorry for them.'

I grinned, ruefully. 'Yeah, I'm sorry about the tears.'

'You're not a sad fuck. Or at least not a permanently sad fuck, just so long as your Kim gets preggers.' I was touched that Sophie had remembered Kim's name.

'Do you fancy a quick FPS?' asked Sophie.

'FPS?'

'You remember – full personal service.'

Actually, I couldn't think of anything nicer. After all the sexual angst with Kim, an uncomplicated, reassuring tumble with Sophie was just what my battered libido needed. What Erica Jong once called the zipless fuck. Then I remembered my finances.

'I'm afraid I'm spent up.'

'You never 'eard of a tart with an 'art?' said Sophie,

suddenly laying on the cockney with a Barbara Windsor-sized trowel. 'I don't want you thinking I'm soft, and Henrietta would be furious if she knew I'd given you a freebie, so I'll take the thirty-five basic for the straight massage, and if you give Henrietta a tenner tip, you'll earn me a few Brownie points too. But anything else you fancy is on the house. You need a bit of a cheer-up.'

I thought of Kim, doubtless back in the ward by now and sleeping peacefully under the anaesthetic. A quick FPS was strictly surplus to requirements. On the other hand . . .

She moved thrillingly beneath me. Surely prostitutes never came, I thought. But the intensity of her response as she pulled me deep inside her seemed absolutely genuine. I felt a great wave of gratitude for Sophie as I came myself. In recent months I'd felt like little more than a sperm machine, a defective, unreliable sperm machine. The idea that I might have sexually gratified Sophie was an immense boost for the battered ego. And even if she had been putting it all on, it was an act of real charity.

'Thank you for that,' I said.

'The pleasure was all mine,' said Sophie as she neatly plucked off the condom, wrapped it in a Kleenex, and threw it in the bin. 'But it'll still cost you thirty-five quid.'

She was brilliant at hitting the right note, at skilfully lightening the mood just as I was about to get maudlin.

I went over to my jeans, counted out £35, and handed the notes over. Sophie, already back in her towelling dressing gown, put the money in her pocket and smiled conspiratorially.

'Perhaps you ought to have a shower before going back to that clinic. You'll be ponging of musk-oil otherwise and your Kim might get suspicious. Take your clothes into the bathroom with you, and don't forget your little jar whatever you do.'

I gathered up my things, had my shower and got dressed. I was just putting on my hideously creased, sweat-soaked linen jacket when the doorbell rang. Sophie came in and told me to keep quiet until she'd got the next punter into the bedroom and gave me the all clear.

'It can spoil it for 'em if they know someone has been here just before,' she said with her usual unsqueamish honesty. It slightly spoilt it for me too, as I sat on the edge of the bath, and heard the footsteps going down the passage. I told myself not to be silly; I'd only met Sophie half an hour earlier. Was I expecting fidelity from a call girl? Was I turning soft in the head?

Sophie came in, gave a thumbs-up sign, hesitated for a moment and gave me a quick kiss on the cheek, a greater intimacy, I realized, than any she had previously allowed me.

'I'd like to know how it all works out. If you feel like telling me, that is,' she whispered, and then she was gone. I waited until she was safely in the bedroom, and walked down the corridor into the parlour (it was the only word that captured its suffocating tweeness) and received a radiant, gap-toothed smile from Henrietta.

'All well, I trust? And I hope we can look forward to seeing you in our little establishment again soon, sir?' she said. Sophie was right, Henrietta liked winding up the punters, and I liked her the better for it.

'First class,' I said, entering into the spirit of the game with a strangulated upper-class accent, and handing her a tenner. 'Absolutely A1 if I may say so, though the video might prove a little too gamey for some tastes.'

'I'll bear it in mind, sir,' she said, ramming a Senior Service into a cigarette holder and taking a deep drag. 'You have our number, I think?'

I took the card out of my pocket and waved it at her, and she opened the door and let me out. Going up the steps I became nervous that everyone in the street would know I'd just been to a massage parlour, but, in a sudden burst of high spirits, I realized I didn't give a toss if they did. My headache had gone, the mental clouds seemed to

22

have lifted and even the burning, blinding sun was suddenly all right by me.

It was still short of eleven-thirty. I decided to have a quick drink at the flower-bedecked pub. As I ordered my pint of Pedigree, I had an irrational flash of conviction that this time the treatment would work, and I began to smile like an idiot.

'Won the pools, mate?' said the barman.

'I might have done just that,' I replied.

I'd warned them at the office that I might be a bit late, but I was now going to be very late so I rang Brian Waynefleet, art director and production manager at my new job, to tell him I'd be on my way soon.

'Trouble getting it up this morning? All the little spermy-wermies jump out of their jar, did they?' he leered. Over a few pints (I tended to get through most of my weekly supply of units in one session with Brian), and much to my subsequent regret, I'd foolishly told him about the infertility treatment soon after joining the firm.

'One way and another I've had quite a morning of it,' I said. I was not, I was emphatically not, going to tell him about my visit to Sophie's. It would be like giving a great juicy bone to a dog and he'd gnaw at it continuously and never let me forget it. I wouldn't even put it past him to drop heavy hints to Kim, if they ever met (something I was at great pains to avoid), and with that thought all the erotic and sentimental shine went out of the morning's activities.

Had we stopped at the hand relief, and I'd packed up my jar and gone my way, it would have been fine to tell Kim about Sophie; indeed, knowing Kim's generous nature, she might even have found the story funny. But the full personal service had been different. It had been more than cold, rubber-insulated sex. On my part, at least, it had been accompanied with real emotion, not just gratitude but affection too. And Sophie's goodbye kiss and final words seemed to suggest an involvement, however shallow and short-lived it might prove, on her part too. I had betrayed Kim, and the belated realization of the fact was like a sickening kick in the solar plexus.

'What's the matter with you, mate?' came Brian's insufferably chirpy voice down the phone. 'Got your tongue stuck down someone's throat?'

'No, I'm fine,' I said. 'See you soon.'

'Right. Oh, by the way, Will, what do you get when you put a baby in a Magimix?'

'I don't know, Brian,' I replied – he always tediously insisted that you went through the motions when he was telling one of his jokes. It saved time if you did it at once – 'what do you get when you put a baby in a Magimix?'

'An orgasm,' he yelled triumphantly, and slammed down the phone before I had time to tell him what a loathsome little prat he was. Not that I would have done. He was senior to me, and in between his bouts of obscenity and boozing he had a habit of letting you know the fact. Also, and this was the really worrying thing, I rather liked him.

I finished my pint in double-quick time and walked briskly back to the clinic. I was prepared to bluff it out if necessary, but it would be less bother all round if they thought I'd produced my sperm on the premises. There was no one about, and I crept back into the wanking room undetected. I sucked an extra strong mint to cover the smell of the booze, then opened the door with a flourish and advanced on the reception desk.

'Oh, there you are, Mr Benson. We'd virtually given you up for lost,' said the *Gauleiter* on duty. 'We knocked on the door twenty minutes ago,' she added, a distinct edge of suspicion in her voice, 'but there was no reply and the room turned out to be empty.'

Emboldened by the pre-lunch drinks, which seemed to have got the remains of last night's malt whisky kicking in nicely again too, I told her, rather loudly, that I'd had trouble coming that morning, if it was any business of hers, and that I'd gone for a walk in the hope of finding stronger pornographic fare than that provided by the clinic. I tapped my plastic bag significantly, and triumphantly produced my brown paper envelope with the sperm sample inside.

Then, with a stab of remorse, I remembered Kim and asked how she was.

'You'll be glad to hear that Dr Lefevre collected three eggs from her.'

Wow. Two had been our previous maximum, and that had only been on one occasion. Despite all the pills she took, the injections she suffered, the inhalants she sniffed in the course of every treatment, Kim normally only produced a single egg.

'You didn't tell her I'd gone missing, did you?' I asked anxiously. 'I don't want to cause her any worry.'

'There hasn't been a chance. She's not come round yet,' said the receptionist with a kindly tone that made me regret my previous aggressive swagger. 'She'll have no idea that you had any problem this morning unless you choose to tell her. And I wouldn't if I was you. She needs to keep calm.'

'Thanks,' I said. 'You're absolutely right. Can I go and see her?'

The receptionist nodded. I walked down the corridor and into the small ward. Only two of the six beds were occupied. Kim was sleeping peacefully in one of them, and my new friend, Isaac, a Hasidic Jew, was sitting on a chair besides the other, gazing tenderly at his own sleeping wife. He got up and shook me warmly by the hand.

'Everything OK?' I whispered.

'More than OK. Superb,' he said.

We'd met that morning, waiting in line to pick up our sperm pots at reception.

'My name is Isaac,' he'd said. 'This is my, our, first time. My wife Leah and I have been trying to have a child for the past ten years. It has now come to this,' he explained, with moving simplicity and a complete absence of self-pity. 'What has been greatly worrying me is how I am to produce the sperm,' continued Isaac. 'I cannot call on my wife's assistance in such a place. And I am so nervous I am not sure I can achieve an erection. I could not bring myself to tell the lady at the counter this. Have you any advice to offer me, please?'

The same anxiety had of course been dogging me since I'd woken up, but I had a hunch Isaac wouldn't be as inured to soft porn as I was.

'There are magazines,' I said, 'in the rooms where you are sent to produce your sperm. With pictures of naked women. Lots of them.' I couldn't bring myself to tell him that I worked for such publications myself.

He smiled with delighted incredulity. 'They actually supply these magazines? Often I have seen them in newsagent's and thought they might help Leah and me with our trouble. But I've always bottled out when I actually got into the shop.' He'd thanked me warmly and rushed with almost indecent haste to one of the wanking rooms. He was a lovely man.

'I have been watching my wife all morning,' he said now, fondly. 'And while I was here the staff seemed to be a little worried about your whereabouts. Did things go all right with you, too?'

'Eventually,' I replied.

'And how many times have you been through this terrible business?'

I told him and he nodded sadly.

'Six times. That is hard. But they say there's only ever a twenty per cent chance of success. At best.'

It was my turn to nod sadly.

'Will you continue if it doesn't work this time?' he asked.

'I want to stop but Kim, my wife, is desperate. I think we'll have to keep trying.'

He produced a card from his wallet and asked me if I had one too. He was a jeweller in Hatton Garden and I was glad that my own card gave no clue as to the nature of my business. 'Botticelli Fine Art Publications, Ltd' it announced blandly, with a tasteful little engraving of *The Birth of Venus*.

'You are an expert on art?' he asked.

'I suppose you could put it like that,' I said shiftily.

'If you are successful this time, you will let me know? And if my wife and I are successful, can I ring you? It wouldn't hurt too much if you had failed? My own view is that to learn of anyone's success might be encouraging.'

He was right. We shook hands on it. I reflected that in all my previous visits to the embryo factory, I'd never exchanged more than a tentative nod with any of the other clients. Couples always seemed to be locked inside their own little cocoons of anxiety and febrile hope. There was something admirable about Isaac's openness.

Leah was beginning to stir.

'I feel I must confess,' said Isaac conspiratorially, before looking anxiously at his wife. 'I have stolen one of the magazines. *Hustler*. It was very good. You don't think they'll notice, do you?'

'I'm sure they won't,' I said. I was rather taken with the idea of Isaac reading *Hustler*.

He nodded, and smiled happily and went to join his wife, who was definitely beginning to come to. Kim still seemed to be spark out, cosily tucked up and snoring gently. As I watched her, I realized that I loved her far too much to tell her about Sophie. A typically shabby piece of male equivocation, you might well mutter. We'd both always said there should be no secrets between us, and until now, on my side at least, there were none. But surely one of the signs of real love is to keep your own messy guilt to yourself. Nevertheless, I had a strong urge to confess. I'd undoubtedly feel better if I got my experiences with Sophie off my chest. Kim would almost certainly feel worse, though, and there was no telling how much worse. And at the moment she needed serenity more than anything.

She rolled over on to her back and after a couple of minutes her eyes opened.

'Hi, Kim,' I said. 'Welcome back to the land of the living.'

I picked up her hand and cradled it in mine. 'You won't believe this,' I said, 'but they've got three eggs.'

'Great!' she said, her voice still thick from her chemical slumber. 'And I forgot to say, because we were in such a hurry, but I spotted a black cat just before we came into the clinic.'

'We're home and dry, then.'

'You never know,' she said with a sleepy smile, and then she began to sit up and take notice. 'Why are you still here?' she asked. 'You normally go straight to work after you've handed over the jar. That booze didn't put the kibosh on things, did it?' There was a note of real anxiety in her voice.

'Everything was fine,' I said. 'I just thought I'd hang around this time. But I ought to be getting on now I know everything's OK. How are you feeling?'

'A bit sore and a bit sick, as usual. But *Neighbours* will be on the telly soon. That always cheers me up.'

'And have a chat with Leah in the other bed. I've been talking to her husband Isaac and he's very nice. And you'll get a taxi to take you home when you're allowed to go?'

'Yes of course, Will. Stop worrying. Go to that horrible job of yours and earn some money in case we have to go through all this yet again.'

She looked happier and more relaxed than she'd been for ages, and I thought of her eggs and my sperm, sitting in their specimen jars and waiting to be mixed into life by white-coated technicians, and didn't know whether to laugh or cry. I kissed Kim on her snub nose, sketched a wave at Isaac and Leah, and went off to my horrible job.

28

Wednesday 19 July

Child Roland to the dark tower came,
His word was still, Fie, foh and fum,
I smell the blood of a British man.
King Lear

I sat on the Tube in a state of wonder, marvelling all the way from Victoria to Borough. Two of Kim's three eggs had fertilized successfully, and before returning them to the womb that morning, Dr Lefevre had shown us the tiny embryos, blown up to hundreds of times their real size on a medical epidiascope. They consisted of four cells, each with a dark nucleus at the centre and what looked like a blob of jelly surrounding it. It seemed frankly incredible that each of these alien, amoeba-like creatures held the potential for human life, that those four cells could eventually turn into a new-born baby, a child, a teenager, an adult . . .

'I'm going to call them Bill and Ben,' said Kim, laughing, though I couldn't help noticing there were tears in her eyes. This was as close as she had come to motherhood. Seeing the cells up on the wall made the whole process seem real rather than merely theoretical.

'You mustn't get your hopes up too high. Remember we've placed embryos in your womb on five previous occasions and they haven't survived,' said Dr Lefevre.

'You are pleased, though, aren't you?' asked Kim, with an edge of desperation in her voice.

'Yes,' he replied with a smile. 'They look terrific to me.'

The doctor went off to prepare the embryos, Kim went off to change into her gown prior to having them placed in her womb, and I settled down with a magazine, that Bible of ageing rock fans, Q.

I'd hardly read more than a couple of record reviews when I was told I had to gown up too if I wanted to watch. I felt rather queasy about going into the operating theatre but Kim had pointed out rather sharply that most men came in with their wives for this bit of the treatment. So I put on my green robe, J-Cloth hat and dinky white Wellington boots and went into the theatre. There was no need for anaesthetic when putting the eggs back, only when taking them out, and a wide-awake Kim gave me a comic grimace as I came into the room. I could see why. She was flat out on the table with her legs apart and raised in a kind of kinky stirrup affair. Dr Lefevre was having a quick shufti down below, so I sat at the top end and held her hand.

'Does it hurt, this bit?' I asked.

'Not really. Bit uncomfortable sometimes. He just pushes a thin tube into my uterus, and squirts the embyros up with a bit of culture fluid.'

'Feeling all right up there?' asked Lefevre. Not so much a room with a view in his line of work, but endless views of a womb.

'Fine,' said Kim, and a moment later he announced that the mission was accomplished.

'All we've got to hope now is that they implant satisfactorily and develop properly,' said Dr Lefevre, whom both Kim and I had come to trust increasingly, despite the months of failure. He never buoyed up your hopes with false promises and he was immensely sympathetic when a treatment didn't work.

I changed trains at Stockwell, dreaming about a massively pregnant Kim and a buggy made for two standing in the hall. I normally tried to repress paternal feelings, believing I could be far more help to Kim if I seemed to be relatively unscathed by the emotional traumas of IVF, but occasionally I felt a sharp stab of longing, like a raw wound. When you are trying and failing to have a baby, they seem to be everywhere. Grizzling in shops, smiling cutely on advertising hoardings and, most harrowingly of all, suffering on television screens. In Bosnia, in the famine-lands of Africa, in cases of almost unimaginable cruelty and neglect at home, the whole world sometimes seems to be reduced to the scream of a crying, inconsolable child. Such horrors made our own pain seem like frivolous self-indulgence; there was hardly a shortage of children, indeed the very reverse was true. Yet somehow that knowledge only made our barrenness hurt more.

I almost missed my stop at Borough, and bounded out of the carriage just as the doors were closing. The clock on the church of St George the Martyr, one of the few handsome buildings in a neglected, decaying corner of south London, said it was 10.35 a.m. I was going to be late for work, for the second time that week. And I'd only been there just over a month.

As I walked down Tabard Street, past the public school mission building, the bleak Peabody estate and a tiny dairy run by ancient Welshies who seemed to have survived from the world of Ealing comedies, I realized how much I was missing *Theatre World*. I'd made it to deputy editor by the time I left, but the paper was a notoriously bad payer, and our combined salaries wouldn't sustain a succession of failed IVF treatments. Needless to say, there didn't seem to be a prayer of free treatment on the NHS, or not until Kim was long past the menopause. Somehow, we'd had to find more money. Kim had done a few subbing shifts on the nationals, but she was meant to be keeping calm to give the IVF the best chance of working, and nine hours on the *Sunday Mirror* was hardly conducive to that. I'd flogged a few arts features to some of the quality papers, but the money still wasn't anything like enough – hundreds when thousands were needed.

And then I'd run into the comedian Joe Johnson and his

personal manager Harry Meadows at some ghastly show-biz awards ceremony. Over the past three or four years the comic who had once been notoriously billed as the Big Cunt had transformed himself into a much-loved national institution. His act wasn't nearly as filthy as it used to be, and since he'd gone on the wagon, both his material and his timing had become much sharper. He hosted his own quiz show on ITV, played the blearily lugubrious landlord in a BBC sitcom and had become the best pantomime dame in the business. In short, he'd turned respectable. It was only a matter of time before he went to Buckingham Palace to collect his OBE. I was pleased for him, but I missed the dirty old bugger of old.

Meadows and I had once had a nasty run-in, with me on the receiving end, and the manager had felt he'd owed me ever since. Chatting after the awards (Joe Johnson having been announced as TV Personality of the Year) I'd told Meadows about the infertility treatment.

'Tough on your *Theatre World* wages, I'd guess,' he said, as Joe Johnson was pictured 'sharing a joke' with Michael Portillo and Gillian Taylforth. 'Would you be interested if I pointed you in the direction of more lucrative employment?' As always when Meadows was at his most serious, his eyes were disconcertingly dead.

'Anything legal gratefully considered,' I'd replied. 'Anything illegal considered too, if there's a good chance of not getting caught.'

I feared he'd probably forget all about it, though those dead eyes were a hopeful sign. And sure enough, the following day he'd phoned to say I had an interview with Botticelli Fine Art Publications, that Friday morning, eleven sharp, with the proprietor and managing director, Mr James Wintour.

'But I know bugger all about painting,' I'd protested. 'And I can't believe art magazines will pay much better than *Theatre World*.'

'Fuck the art,' said Meadows sharply. 'They're soft-porn

mags and they pay very well. You're not a prude, are you, Will?'

'What's the job?'

'Wintour didn't say what he had in mind, but turn up in your best suit, look intelligent and don't take the piss, and I'm pretty sure he'll have something for you.'

I wondered what kind of relationship Meadows had with Wintour, but decided it would be best not to ask. Take the money and run was my guiding principle of late.

Botticelli's HQ was a grimy brick warehouse with a few offices on the first floor. The warehouse was the heart of the operation because, as I was to learn during my interview, the bulk of Wintour's profits came from a thriving mail-order business based on the ads at the back of all three publications. The magazines themselves were little more than the shop window for a brisk trade in dodgy erotica dispatched in plain brown paper envelopes and parcels.

On the morning of my interview, I'd negotiated my way through the fork-lift trucks and the stacked-high pallets down below, and gone through a door at the back marked Reception. At the top of a flight of uncarpeted stairs, in a small but surprisingly smart room, an enormously fat woman sat behind a desk. There was no evidence of any of the Botticelli publications on the coffee table, I noticed, but *Time Out*, the *Spectator* and *Literary Review*. I'd announced myself, and she'd sighed and helped herself to a handful of chocolate biscuits from a tin on the desk, before leading the way through a door behind the desk. We walked down a grubby, lino-floored corridor, with a few closed doors, and she knocked at one at the end, opening it without waiting for a reply.

'Will Benson to see you, Mr Wintour,' she said through a mouthful of biscuit, then gave a sudden grin as if to apologize for her initial surliness and waddled off again.

'Thank you, Daphne,' said Mr Wintour, who appeared to be cardigan-man incarnate. He was wearing a particularly shaggy, shapeless number, a perfectly vile mixture of ginger and olive green wool with lots of fancy ribbing which must surely have been knitted by his wife or his mother. Only great loyalty could have made a man sport that revoltingly homely garment in public. He smiled broadly, revealing immaculate teeth, and his eyes twinkled merrily behind horn-rimmed spectacles. As he got up to shake my hand and thump me heartily on the back, I was delighted to discover that he was also wearing tartan carpet slippers.

'Welcome, welcome to Botty Publications,' he beamed, his rich fruity tones indicating that this was a preposterous joke we could both share. 'Draw up a chair and sit ye down.'

His expansive office looked more like the room of an Oxford don with private means than that of the proprietor of a soft-porn outfit. A log fire burned brightly in the grate – gas effect, surely, I thought, but no, the logs were real and the room was delightfully tinged with the smell of burning apple wood. There were some choice items of lovingly polished antique furniture, a venerable grand-father clock ticked soothingly, and one wall was entirely covered with shelves filled with handsome leather-bound volumes.

He went and selected three volumes, and put them down at my side of the desk. 'Perhaps you would care for a quick browse before we get down to our little chat. You've probably never seen them before,' he added with a kindly smile. 'It is a remarkable fact that although glamour magazines sell many hundreds of thousands every month, no one you meet ever seems to have read one.'

I didn't own up to being something of an expert on the subject. Nor did I tell him that rival publications were favoured by the IVF clinic. Mr Wintour made his way to an eighteenth-century side-table which somehow sup-ported a huge and elaborate chrome coffee machine.

'Espresso or cappuccino?' he asked, banging in the coffee with all the fluent skill of an Italian waiter.

'Espresso, please. No sugar.'

'But perhaps just a small slug of this excellent grappa? I find the mixture very reviving at about this time of the morning.' He sounded like a kindly uncle offering sweets. His face was eerily bland and unlined. It was impossible to guess his age; he could have been anything from thirty-five to fifty-five.

'Well, if you're having one. It sounds delicious,' I said, and opened the first leather volume, which turned out to contain the past year's issues of *Crumpet Corner*. The magazine consisted entirely of photographs of models in various stages of undress, accompanied by racy captions, many of them written in breathless, first-person prose. *Hi, I'm Tracey, and I never thought it would be possible to feel as horny as I did when I posed for all you salivating men reading (or should that be ogling??!!) Crumpet Corner. Who'd have guessed that demure little Tracey (I only left my convent school six months ago, fellas!!!) was really such an exhibitionist. My love juices really started flowing, I can tell you, when I allowed a zoom lens to probe all my secret places, and I'm just glad the photographer was gay (he was ever so nice, though) or I don't know what would have happened in my luxurious Mayfair apartment. As it was, I had to finish myself off with my twelve-inch vibrator when he'd gone. Why don't you write to me, fellas, c/o good ol' Botty Publications, and tell me just what you'd like to do with me on the fur rug in front of my roaring fire. I just know you could light my fire!!! Come on, guys, give Trace a treat!*

I opened the second volume, which contained copies of what Mr Wintour told me was their biggest seller, *Luv Bytes*. This one looked as though a bit of effort went into it on the editorial as well as the photographic side. There were naturally lots of pictures of naked girls, and the same cheerily bawdy fragments of autobiography to accompany them. But there were also articles assumed to be of general interest to men. Lots on cars, naturally, and travel, pieces on fashion and even record reviews. And a large chunk towards the back of the magazine was concerned with computers, CD-ROM, and the latest video games, an area of late twentieth-century life that had somehow passed me by. I'd always suspected that the propeller heads who got a kick out of computing would be into sex mags too. All that time spent alone in the bedroom. The pursuit of solitary pleasure. No doubt about it, *Luv Bytes* was a brilliant piece of niche marketing. Play with your computer, then play with yourself.

The other big feature, apart from a smattering of risqué jokes and Donald McGill-like cartoons (in many ways *Luv Bytes* resembled a children's comic for adults), was page after page of erotic short stories and sexy, confessional letters that purportedly came from the readers. Oddly for a magazine aimed at men, most of them appeared to be written by suburban nymphomaniacs, a surprisingly large number of whom seemed to have discovered the delights of lesbianism for the first time. As Mr Wintour brought over my cup of espresso and grappa, I asked him about this apparent paradox.

'Well, we do get some letters from women who enjoy looking at the magazines with their boyfriends and husbands,' he said, with the benign smile of an Anglican vicar explaining the mysteries of the Holy Trinity, 'and some of the men write in too. But for the purposes of variety,' and here his face assumed the expression of a mischievous small boy confessing to scrumping apples, 'we do, ahem, make quite a few of them up. As you might imagine, not many of our readers are exactly D. H. Lawrence when it comes to wielding the pen for the purposes of erotic prose. And men seem to enjoy reading the confessions of liberated women rather than the bragging accounts of their fellow males. Lesbianism and troilism seem to be particularly popular.'

I nodded in what I hoped was a suitably man-of-the-world manner, muttered that I could absolutely see his point, and opened the third volume. At this point, try though I might to keep a poker face, my jaw visibly dropped. *Luvverly Blubberly* was the title, a publication I'd somehow missed in the past. It was entirely devoted to enormously fat women. Great rolls of white flesh bulged out of outsize lingerie. Breasts the size of fully-blown balloons hung pendulously. These were women with a spare tyre on their spare tyre and thighs the size of the trunks of mature oaks. Yet oddly, what might have been a grotesque freak show was surprisingly endearing. Unlike the glammed-up models in the other mags, with their flawless bodies and expressions of simulated desire, these were unmistakably homely types who looked as though they found the whole business of stripping for a prurient lens a huge joke. Many of them were old enough to be grandmothers, one or two indeed proudly announced that they were, and almost all of them had outsize grins on their chubby and often strangely beautiful faces. The effect was at once comic, touching, and I suddenly realized to my intense surprise, arousing.

I turned the pages under Mr Wintour's twinkling gaze, and suddenly let out an involuntary gasp. There was Daphne in all her fleshy glory, disporting herself on a sofa that looked in danger of collapsing under her vast weight.

'Um, isn't this . . .?' I asked hesitantly, showing him the double-page spread. She had a trick of pushing one of her breasts up into her face and sucking her own nipple.

'Yes, dear old Daphne,' said Wintour indulgently. 'She came to us as our receptionist and switchboard operator, and naturally I wouldn't have dreamt of asking her to pose for us. Up before an industrial tribunal for sexual harassment quick as a flash if I had. And one thing you will learn about me, Mr Benson, should you come and work here, is that I always stay rigorously within both the spirit and the letter of the law.' For a moment it was as though a different man was speaking. The fruity *bonhomie* had been replaced with real authority. But within a couple of seconds, Wintour had reverted to his old cosy self.

'Anyway, as I was saying, after a couple of months Daphne came in for a bit of a chinwag and very shyly inquired whether she might pose for one of our photographers. Naturally I said yes, and she has become one of our most successful models. She certainly receives a great deal of fan mail. And though the extra money obviously comes in useful, I think old Daphne really rather enjoys it. Lovely girl, lovely girl.'

Mr Wintour, in a manner that seemed to indicate extreme reluctance to end our amiable preliminary chat, suggested that perhaps we had better get down to business. 'Harry Meadows speaks extremely highly of you,' he said. 'But I was wondering what had made you decide you wanted to move into, um, our particular area of publishing. Rather off your usual showbiz beat, I would imagine.'

I wondered whether to lie, and come out with some guff about how I had always had a secret hankering to work on girlie magazines, but after his comment on the strictly legal nature of his business it was clear that he was a great deal sharper than the avuncular, donnish manner suggested.

'To be frank, I need the money,' I said. 'Harry indicated that the pay here was much better than at *Theatre World*.'

'And may I ask why you need the money?' he asked, again with the faintest hint of steel behind the solicitude.

'It's a rather personal matter.'

'Come, come, Mr Benson, you will appreciate that I need to know that your financial difficulties are, how shall I put it, unlikely to bring the old firm into disrepute.'

'I'd appreciate it if this went no further.'

'You can be assured of my discretion,' replied Wintour.

I told him about the ruinous cost of IVF treatment and he looked genuinely sympathetic.

'A great blessing, children,' he said, looking at a photograph of two mischievous looking schoolboys in an elaborate silver frame on his desk. 'I don't see them as often as I would like. My wife and I are unfortunately divorced.'

I wondered whether his line of work had had anything to do with it, and, indeed, how it would affect my relationship with Kim. She'd wished me good luck with the interview, and she knew we needed the money, but I got the impression that she wouldn't be exactly heart-broken if I failed to get the job.

'If you did decide to take me on,' I said, 'what sort of work would you expect me to do?'

'Can I take it you're still keen? After seeing our product? You wouldn't mind, erm, paddling in what some might consider murky waters?'

'No, not at all. I mean I'd certainly react differently if it were hard-core stuff, anything involving children, for instance, or physical cruelty.' I'd once had an eyeful of some S and M magazines, and hadn't liked it a bit.

Mr Wintour pursed his lips and shook his head and looked appalled at the very idea that such material existed.

'But your stuff, if you'll forgive me saying so, is almost good-hearted. I mean jokes pages and the like. And those jolly fatties. I mean, the pictures aren't even that strong, from what you might call the gynaecological point of view, are they? What did Kingsley Amis say? That very explicit porn, you know with the legs open and the labia parted and all that, was a bit like looking into the inside of a giraffe's ear?'

'Ah, yes, our old friend the open pussy or beaver shot,' said Mr Wintour, for the first time actually getting right down, as it were, to the nitty-gritty of his profession. 'Yes, quite legal, but the wholesalers aren't too keen on them and you can have trouble getting distribution through the big chains of newsagents. But I am delighted to hear you aren't offended by the magazines. I tend to adopt a rather missionary position about soft porn.'

I assumed that this was meant to be a joke, and, in grovelling interview mode, giggled accordingly. This was a mistake. Mr Wintour regarded me with a pained expression.

'I am absolutely serious,' he said. 'It seems to me that men looking at our magazines and having the occasional crafty hand-job are less rather than more likely to indulge in extra-marital affairs or, more seriously, sexual offences. It gives their life the slight extra *frisson*, the hint of illicit fantasy, they need. I suspect that most of the people who buy our product would run a mile if one of our models rang at the front door and propositioned them. Or an amorous neighbour come to that.

'Then of course there is the feminist objection that we are exploiting women. I prefer to say that we are celebrating them. Moreover,' he continued, sounding more and more like a wise old university lecturer, 'just who is exploiting whom? No one forces the models to pose, but there is never any shortage of willing recruits. They are well paid, and the men, surprisingly large numbers of men, are more than happy to part with a couple of quid to look at them. It seems to me an entirely legitimate and not dishonourable trade.

'Now, as to the job. What we are really looking for is a staff-writer. One of the great joys of our line of work is that you don't have to bother too much about the wordies. It's the pictures that count. Inspiration fails? Bung in another four-page spread. As you've seen, *Crumpet Corner* contains just a few captions. Do you think you could manage that kind of thing?

'Then there are the short stories and "readers' letters" in *Luv Bytes* and *Luvverly Blubberly*,' he went on. 'As I said, quite a few of these are genuine, but we get through an awful lot of them, and the feature-length "confessions" need a professional touch. We lost our regular staff-writer six months or so ago, went on to higher things, if you can call *The Times* higher things these days, and so a lot of the writing has been contracted out to freelances. We often buy in from other magazines anyway. And all the computer stuff at the back comes as an entirely separate package from a specialist firm we sub-contract to. They produce it all themselves, right up to the design and the finished pages. But we like to keep the soft porn element in house as much as possible. It makes for consistency of style as much as anything else, and although it's a trick you can pick up pretty quickly, even the most versatile freelances sometimes have trouble with the steamy sex scenes.'

'I've never written anything like that myself. I'd probably need a bit of help at first. But,' I added quickly, 'I'm sure I'll be able to manage.'

'I'm sure you will, Mr Benson. Knowing you were coming to this interview, I bought *Theatre World* yesterday. If you can make the opening of a new arts centre in Basingstoke sound interesting, you shouldn't have too much trouble with our little fictions here at Botticelli.'

'I've brought a few cuttings along with me, plus my CV,' I said. 'Would you like to see them?'

He nodded. I handed them over and he studied them for a few minutes.

'There's some nice stuff here,' he said generously. 'You'll miss *Theatre World*, I would imagine. How much were they paying you?'

I told him the pitifully low figure.

'Well, I think we should be able to double that,' he said.

I gasped. 'That's terribly generous.'

'Not at all, not at all. Wages are on the generous side here, because it's not the sort of job everyone would feel happy with and Botticelli is an extremely successful enterprise.' He went on to explain how more than half of the firm's profits came from the mail-order business, and from the telephone sex lines that charged eighty-four pence per minute (cheap rate) for the privilege of listening to tape recordings of women describing their sexual fantasies and faking noisy orgasms. I'd rung one myself once, in a spirit of idle curiosity, and found that you had to wait a very long time indeed for the recordings to reach their pre-destined climax. And with every minute of whispered foreplay that passed, the cost of the call was clicking up like a taxi meter.

'So you think you might be interested?' said Mr Wintour. 'The work load is pretty intensive and we operate with a very small staff. But I think you might be happy here. And I would be delighted if you felt you'd like to do some show-business interviews for *Luv Bytes*. I increasingly see it as a general interest magazine with a soft porn element, and any culture you might bring to our pages would be very welcome indeed.'

I thought about phoning the director of the National Theatre for an in-depth interview and then explaining that I no longer worked for *Theatre World* but for a fascinating publication called *Luv Bytes*. The proceeding seemed fraught with embarrassment, but Wintour seemed genuinely keen on 'raising the tone a little' as he put it.

We shook hands on the deal, and after working out my notice at *Theatre World* and bidding it a sad farewell, I joined Botticelli Fine Art Publications Ltd with the inflated title of Chief Staff Writer and an even more inflated salary.

I'd been so lost in remembering my interview with Wintour that I walked right past the open doors of the Botticelli warehouse. The two middle-aged and splendidly beer-gutted men responsible for dispatching the sex goods brought me back to the present with cheerful cries of 'Wanker!' accompanied by appropriate arm movements.

Brian Waynefleet was of course the reason everyone knew about the indignities of IVF treatment.

I retraced my steps, grinned ruefully and told them we'd all be out of work if wanking went out of fashion.

'True enough,' said Alf, the friendlier of the two. 'Though speaking for myself I'd prefer a game of pool and a few pints any day. Pub at lunchtime?'

'I've had my units for the week,' I said. They nodded

sympathetically. They knew about the booze rules too. 'But perhaps I'll come over for a Perrier.'

I climbed the stairs, blew a kiss at Daphne, who had been pictured that month in the pages of *Luvverly Blubberly* bursting out of an outsize St Trinian's school tunic, and went into the main office. Wintour had been right about the low staffing levels. Apart from the boss himself, Daphne who doubled as receptionist and secretary, and the chaps in dispatch, there were only five of us on the permanent staff, and one of them, Graham Gates, the company accountant and advertising manager, had an office of his own. He was built like a rugby prop forward, put away impressive numbers of pints at lunchtime and occasionally, I was told, treated the whole staff to lunch at Le Pont de la Tour on the Thames.

Foul-mouthed, cynical, and a compulsive sweet-eater, Brian Waynefleet, with his flushed, acne-scarred face, greasy pudding-bowl haircut and hideous cerise corduroy jacket, two sizes too tight for his short but bulky frame, was top dog in editorial. He must have been in his early thirties, like me, but in his moodier moments he was more like a sulky adolescent. He selected the pictures for publication, designed the layouts and put the magazines together on his snazzy computer system, which sent the finished pages straight down the line to the printer's. After the pen and paper days of *Theatre World*, I found it bewildering, but mercifully didn't have to get involved in much of the technical stuff myself. I just had to learn to use my own computer, little more than a word-processor, though that didn't stop me losing endless stories in the electronic ether during my first few days.

Then there was Linda Belling, to whom I was rapidly becoming devoted. She commissioned all the general interest features, liaised with the freelance photographers, and occasionally helped out on the writing side. She was boyishly pretty, had a laugh like a noisy soda-syphon and offered convincing proof that a dirty mind is a joy for ever.

She was, in her own words, a 'lesbian through and through', a phrase that occurred with remarkable regularity in the 'true confessions' in which bored housewives or nubile young students described how they had been seduced by another, more experienced woman for the first time. Linda really put her heart into these, and they were easily the sexiest read in the magazines. But she was good on the heterosexual stuff too, with a special penchant for man-devouring redcoats at holiday camps, and sex in unusual places, like the London Underground and, more titillatingly implausible still, jammed lifts in multi-storey car parks. She taught me the crucial trick that it is the specific detail that brings sexual fantasies to life. 'You can't just have handsome hunks and horny women rutting away in a vacuum,' she explained patiently. 'You've got to create an impression of their lives and their surroundings so that readers can picture them in their mind's eye. It's the little quirks that are usually the turn-on.'

She was quite a turn-on herself, but appeared to live a quiet and by all accounts happy domestic life with the middle-aged headteacher of a Southwark primary school, who sometimes came to pick Linda up after work. She looked more like her mother than her lover. Linda had been particularly interested in the IVF treatment. She was considering it for herself, as both she and her partner wanted a child of their own. It was the kind of story with which the tabloid press would have had a field day if they ever got wind of it (*Lesbian Headmistress in Test-Tube Baby Storm with Sex Mag's Luscious Linda*), but in my view the couple would make more stable and loving parents than most.

The fourth member of the editorial team was Janice Cockett, invariably known to Brian as Mrs Cock-up. This was unfair, as Janice, sour, middle-aged, and apparently born without the facial muscles required for smiling, was a sub-editor of ruthless efficiency and terrifying pedantry. She clearly regarded Botticelli Publications with complete contempt, but was damned if she was going to let a split infinitive or a hanging participle go through unchallenged, 'You can't have cunnilingus,' she'd exploded on my first day after I'd nervously submitted my first attempt at an erotic short story for inspection. 'Most of our readers wouldn't have a clue what that is. House style here is suck, lick, tongue, sixty-nine, blow job or go down. Got that? And you've got throbbing cock in two successive paragraphs. I'm changing the second to massive manhood. And I'm getting very tired of the phrase mega-melons. Do try and ring the changes a bit for heaven's sake.' I was scared of Janice. She knew her job and she could see that I was a blathering incompetent. Mercifully, kindly Linda gave my pieces a quick read before I sent them over to the gorgon, so I didn't get bollocked too often.

Brian looked at his watch as I walked in, then gave one of the rare generous grins that persuaded you he wasn't so bad, after all.

'How were the eggs?' he asked. 'Scrambled or sunny side up?'

'Two of them were fine. They showed them to us projected on to the wall.'

'Something to celebrate, then,' he said. 'Pub at lunchtime.' When Brian said pub at lunchtime it was an order rather than a suggestion. But why not? Screw the units for once, Kim had got two embryos inside her. Perhaps we really were going to be parents.

'Great,' I said, and Brian took another bite of that day's pile of horrible confectionery. He was an aniseed twist man at heart, but was trying to cut down on his usual half pound a day because the hard-boiled sweets were playing merry hell with his already terrifying teeth. He couldn't resist crunching them, so now, like a heroin addict doing the methadone treatment, he was trying to limit himself to edible knickers. These had been one of Mr Wintour's less successful mail-order lines, made out of red and black licorice and rice paper. They tasted vile and the idea that anyone might actually wear them beggared belief.

I sat down at my desk, and bashed out a few captions for *Crumpet Corner*. The last pages of *Luv Bytes* had gone the day before and this was a slack period. I was rather taken by the photos of Felicity, a curvy brunette dressed up as a traffic warden. *I love to book 'em, then bonk 'em, admits our lovely meter maid*, I wrote. *First they're furious, then they start to get turned on by my uniform, which shows off my massive mams to best advantage. I always make sure I leave a couple of my blouse buttons undone so they get tantalizing glimpses of my cleavage. My biggest fantasy is giving gorgeous Melvyn Bragg a ticket and then slipping him my phone number just as he's about to go ballistic. Why don't you come and read my meter, Melv?*

Thoughts of Melvyn reminded me that I ought to try to fix up a celebrity interview to 'raise the tone' of *Luv Bytes*. Perhaps I'd try him. He went in for erotic writing on his own account. On second thoughts, though, perhaps I'd try after lunch, with a few units inside me. I'd been rudely turned down by Jeremy Beadle the day before, who had positively salivated over the idea of a three-thousand-word interview until he'd finally got round to asking exactly what titles Botticelli published. The phone had been slammed down by a man who very evidently wasn't game for a laugh. He would be appearing in one of the *Crumpet Corner* captions very soon.

Brian, Linda and I went over to the Pride of the Borough at noon (Janice never joined such jaunts, preferring to spend her lunch-hour with sandwiches and Proust) and we were soon joined by Graham and the chaps from dispatch. I tried, heroically I thought, to alternate halves with Perrier water, but people kept buying me pints and it seemed churlish to refuse. There was an excellent jukebox, jam-packed with classics and rarities from the sixties and seventies. With three pints and an all-day Big Breakfast (including black pudding) inside me, and Wizzard's 'See

My Baby Jive' blaring out of the speakers, I should have felt at peace with the world. As so often, however, I was actually feeling guilty about breaking all my own rules. But at least Brian seemed to be in unusually amiable form. After only one of his beloved child abuse jokes ('What's black and blue and knocks on the window? A baby trapped in the washing machine') I managed to get him on to the less dispiriting subject of pop music: he was a mean selector at the jukebox. To my astonishment, it turned out that he was a fanatical devotee of the Grateful Dead. This was worrying, because Deadheads are usually nice if infuriatingly laid back. Brian was obscene, paranoid and about as nice as a going-over in the back of a police van.

'Yeah, they're gradely, the Dead, really gradely,' said Brian, who as far as I knew had spent all his life in London, but for mysterious reasons sometimes lapsed into broad Yorkshire. 'I've just bought a nineteen sixty-eight import of them performing at the Winterland Ballroom. It's got a version of "Dark Star" on it that's even better than the one on *Live/Dead*.'

'You couldn't tape it for me, could you?'

Brian had a better idea. I could come round to his place after work, he'd play the whole album and tape it for me at the same time. The idea of a night *chez* Brian wasn't exactly irresistible. Nevertheless, this was obviously more than a casual suggestion. Brian never spoke about his life outside the office, and though his tone of voice was studiously casual, there was something beseeching and spaniel-like in his bloodshot eyes. Perhaps he was lonely. At any rate, I got the distinct impression that this was an offer he'd bitterly resent my turning down, and a bitterly resentful Brian was something to be avoided.

Back at the office, with six pints inside me, I tried to explain all this to Kim without him overhearing me. This meant I was talking in a slurred whisper, and Kim asked me if I was ill.

'No, just trying to be discreet. I'll try to get home as soon as I can.'

'You're bound to be late with Brian,' said Kim. 'But don't worry. I can see he's someone you've got to keep in with.'

'You're an angel,' I said, putting the phone down.

'A night with our Bri, eh?' said Linda with a grin. 'You are privileged. Watch out, Will. He might be after your body.'

'I rather fancy him, actually,' I said, and she shuddered.

It turned out that Brian lived only a couple of streets from the office. It was typical of his twisted personality that he'd never mentioned this, even though the Pride must also have been his local in the evenings too. With Botticelli Publications' generous salaries, he could have had some modishly converted loft apartment on the Thames, but instead he led me into the heart of a vast, run-down sixties council estate dominated by two twenty-storey tower blocks.

'They're called Burwash and Simla,' he said as he led the way into the lift that smelled horribly of old urine, 'but everyone round our way calls them Bagwash and Bloody Identical.'

The lift shuddered to a halt on the eighteenth floor, and Brian opened the door to one of the four flats in the communal hall. Once upon a time, it might have been a cosy home. But not any more. The stench of old food in the living room made you gag, the carpet was littered with half-finished Indian and Chinese takeaways, and there was a thick layer of dust all over the furniture. Brian went into the kitchen to get us drinks, but one look at the place persuaded me that I'd be safer in the living room. The view from the windows, though, once I'd wiped a clean patch with my handkerchief, was stunning, with Tower Bridge and the Thames in the foreground and London stretching for miles in every direction beyond. But even in the clear, summer-evening sunlight, there was a pall of pollution in the air that turned the horizon into a grubby smudge. I began to wonder what Brian, a man of handsome means with, as far as anyone knew, no wife or children to support, was doing in a council flat.

He came over with an enormous Scotch in a greasy glass. I wiped it clean as best I could as he went over to the hi-fi, which looked as if it must have cost at least a couple of grand. There were also hundreds of compact discs, all neatly stacked in racks, the only evidence of order in the entire room. He slipped a tape into the cassette, loaded the CD player and pressed the right buttons. Jerry Garcia's guitar came soaring out of the magnificent speakers.

We grinned at each other with shared pleasure and if it hadn't been for his rotten teeth, Brian would have looked about twelve years old. He needs a friend, I suddenly realized, he desperately needs a friend.

'Sorry about the mess,' he said, as if it were just the ordinary disorder of a busy life rather than a stinking cess pit. If you lived with it for long enough, presumably you didn't notice the smell.

'Smashing view,' I said. 'How did you come to live here?'

'I've lived here most of my life. My mother was rehoused here when I was six, back in nineteen sixty-nine. I've been here ever since, apart from my time at university. She died a couple of years back.'

'I'm sorry,' I said.

'It was for the best, really. She was in a terrible state by the end. Alzheimer's, double incontinent . . .'

'And did you look after her?'

'Yeah, as best I could,' he said, trying and failing to sound off-hand. 'Lot of help from the social services. You know, cleaners and the like, a community nurse.' He seemed to be embarrassed about this evidence of decent behaviour and his voice sounded suspiciously choked. So as not to embarrass him further I wandered over to the sideboard. There were pictures on it of Brian as a young child, riding a kiddies' roundabout at a fairground, sitting on a donkey on the beach with the Blackpool Tower in the background. There was a peculiarly touching one of him holding his mother's hand and smiling up at her with a broad grin on his then cherub-like face, while his mother stared, bleakly, into the camera.

'My dad died shortly after that was taken,' said Brian. 'It was then that we came here.'

I couldn't understand why Brian didn't move out of this little flat with its suffocating memories, or at the very least clean it up and give it a fresh coat of paint. Perhaps life had lost most of its meaning for him after his mother died. Perhaps that explained the obscene cynicism and the moments of cruel bad temper. I suddenly found myself feeling sorry for him, and liking him a great deal more.

'I'm sorry, Brian, you must have had a tough time.'

'Sod it,' he said. 'Have another drink.' He topped me up generously, poured a quadruple for himself and then asked, terrifyingly, if I fancied something to eat. The idea of eating anything from that nightmare kitchen made me feel sick. I told him I was fine and that the Big Breakfast at lunchtime would see me through.

'So tell us what happened the other day,' said Brian. 'When you went to give your sperm sample. You sounded right excited on the phone. Some nurse come in to jack you off?'

Oh God. The last thing I wanted was an inquisition. I was damned if I was going to tell him about Sophie, though just the thought of her made me smile affectionately.

'No, nothing happened,' I said.

'Garn,' he replied. 'What was that sly smile in aid of just now?'

'Just a smile of relief, that's all. It took me ages to get it together.' I tried to change the subject. 'I mean the magazines the clinic supplies to help you along don't work that well when you're actually producing the bloody things yourself. Don't you find that?'

Brian looked offended that he might take anything other than a purely professional interest in soft porn.

'My sex life's my own affair,' he said with a sudden edge of fury, his acne-scarred face flushing ominously. 'I do all right on that score thank you very much. I've no need for a crafty wank, I can tell you. OK?'

I'd hurt him. It seemed to me highly unlikely given his personality, not to mention the state of his flat, that Brian had a steady girlfriend. Nevertheless, although I pitied him, I also felt peeved. What right had he to come over all coy about his own love life when he was constantly making nasty cracks about the IVF treatment, and was at that very moment grilling me on how I'd come to produce a sperm sample two days earlier?

'Look, Brian, let's forget it, OK. Let's not spoil an enjoyable evening.'

He had the grace to look faintly sheepish. 'Yeah, OK,' he said. 'I'm sorry. I can see this test-tube baby business must get you down. I've been a prick to give you so much grief over it.' He grinned and offered his hand. 'Shake on it?' he asked. 'Eeh, bah goom, I'm reet sorry, lad,' he added in broad Yorkshire. I shook his hand, noticing that the fingernails were bitten to the quick.

'Gradely,' I said.

Brian nodded, went to the sideboard and brought out a little polythene bag.

'Want a spliff?' he asked, as the Dead cranked themselves into the sonic madness of 'Dark Star'. I didn't, I wanted to get out of this sad and terrible place as quickly as possible. But it seemed a rejection of his hospitality to deny him yet again, so I nodded, and watched as he rolled a joint with what appeared to be pure grass. He took a couple of hits himself and passed it over. There was something so unwholesome about Brian that I found myself reluctant to put my lips where his mouth had been, but there was no help for it. I took a big swig of Scotch, dragged down three or four deep lungfuls, and then returned to the Scotch, washing it around my mouth and licking my lips with a whisky-drenched tongue. I had an idea at the back of my mind that alcohol killed almost as many known germs as Domestos. Nothing much seemed to happen at first, but then my head suddenly seemed to be exploding to the sound of the Dead, and I found I could hardly lift my arm when I tried to get another slug of Scotch to my lips. I was still relatively unused to large quantities of alcohol, and the dope had knocked me over the edge.

'You know the Grateful Dead are coming to London in a couple of weeks?' said Brian. I nodded and found that I couldn't actually speak. 'I've bought a couple of tickets.' He passed the joint over, and as I took another lungful, the grass burnt like fire at the back of my throat and the sickly-sweet smell of the burning leaves made me feel nauseous. My skin turned cold and clammy and it was only by an immense effort of will that I managed not to throw up on the carpet. Mind you, it wouldn't have made much difference if I had.

Very carefully, I continued to nod my head to show I'd heard. It felt enormously heavy, an intolerable burden on my shoulders. I really wanted to lie down on the floor, but even in the fog of marijuana and booze I realized that I couldn't face the horrors that lurked there. I'd got to get out of here soon, out of the flat and Brian's disconcerting company, and get some fresh air into my lungs.

'SO WOULD YOU LIKE TO COME?' Brian shouted at what suddenly seemed enormous volume, and in the distant recesses of my memory I remembered that some time ago, several hours or days ago, he'd asked the same question, twice, and I'd been incapable of answering. I nodded and held tightly to the arms of my chair.

I don't know how long I sat there. At some stage Brian must have changed the record, for the next time I made a temporary touch down in reality, the Dead weren't playing any more, it was the Smiths. I sat and listened and began to feel a great deal better as the daylight slowly turned to rosy dusk. I could have killed for a glass of water, though. Brian stubbed out another joint, and I saw there were now four dog-ends in the ashtray. If my own experience was anything to go by, he must be completely off his face, but then I was a very occasional dope-smoker and Brian possibly passed his lonely life outside the office with only Mary Jane as companion and comfort. I got tentatively to my feet and found I could walk, a matter of huge relief. I picked up my empty Scotch glass and tottered into the kitchen, the need for water in my parched throat now stronger than my dread of the squalor. I nearly changed my mind as I turned on the light switch. There was a scuttling noise and a dark shape disappeared under the cooker: a cockroach.

I advanced nervously towards the sink, trying not to look at the filthy saucepans and coffee cups sprouting hairy growths of green mould. I let the tap run for several minutes, and then drank, greedily at first, then more slowly and calmly, six glasses of water. It made me feel so much better that getting out of the kitchen again became an urgent priority.

Back in the sitting room, Brian was completely lost to the world, now slumped in his armchair with a burnt-out joint between his gnawed fingers. I shook him, and he stirred and mumbled something that sounded harrowingly like 'Mammy', and it seemed a shame to bring him round. Wherever he was now, at least he wasn't aware of this wretched flat, and his grief over his mother, and doubtless countless other miseries and nagging obsessions.

I found a piece of paper on the desk in the corner, and wrote a note thanking Brian for his hospitality, wishing him sweet dreams and telling him I'd love to come to the Grateful Dead. I wondered who had stood him up if he'd got two tickets, then wondered if he'd meant to ask me all along. Either way, it seemed a little sad.

I was dying for a slash after all that water. There were

three doors out in the hall. The first I tried was Brian's bedroom. One look at the grey sheets, the great pile of magazines by the bed and the crisp discarded Kleenex that littered the floor told me far more about Brian's private life than I wanted to know. In the corner was a large work station, with a mass of expensive computer equipment and a classy laser printer.

The next room was a very smelly, very dirty bathroom and loo. I held my breath and shut my eyes as I peed, before racing out and slamming the door behind me. I should now have left the flat and gone home, but curiosity got the better of me. I nipped quickly back into the sitting room to check that Brian was still crashed out and opened the third door. It was like entering a different world. It was another bedroom, smaller than Brian's but immaculate. The carpet was hoovered, the bed neatly made. There were freshly cut roses on the dressing table, a dozen of them, and a silver backed hair-brush and mirror that looked old, beautiful and fearfully expensive, though Brian had probably reduced the value by having them engraved. Each bore the discreet legend 'To Mammy on her 70th birthday. With all my love, Bri.' There was a framed photograph of his mother, looking frail but aware, perhaps the last one taken before Alzheimer's got her in its grip. In front of it was a candle, half burned. The room was a shrine, the rest of the flat a graphic self-portrait of all the despair and emptiness and possibly guilt Brian had experienced since her death. Perhaps he'd lost his temper with her when she became foolish and incontinent, perhaps he felt he hadn't done enough for her. He'd done more than most, far more. But self-loathing seemed to be eating him from within, like cancer.

Being in that room was an unforgivable trespass on private grief. I shut the door behind me and got out of the flat as fast and as quietly as I could. Brian would be furious if he knew I'd seen that room, livid with himself for passing out and not keeping an eye on me.

Even the urine-soaked lift was a relief after the flat. As I stepped outside, into the mangy estate gardens, it still wasn't quite dark, and a few birds were singing in the stunted London trees. I walked back home through the south London backstreets, and it was only ten by the time I arrived at Rita Road. Kim had evidently been expecting me to stay out until the pubs shut. There was no sign of her in the kitchen, the sitting room or our bedroom, and I thought she must have gone out to see a friend. Then I noticed the light shining under the door of the spare bedroom. I hardly went in there from one month to the next. I thought she'd be pleased and surprised to find me home early, so I walked straight in. It was the second room I shouldn't have entered that night.

Kim was sitting on the bed in her nightie, tears rolling down her cheeks, surrounded by everything the mother could want for the new-born child. She jumped, guiltily, as she heard me come in, then started sobbing uncontrollably. I went over to her and held her in my arms and tried to wipe away her tears with my handkerchief, but she seemed beyond consolation. She just kept gasping, 'It won't work, it won't work, it won't work.'

So I held her, and told her how much I loved her, and she buried her face in my chest and soaked my shirt with her warm, salt tears. There was all the time in the world to survey the contents of the bed. Tiny white all-in-one vests, miniature socks with dinosaurs on them, a hooded towel with a teddy on it, what looked suspiciously like a hand-knitted matinee jacket (where and when had she found time to do that?). I wondered how long she could keep taking all this terrible pain if the treatment failed yet again. Slowly she relaxed in my arms and fell into a deep sleep. I picked her up and carried her into the bedroom, and though she stirred as I laid her down, and covered her with the duvet, she didn't wake fully. I undressed, quickly cleaned my teeth and washed, before climbing into bed and curling myself around her. Like two spoons in a drawer, I thought, remembering our first night together, another chaste night like this one. It had been Kim who tended to me then, though my wounds had been physical rather than emotional, and quickly healed. I kissed her gently on the back of the neck. My wife. Though at that moment she felt more like my child.

Wednesday 26 July

For she had a tongue with a tang.
The Tempest

I was back at the pretty Pimlico pub with the flowers
outside. I shouldn't have been there. I knew that, but the
last week had been pretty hellish one way or another. I'd
half-feared that Brian would be distinctly hostile to me at
work, regretting the fact that he had allowed me such an
insight into his life, but I couldn't have been more wrong.
He was intolerably cheerful, bouncy, even roguishly affectionate, slapping me on the back and muttering northern
inanities like 'Where there's muck there's brass' and 'Tha's
nowt so queer as folk'. The latter was especially worrying.
At times I wondered whether Linda had been right and he
really did fancy me. There was no escaping him. He was
constantly wandering over to my desk to look over my
shoulder as I bashed out the day's required word-count of
sexual fantasies and leery *double entendres*. Lunchtime visits
to the pub became *de rigueur*, and though I tried to bully
Linda into coming as often as possible, she very understandably didn't want to join us every day, pleading
poverty or hangovers or a desperate need to go to the
shops. Luckily the chaps from dispatch and Graham the
accountant were usually there and we wasted liquid hours
playing the jukebox and pool.

The moderation on the alcohol front had, in the last ten
days, gone entirely to the dogs; I'd given up trying to
count the units now I was knocking them back so reck-

lessly. The problem was Kim. After the sad night with the baby clobber, I'd suggested, as gently as I could, that it might be best to make the present treatment our last, whether it worked or not. Kim had stormed out of the flat in silent fury, going to work at least an hour earlier than she needed to. This, I thought glumly, was the time when she was supposed to be keeping calm to give Bill and Ben their best chance of survival. If they were feeling all this anguish, who could blame them if they decided they'd much rather not be born. I had an anaesthetizing belt of malt whisky before setting off to work myself, the start of the slippery slope.

That night Kim had again been slumped in unreachable gloom. She didn't want to talk, she said. She didn't want to be touched, she wanted to be left on her own. And she'd insisted on being on her own ever since. She would come back from work, open a tin of baked beans and eat them cold for supper, and go straight to bed. When I joined her, invariably after drinking too much and watching arid hours of junk telly, she retreated to her side of the bed and made it absolutely clear that I was to stay on mine. The weekend had been a desert of reproachful silence with Kim opting to spend the whole of it curled up in a ball under the duvet. I brought her cups of tea and nursery food, and tried to start anodyne conversations, but she couldn't or wouldn't respond. When I came back for the tray, she'd always pretend to be asleep. Sometimes she'd eaten, mostly she hadn't. I remembered her former voracious appetites – for food and drink, for sex, for laughter – and mourned for the Kim I'd lost.

So here I was at the Pimlico pub. It was 3.30 in the afternoon and I was meant to be at work. Over the lunchtime pints with Brian I'd disgraced myself at pool and felt my whole body being engulfed in great waves of depression. And then, standing at the bar and getting a last pint in, a pint which I knew would merely worsen the dismal gloomies but which I was bloody well going to have anyway, I found Sophie's card, next to a letter from the bank manager about our whopping IVF-induced overdraft. Brian had gone to the gents, so I had a quick look at the card while waiting for the barman to take my order. I had to see Sophie and see her soon. Maybe it was the hectic garbage about a female lorry driver I'd been writing that morning (*Hitch-hikers queued up for a ride in my five-ton truck of shame!*) that had brought on a rare twinge of lust, but beyond the lust was a desire for companionship, for Sophie's good-humoured common sense. I might have been kidding myself, but visiting Sophie seemed more like consulting an agony aunt than going to a tart. An agony aunt who was prepared to give you a blow job, to be sure, but fuck it, I needed a break from the misery.

I brought the drinks over to Brian and realized that the very thought of Sophie was making me grin fatuously.

'Well, thank Christ you've cheered up at last,' he said. 'It's been like sitting next to Queen Victoria this lunchtime.'

'I was just thinking of that joke of yours. The one about the mentally retarded Thalidomide victim with Aids.' Actually this was one of Brian's many jokes that I spent a lot of time trying not to think about but I needed to make him feel kind-hearted, and craven flattery seemed the best approach. 'I was wondering if I could have the afternoon off, actually. Kim was heaving her guts out this morning and I'm a bit worried about her.'

'Morning sickness!' cackled Brian. 'Morning sickness. You've done it at last, mate.'

I tried to keep my fatuous smile intact, and said perhaps he was right but at all events I'd like to get home. Brian took a long draught of beer, chased it down with an aniseed twist that he crunched horribly, and nodded indulgently.

'On your way, then, squire.'

'You're a real pal,' I said, and set off cheerfully for the Tube. There was a long wait for a train and I felt a twinge of guilt as we stopped at my usual station, Vauxhall, but I repressed it and travelled on up to Pimlico. Feeling unaccountably nervous I stopped off for yet another pint I didn't need. Half-way through it I remembered Henrietta and thought I'd better ring rather than just turn up. Henrietta would probably regard an impromptu visit as a dreadful breach of etiquette. I dialled the number from the payphone at the bar and it rang and rang without an answer. I felt a mixture of relief and disappointment. No need for pangs of guilt. But the depressing prospect of more bleak hours of silence in Vauxhall.

I finished my pint, then had a large Scotch. Stepping out into the sultry heat it occurred to me that Henrietta might have popped out for a packet of fags and Sophie might have been busy with a client. Why not just turn up?

I went down the area steps and was surprised to find the front door half open. I rang the bell, rang it again, then called 'Coo-ee', feeling more anxious by the second. Finally I plucked up the courage to go in and find out what was wrong.

Henrietta was lying on the floor in the cosy sitting room, blood seeping from her nose, which looked broken. I went and knelt beside her and asked if she was all right. Silly question, really, but she was conscious and more or less articulate.

'Someone just burst in,' she said, as I held up her head. 'About fifteen minutes ago.' I looked at my watch. It was 3.45 p.m. 'He was wearing one of those horrible rubber masks. Of Elvis Presley. He smashed me on the nose, then smashed me on the knee with a truncheon when I was on the floor. I can't get up.'

'Jesus,' I said.

'Forget it, go and see Sophie. I'm terrified. He was in there for about five minutes with her. There were sounds of a fight, a lot of grunting and shouting and screaming. I haven't heard a thing since he left.'

It was my clear duty and I got to my feet with legs

like jelly. Don't even think about it, I told myself, just do it.

I rushed down the short corridor and into the bedroom. Sophie was lying, naked, on the bed. Her lingerie, cut to shreds, was scattered all over the floor. I only noticed that later. What I noticed first was the blood bubbling out of Sophie's mouth and down her chin and neck. The once clean sheet on the bed was smeared and stained bright red, and she was groaning, quietly but horribly. I went over to her, crouched by the bed, and tried not to look at her mouth too closely. But of course I did look, and almost threw up. It was jammed full of cotton wool, but the blood was still seeping from it. She made noises of unspeakable anguish, and pointed at the carpet, to a spot about six feet from the bed. There was a small piece of stewing steak lying there. But it wasn't stewing steak, it was half of Sophie's tongue.

I was about to rush out and phone for an ambulance when Sophie made more dreadful noises, half whimper, half gurgle, as the blood trickled down her throat. She pointed again, this time to the fridge in the corner from which she'd served me champagne on my last visit. There were two glasses on top of it and, I guessed, an ice box inside. I knew what I had to do. Like most men, I'd shuddered over the dreadful fate of Mr Bobbitt.

'Wouldn't it be better to get an ambulance here at once?' I said, but she shook her head, and grunted with despair. I picked up a tumbler, got the ice tray from the fridge, and bashed out a few cubes. Now for the tongue. I remembered that ice could burn human flesh. I had to wrap it up in something. Sophie had got there before me. She'd managed to pick up a Durex from the basket on the bedside table and open it. I took it from her, seized a handful of Kleenex and, trying to convince myself that it was just a piece of meat that I'd dropped on the floor during a dinner party, got my Kleenex-covered fingers round the inch-long lump of flesh. I opened the Durex clumsily with my spare hand

and eased the tongue into the opening. The rubber closed around it, and I put the monstrous package in the glass with the ice cubes.

There seemed to be more and more blood seeping from Sophie's mouth. 'Is there anything I can do?' I asked. 'We've got to staunch the flow. More cotton wool? A handkerchief?' Somehow Sophie crawled to the other side of the bed, and pointed to the bottom drawer of the chest of drawers. It was open and contained a box of Lillets. Brilliant thinking, Sophie, I thought, and realized she must have one in her mouth already. And that would have to be taken out first. I really didn't think I could face this. But I got a Lillet out of the packet, and went and sat next to Sophie, putting my arm round her bare, blood-stained shoulder. She was shivering violently and I noticed there were livid scores round her wrists. The bastard must have tied her up before he went to work on her tongue. But he'd untied her when he left. A hint of mercy there? Giving her a chance to get help before she bled to death?

'Do you want me to give you a hand? Can you take the old one out yourself?' She shook her head and more blood dribbled down her chin. It was going to hurt whatever I did, so I told her to open her mouth as wide as she could and close her eyes. At the back of my mind was the knowledge that the Aids virus was passed through blood, and prostitutes were a high-risk group. I glanced quickly at my right hand, but could see no scratches. I got a couple of fingers on to the bloody rag and yanked it out as fast as I could and hurled it across the room. She stiffened in my arm as I did so, and her nails dug deep into my thigh. But she managed neither to scream nor shut her mouth and I jammed in the fresh Lillet and told her she was a star. Still shivering, she stroked my thigh as if apologizing for the damage she'd inflicted on it a moment earlier.

'Right. Now I really must get an ambulance,' I said, but Sophie again shook her head with a terrible urgency. She rose from the bed, staggered over to the window and threw it open. She put her arm out and gestured under the window sill, grunting incomprehensibly. I leant out and felt beneath it. Just rough concrete at first, but then I touched a polythene bound package. Drugs? I wondered desperately. Christ, if Sophie was a junkie there really was a risk of Aids. I yanked at it and came up with a package covered in masking tape. Sophie seized it from my hands and began ripping at the polythene. There seemed to be about five layers of plastic bags, and she was getting progressively weaker. I took it from her and tore it open myself. If there had been heroin or cocaine in there I'm not sure that I wouldn't have taken a hit myself.

In fact the package contained a cassette tape in its plastic box. Sophie slipped it into the inside pocket of my jacket and I put the scattered packaging into my Tesco carrier bag. She put her fingers to my lips and shook her head. Don't blab seemed to be the message.

'Ambulance,' I said. 'Henrietta's OK. Just a broken nose and a buggered knee.' She nodded, and lay down on the bloody sheets.

Henrietta had managed to get herself up into a sitting position against the wall.

'Sophie will live,' I said, as I rushed to the phone. 'The cunt cut her tongue out but she'll live.'

As I dialled 999 and waited while it rang twenty times without an answer, I could hear Henrietta bidding a noisy farewell to her lunch. I didn't look. I'd seen enough for one afternoon. I finally got through and gave the details of what had happened and the address, but the guy at the other end warned there might be a delay. A computer was down. They would do their best to be there in fifteen minutes.

'I'll take her to St Thomas's myself in a taxi, you wanker,' I said, to which he replied that there was no need to be offensive but it was probably the best bet.

I went back to the bedroom. Sophie had got a pair of jeans and a T-shirt on, and was sitting on the bed looking defeatedly at an expensive pair of trainers. I knelt before her and put them on. She was still shivering, but I found a cardigan under the bed and helped her into it.

'The ambulances are up the spout,' I said. 'Do you think you could make it up the steps so we can get a cab?'

She nodded. I put my arm round her waist, picked up the glass and the Tesco carrier with my spare hand, and helped her slowly down the corridor and into the parlour. Henrietta, still sitting on the floor, blanched at the sight of Sophie, with her bruising and her blood stains and the already drenched cotton wool in her mouth, but Sophie gave her a tentative thumbs-up and nodded.

I thought I ought to help Henrietta into a chair by the phone, so she could call for help if she needed it. With great difficulty I yanked her weighty body upright, but she screamed with pain and asked to be put down again.

'The phone's got a long lead,' she said. 'Just bring it over here.' She gave Sophie a pitiful stare. 'I'm so sorry, sweetheart. I couldn't stop him. Did you see his face? Did you know him?'

Sophie shook her head, abstractedly. 'I'll phone Jim,' said Henrietta. The ponce presumably, I thought. Where had he been when they needed him? Sophie nodded wanly and I took her hand, led her out of the door and had almost shut it behind us when I remembered the glass I'd put down on the window sill. I went back for it, waved it at Henrietta and told her they could do wonders with microsurgery these days, shut the door and helped Sophie up the steps. We stood in the clammy heat and I took the opportunity of ditching the packaging that had held the tape in a handy rubbish bin. A cab was going up the other side of the road and I hailed it desperately, but with forlorn hope. I'm usually invisible to taxi drivers. But mercifully he turned round and came back to us.

He took one look at Sophie and at my disreputable linen jacket, now spattered with her blood.

'In you get,' he said brusquely. 'St Thomas's Casualty?'

I nodded, helped Sophie into the cab, and sat beside her with the glass between my knees. She took my hand and squeezed it and I squeezed hers back. I thought the driver would be agog to hear what was going on but he appeared to be a cabbie of unusual discretion and closed the glass screen.

'Are you sure you don't want me to tell anyone about this tape? Shouldn't the police be informed?' I asked.

She shook her head emphatically.

'And have you any idea who did this to you?'

She shrugged, then pointed at the inside pocket of my jacket.

'The tape?' I said. 'It might have something to do with this?'

Sophie nodded, then shook her head wearily. She didn't seem to know.

'Does anyone else know about the tape or what's on it?' I asked. 'Henrietta? Jim, was it? Or your colleague, what was she called, the one I tried to see first, the one with the enormous knockers?'

Sophie made a foolish attempt at a grin and winced with agony. Then she shook her head and pointed at me. I seemed to be the only one who knew anything about it. Though perhaps whoever it was that had savaged her knew something about it.

'Are you sure it wouldn't be wiser to take it to the police? I've got a hunch that the hospital will be obliged to get on to them anyway when they realize what's happened to you.'

Sophie began to exhibit signs of real distress, shaking her head adamantly, and putting a single finger to her bloodied mouth.

'Do you want me to play the tape, or just keep it safe?' I said, beginning to feel as if I was caught up in a nightmarish game of Twenty Questions. Sophie nodded and I realized I didn't know which question she was answering.

'Play it?' I said.

She nodded.

'And no police?'

Another, very emphatic nod. We were drawing up outside the hospital, but Sophie began pointing at her nose, then her throat, and drawing little shapes in the air. Then she began tracing what I guessed were letters, very awkwardly, on my thigh with her finger. She was trembling so much it was impossible to make them out. I gave her a pen and a cash dispenser slip, and she scribbled a few letters between the fits of shakes: C.O.U.G.H.

And then she dropped the pen. The taxi had arrived at the hospital now. I picked up the pen to see if she wanted to write any more, but she was virtually overcome by pain and shock, and simply shook her head in blank despair.

'Right, let's get you into Casualty. They'll fix you up in no time,' I said, with a bright confidence I didn't actually feel. The driver decently declined payment as I groped for my wallet, and I told Sophie the pain would soon be over and helped her up the ramp.

The Accident and Emergency Department was mercifully quiet and I took Sophie straight up to the desk. 'This lady has had her tongue cut out,' I said, putting the tumbler with its now melting ice on the desk. 'It's in there, actually, inside a Durex.'

'Jaysus,' said the Irish nurse, who must have encountered more than a few horrors in her time. 'You better come straight through.' As we went into the Casualty Ward, Sophie suddenly buckled at the knees, though she was still conscious. I managed to stop her falling on the floor, and picked her up in my arms. A junior doctor, his face waxy with fatigue, hurried over and I told him what had happened in a single breathless sentence, Sophie still in my arms.

'When did the attack take place?' he asked.

'About half an hour ago, I think.'

'Right,' he said, taking Sophie from me and laying her gently on a bed in the recovery position. 'There should be a good chance of repairing the damage.' He then looked at me with an expression of disgust on his face.

'You didn't commit this atrocity yourself, did you?'

Oh Christ, I thought, this was going to be first of many questions. 'No, I bloody well didn't,' I said. 'She's a hooker if you must know. I was a potential client and I blundered into this mess quite by chance.'

'Right, sorry,' he said, very decently. 'She seemed to trust you. I suspect a lot of other people would have buggered off under the circumstances. Now, there's no time to waste. If you will go and wait in the reception area, we'll get Miss . . .?'

'Sophie,' I said.

'We'll get Miss Sophie straight into the theatre. Stay put. There will be a lot of forms to fill in and questions to be answered.'

They drew the curtains round Sophie and I made my way back to the waiting room, feeling decidedly shaky now that I had shifted the burden of responsibility on to someone else. I tried not to think about what was going to happen next. Questions, certainly, and probably the police, and a great deal of anguish for Kim.

I sat there for about twenty minutes and my heart lurched as I saw two uniformed policemen coming in through the main entrance. I then did two things, one sensible, the other exceptionally stupid, in quick succession.

By my chair there was a mournful-looking palm plant in a pot encased by a square wooden container. I surreptitiously removed the tape from my pocket and dropped it in the gap between pot and container. I then looked up to see if the police had seen anything. They were deep in conversation with the Irish nurse at reception. That was when I made my blunder. The idea of endless interviews with the police, of a visit to the cop shop, of Kim finding out all about my visits to Sophie, suddenly brought on a massive panic attack. They would undoubtedly see me if I made my way to the main entrance, but not far from my chair was a door with a sign saying Out-patients' X-Ray Department. Perhaps there would be another way out from there and I could quietly disappear. I got to my feet, gazed around the palm at the cops who were still talking to the nurse, and shuffled quietly towards the door. There was a shout of, 'Hey, you!' and I put a sprint on. Once through the door I discovered I was in a long corridor and I ran down it at full pelt. There was another corridor forming a T-junction, and I turned right and saw that at the end there was a door marked Emergency Exit with one of those push-bar arrangements they have in theatres and cinemas. I hurled myself against the bar, looked over my shoulder to see the two uniformed policemen racing along behind me with their helmets in their arms, and stumbled down some concrete steps. I turned left towards the river. By now my chest felt as though it was going to explode like an ancient, overheated boiler. I took another flight of steps two at a time and found myself on the Embankment river-walk. Instinctively I turned west, towards home in Vaux-hall, and a quick backwards glance revealed I was putting some distance between myself and the police. Perhaps I'd manage to escape them, after all. It was then that I met my own have-a-go-hero. Have-a-go-heroes had featured prominently in the *Bridport News*, where I'd begun my career, usually pictured bruised but bravely smiling in their hospital bed after foolishly tackling a burglar or a mugger. My own hero escaped entirely unscathed, and didn't even have to move from his bench with its agreeable view of the Houses of Parliament. He simply stuck out his walking stick and tripped me up. I hit the deck like a large sack of potatoes, doing grave damage to both hands and knees, and lay there, winded and sobbing with frustration. The police soon had the cuffs on me and yanked me to my feet. I looked my nemesis in the eye. He was a Chelsea pensioner, eighty if he was a day, with a silver beard and medals on his scarlet coat. I couldn't even find it in my heart to hate him. Indeed his solid, ancient decency filled me with a sense of shame, before I realized I hadn't actually done anything wrong. Well, not that wrong.

'Nice work,' I said.

'Best fun I've had all week,' he replied. 'Not too badly hurt, I hope? And not in too much trouble either?'

'Enough trouble to be going on with,' I said, and he replied that he was sorry to hear it and wished me good luck. I felt like shaking him by the hand. English fair play and all that. Unfortunately I was handcuffed. He started ambling off down the Embankment.

One of the cops was talking into his radio. The other, pustular and ludicrously youthful, bellowed, 'Hey, grandad, we might need you as a witness,' at the pensioner's retreating back.

The old soldier's step didn't falter. 'Well, you know where to find me,' he yelled over his shoulder. 'Stanley Thompson's the name, and it's time for my tea.'

I was led slowly back to the hospital, manacled and trying to avoid the curious gazes of those we passed, then told to get into a police car parked near the entrance to Casualty.

'I'm innocent,' I said, as we drove from the hospital. 'I was a fool to run away like that.'

'Save it for later,' said the young cop with the zits. As we passed Big Ben I realized it was only forty-five minutes since I'd left the Pimlico pub.

The police station was an undistinguished modern brick building with a large coat of arms on the outside. I was taken through a side door and into the charge room and told to sit down and wait. There were a couple of chairs, a table and a large sign saying No Smoking. I was dying for a fag, but it would have been difficult to roll one with the cuffs on. The young cop sat opposite me. There didn't seem to be a lot to say. He looked as though he ought to be doing his homework.

A middle-aged sergeant came in, and told me he was

the custody officer. He read me my rights and added that I was allowed a phone call, to a friend, a relation or a solicitor. I said I'd think about it. Kim wouldn't be home from work yet. More importantly I couldn't face telling her what was going on. Not yet. I still didn't know whether I was merely up to my neck in the shit or whether it had already closed over my head.

I told the sergeant my name, age, address and occupation – just 'journalist' at first, but he wanted more detail so I mentioned Botticelli Publications, which produced a smirk, quickly suppressed, from the young constable. He must have been one of our readers. Mercifully the older policeman missed it and just asked me to spell Botticelli. The sergeant then asked the constable what had happened and he described going to St Thomas's after receiving a call from the hospital about a woman who had had her tongue cut out.

'Oh dear, oh dear,' said the sergeant, writing laboriously with his biro. 'And what part is our suspect here supposed to have played in all this?'

'The nurse at reception had just identified him as the man who'd brought her in when he gets to his feet and does a runner. We caught up with him on the Embankment.'

'With a little help from a Chelsea Pensioner,' I said.

The young cop had the grace to blush. 'I'm afraid that's true, Sarge. This old guy tripped him up with his walking stick. Not that we wouldn't have got him anyway.'

'*The Sweeney* rides again,' said the sergeant. 'So Sunny Jim here is suspected of assault, by virtue,' the sergeant seemed to savour the phrase, 'by virtue of the cutting out of a woman's tongue. Nasty, very nasty indeed.' He gave me a stern look, and then unaccountably asked if I'd like a cup of tea. I'd expected to have been beaten up by now.

'And we'd better get the police doctor along to have a look at those cuts,' added the sergeant. He'd be offering to give my shoes a polish if I left them outside the cell door next.

The constable went away for the tea, and with luck, to summon the doctor. My hands were really hurting now and I became morbidly convinced that all that Thames-side grit was going to infect the wounds. Then I thought of Sophie and all her blood.

'I'm innocent,' I told the custody sergeant, who sighed as though he'd heard it a thousand times before, which he doubtless had. He, too, told me to save it for later: for the CID, who would be along soon. Suddenly I remembered Henrietta. Perhaps she was still at the flat. Probably, like Sophie, she wouldn't welcome police involvement, but sod that, I needed someone to clear me and she was the only person who could do that until Sophie became capable of speech.

'Listen,' I said urgently to the sergeant. 'The woman I took to the hospital was a prostitute. Whoever was responsible beat up her maid before going in to attack Sophie. The maid might still be there. She couldn't walk when I left her.'

The sergeant was writing fast. 'Address?' he asked. I gave it to him, and he went out and locked the door behind him. I sat there, glumly, trying not to think about anything at all, and then the sergeant and the constable returned to search me. They took away my wallet, my watch, shoes, lighter and blood-stained jacket, all of which I had to sign for. They let me hang on to the packet of Old Disgusting and my cigarette papers though, and the constable then escorted me to the smoking room where there was a cup of tea waiting for me. I struggled to roll a cigarette, but my hands were shaking so violently the handcuffs jangled. As the tobacco spilt on to the floor I almost cried with frustration, and in the end the constable did it for me and gave me a light.

'Thanks,' I said, and meant it, and he nodded with a blank face. Who'd want to make any kind of human contact with a man who might recently have cut out a prostitute's tongue? I finished my fag and tea and thought I'd better phone Kim. The constable led me back to the custody room. I dialled the number and got only my own voice on the answering machine. I didn't speak. Anything I might have to say would be a dreadful message to come home to, and I wasn't sure if speaking to an answering machine would count as my one permitted call anyway. So I shrugged, and put the phone down, and the young constable led me to a windowless cell with a bare, fixed bench, a lavatory and a tiled floor. He took off my handcuffs before locking the door behind him and I lay on the bench and chanted my transcendental meditation mantra to myself. It didn't do much good, but then it rarely did.

The boredom was broken by the police doctor, who silently removed the grit from my wounds with tweezers and a cotton wool swab, applying liberal quantities of disinfectant which stang like hell. He asked if there was anything the police ought to know about my medical history and I shook my head while he applied the sticking plaster. When he left, I went back to my mantra.

The two CID men, Sergeant Darbyshire and Constable Fox, looked pale and overworked, guarded but surprisingly unthreatening. I met them in a scruffy interview room and the young PC was there too, taking notes, even though the interview was being recorded. Once again I was asked to tell them everything that had happened in my own words. I went right back to the circumstances of my first meeting with Sophie, and stumbled through the narrative. 'Finally, I got a taxi in the Belgrave Road, and took her to St Thomas's,' I concluded. 'I'd hardly have done that if I'd taken a knife to her myself.'

'How do you know it was a knife?' asked Darbyshire.

'Why did you do a runner at the hospital?' added Fox.

I floundered around. I said I assumed it was a knife, and that I'd run away because I didn't want to upset Kim.

'Are you sure you're not Sophie's ponce, Mr Benson?'

asked Darbyshire. 'Sounds like pretty poncey behaviour to me. Mutilating her, dumping her at the hospital and getting the hell out. Had she upset you? Not paying out her full share? Doing too many drugs?'

'I'm not her ponce,' I said, increasingly rattled. 'Have you been round to the flat yet and spoken to the maid? She can clear me.'

They ignored this question. 'Or perhaps you're just a nasty little kink,' said Fox. 'All that porn you write must rot the brain. The hospital said there were marks on her wrists, as though she'd been tied up. What happened, Will? Was it a bit of consensual S and M, only this time you got carried away?'

'I'm not into S and M,' I said. 'And anyway, Sophie doesn't offer any of that kind of stuff.'

'Bit of an expert are you, Will? Been paying for it for long?' asked DC Fox, undoubtedly the nastier of the two.

'I went for the first time last week,' I said, trying to keep the fear and the anger out of my voice. 'Like I told you, I had to produce a sperm sample in a hurry.'

'And yet you didn't tell your wife, even though you claim it was all legit, a matter of necessity. Not very trusting of you, was it?'

'Well, would you have told yours?' I asked, riled.

'I wouldn't have to, William, would I? I don't go to prostitutes.'

'I don't go to prostitutes,' I shouted. 'It was a matter of necessity.'

'So why did you go creeping back? Felt consumed with guilt, did you, and wanted to take your revenge in some kind of pervy way?'

'I wanted to talk to her.'

Fox laughed sarcastically.

Darbyshire took over. He asked me to describe the scene at the Pimlico basement when I arrived, and whether I'd seen anyone leaving as I went in. I hadn't, I said.

'And when you talked to Sophie, the first time, did you

get the impression that she was in any kind of danger, that she feared anyone?'

'Not at all. She seemed kind, well balanced and normal. She even seemed happy in her job.'

'Slag,' said the callow Fox, under his breath, but still clearly audible. Darbyshire threw him a nasty look.

'I realize,' said the sergeant, 'that Sophie couldn't say anything this afternoon. But did the maid give any indication that she knew who might have done it?'

'No. I heard her ask Sophie if she knew who it was. Sophie didn't seem certain. As I said earlier, he was wearing a mask. Elvis Presley.'

'So do you have any ideas at all about who might have done this? Assuming you're innocent, as you claim.'

It was the crunch question. Did I betray Sophie and mention the tape? But I didn't even know what was on the tape yet.

'None at all,' I lied with a fluency that surprised me. 'I was just in the wrong place at the wrong time, I think.'

'Or doing the wrong thing,' said Fox.

I ignored him. 'Have you found the maid? She's a crucial witness,' I asked desperately.

'That's for us to bother about, not you,' said Darbyshire. 'Now we need to send someone round to your place to confirm that you really live where you say you do. I gather you haven't got through to your wife. Do you want to try phoning her again, or let a policewoman break the news to her?'

I dreaded talking to Kim but knew I couldn't shirk it.

'I'll phone her myself,' I said. 'I suppose one of you has to stay in the room?'

Darbyshire nodded and the unpleasant Fox and the constable at least had the grace to withdraw. I dialled and Kim picked up the phone on the second ring, her voice announcing the number with the lifeless tone that had become so depressingly familiar. There was, I thought, no point in beating about the bush.

74

'Kim, it's me, Will. I'm at Belgravia police station. I went to a massage parlour this afternoon and discovered the girl with her tongue cut out. I took her to the hospital and the police now think I may have had something to do with it.'

There was a worryingly long silence and then Kim said, 'Oh, poor Will, I'm sorry,' in the affectionate husky tone she used when we were making love. She sounded, at this darkest moment, as though she might have come alive again.

'Do you want me to come over?' she asked.

'No, I'm OK. They want to send a policewoman over to check the address and everything.'

'Right,' said Kim. 'Try not to worry, Will. It'll be all right.'

'Thanks, Kim. I love you.'

'I love you too,' she said. 'Keep me posted, if they let you, and I'll ring myself if I don't hear anything.'

'Right. Hope to see you later then.' It was only as I put the phone down that I realized she hadn't even offered a single word of reproach, still less asked whether I'd done it or not. At that moment, stuck in an interview room at the Belgravia nick with a suspicious detective sergeant, I felt happier than I had done for months.

I grinned at him. 'She's OK,' I said. 'She'll be expecting the policewoman.'

'Sounds as though you've got a good 'un there,' he said.

'Yes, I have,' I replied smugly.

'I just hope you haven't let her down, then,' he added sternly.

I was allowed another snout, as we prisoners call them, in the smoking room, which was crowded with several coppers now, some uniformed and some not, looking companionable and friendly, but slightly furtive, as the inhabitants of smoking rooms always do. They regarded me with a lack of curiosity which was oddly reassuring, and when I'd finished my crooked little roll-up one of them took pity on me and proffered an Embassy. Then I was taken back to my cell, given a surprisingly good lasagne and another cup of tea, and left to cool my heels.

The time passed slowly but not nearly as miserably as it had the last time I'd been banged up. I felt an enormous sense of relief about Kim's faith in me and, though cool and sceptical, my interviewers weren't the brutal thugs I half expected them to be. Indeed I had the impression that the sergeant was probably beginning to believe my story.

I was given another cup of tea at eleven, and the chance, gratefully taken, of a last snout, before being ushered back into the interview room. Constable Fox was looking very tired indeed. Sergeant Darbyshire, twenty years his senior, looked fresh as a daisy.

I asked them if they had any news about Sophie.

'She's had the tongue sewn back on and she's come round safely from the anaesthetic. It's far too early yet to know whether everything will heal satisfactorily and she'll regain the full use of her tongue,' said Darbyshire.

'Rather important in her line of work,' smirked the egregious Fox, and his superior gave him another of his baleful stares before asking me to go through my story yet again. I was more fluent this time, and made a point of looking them both in the eye.

'How much did she charge?' asked Fox at one point, so I guessed he'd seen, or heard about, the à la carte menu on offer at Sophie's. I reeled off the prices accordingly.

'Quite reasonable, really,' said Constable Fox, and I suddenly found myself warming to him.

'We've had forensic and the fingerprint boys in there,' said Darbyshire, 'and your dabs are all over the place. On the phone, on the fridge . . .'

'Well, they would be, wouldn't they?' I said. 'Doesn't that fit in with what I've been telling you?'

'Yes, but they were also on the window sill and the window was open. Why was that?'

Think carefully, Benson, I told myself.

'You mean did I throw the knife, or whatever it was, out there, I suppose?'

'I'm not supposing anything. I just want an answer.'

'Well, after I'd seen what had happened to Sophie and put her tongue in the glass I didn't feel too bright. In fact I thought I was going to throw up. So I rushed to the window and opened it and after a few deep breaths I felt a bit better.' I was rather proud of this. I'd come within an ace of saying I'd been sick, and they would no doubt be conducting a careful search of the tiny courtyard outside the basement flat.

I was asked to describe Henrietta in as much detail as I could – 'Ugly cow with a voice like Princess Margaret' didn't seem to be detailed enough – and I mentioned Jim, who I assumed to be the ponce.

'From the fact that you're asking me to describe Henrietta, I take it that you found the flat abandoned by the time you got there?' I enquired.

Darbyshire nodded wearily. 'I'm afraid so. These cases can be a bugger. The flats are usually sublet and sublet and sublet, and by the time you get to the landlord it turns out that he has no idea who his tenants were or what his flat was being used for.' He chuckled. 'You may remember that Norman Lamont of blessed memory had a similar problem.'

Fox again asked if I thought Sophie was into S and M. I was at least relieved that he was no longer asking if I was fond of hurting people myself. Presumably Kim had given me a clean bill of health on the sexual kink front when the policewoman came round. I told him that as far as I could see there were no chains, cages, hoods or whips.

'What does the fact that Sophie's tongue was cut out suggest to you?' Darbyshire asked in a friendlier manner.

I was wondering when he'd get round to that. 'Well, it could have been a particularly cruel form of mutilation by some pervert they were unlucky enough to let into the flat. Or possibly someone was trying to stop her talking. Literally in the short term. But more probably as a warning, if she blabbed about whatever it was she had to blab about.'

'Right,' said Darbyshire. 'Now you were the last person to see her. Did she try to communicate anything to you in the cab?'

Again, I was tempted to tell him about the tape, but my duty lay with Sophie.

'There was something,' I said. 'Just before we got to the hospital she scribbled a few letters on a bank slip. They spelled "cough".'

Darbyshire produced it from a file. They'd obviously been through my wallet very thoroughly.

'Cough?' said Darbyshire. 'Mean anything to you?'

'Perhaps her attacker had a cough.'

'Who knows?' he said. He suddenly looked old and tired and his investigation had hardly started.

'Can I go home now?' I asked. 'And if I can't, is there any chance of giving Kim a ring? She'll be getting worried.'

Darbyshire thought for a few seconds. 'You've been here almost six hours. We have to have a review soon to decide whether we can keep you any longer. No, you might as well go. On police bail, mind.'

There were forms to fill in, and I had to pledge that I would report to Belgravia police station in a month's time. My belongings were returned, I signed for them, and Darbyshire himself showed me out of the side door, taking the opportunity to have a few puffs on his pipe. 'They even complain about my tobacco in the smoking room,' he grumbled cheerfully. I wasn't surprised. It smelt like smouldering old socks, and his pipe made grotesque bubbling noises whenever he took a drag.

'You'll give me a ring if anything occurs to you,' he asked, and feeling a heel, I promised him I would.

'And give my regards to your wife. WPC Garrett spoke very highly of her. I gather that the test-tube baby treatment has been getting you both down badly. I hope it works out for you.'

I was very touched.

'If I were you, Mr Benson,' he added, like a stern housemaster, 'I'd give the massage parlours a miss in future.'

I promised him I would and caught a cab back home.

Kim was waiting up for me and gave me a hug as I came through the door.

'I must try getting arrested more often,' I said. 'I thought you'd have my bags packed and left on the doorstep.'

'You're a whoremongering bastard, Will Benson, but I can't altogether blame you. I'm sorry for the last few months, and especially for the last week. I think I've been through a process of grieving. I was so convinced that it wouldn't work I was mourning for those two tiny embryos we saw on the wall. And when you rang and were obviously in trouble I suddenly realized that if we don't have kids we'll still have each other. You were right about stopping the treatment. If it doesn't work this time we should call it a day and try to get on with our lives.'

I kissed her nose and her mouth and her eyes, and hugged her hard, and then we went into the sitting room. She poured a large malt for me and had a small one herself, her first alcoholic drink for over a year.

'And now,' she said, raising her glass. 'You've got some explaining to do, Benson.'

So I told her the tale, of my panicky impotence while trying to produce a sperm sample, and my visit to Sophie.

'She was really nice,' I said, realizing that if the truth wasn't told now it would never be. 'I should have left after I'd got the spunk safely into the jar but she offered me a full personal service on the house, and I'm afraid I accepted.'

'Full personal service?' said Kim. 'Does that mean what I think it means?'

'I'm afraid so,' I said.

'And did you enjoy it?'

'Yes, very much. Though I soon started feeling guilty—'

'But not guilty enough to prevent you paying an entirely unnecessary second visit,' said Kim, sounding worryingly severe.

'I was lonely, Kim. And pissed off. And wondering what the hell was going to happen to us.'

'It's all right, Will,' she said. There were moments when she seemed to glow with grace. 'But you'd better not even think of doing it again.'

'Anyway,' she continued, 'you went back today and found her with her tongue cut out. Christ, the poor cow. Any idea how she is?'

'She seems to be OK; though it's too early to know whether the tongue will heal properly again.'

'God, it must have been grisly. How did you bring yourself to pick it up.'

'Tried not to look,' I said, and told her the rest of the story, and the fact that I was only out on bail, though the police seemed to believe I was innocent. 'Largely thanks to you, I gather. Apparently you made a big hit with the WPC.'

'She was nice, she really was. I said they were mad to think it was you, great soft 'aporth that you are. I told her I could understand why you'd gone to the massage parlour because things were so miserable at home, and I had a bit of a weep and told her all about the IVF, then felt a lot better. Come on, let's go to bed. I can't offer the full personal service just in case Bill and Ben are still hanging on in there but would you settle for a quick ... how do they put it?'

'A reverse massage,' I said. 'And a spot of mutual oral relief.'

'You're on.'

Afterwards, Kim gave me one of her sly, crooked grins and said she felt very relieved indeed. I was too, but Sophie was on my mind.

'How do you feel about a quick visit to the St Thomas's Casualty Department?' I said.

'What, at this time? It's almost one in the morning.'

I reminded her about the tape and Sophie's insistence on not telling the police.

'You feel you owe her, don't you?' asked Kim. 'You're emotionally involved?' It didn't sound like a rebuke.

'I suppose I do. She gave me back some badly needed self-confidence, and handing me the tape was an act of trust. I don't think we can just leave it to moulder in a hospital pot plant. The trouble is the police are probably keeping an eye on the place and it would look very suspicious if it was discovered I'd gone creeping back. They'd probably suspect I'd gone to finish her off properly. And I don't fancy spending the rest of the night in a cell.'

'Right, let's go,' said Kim at once.

On the short journey to St Thomas's, Kim drove and I explained where the potted palm was. 'You can't miss it,' I said. 'One of the leaves is dead and they haven't bothered to prune it.'

I stopped the car fifty yards from the entrance to the Accident and Emergency Department and said I'd cruise around and return every five minutes or so to see if she was back.

'Right,' she said. 'And if anyone asks me what's wrong, I'll tell them I've got a bit of a frog in my throat.'

'Just been giving Charles Aznavour a blow-job,' we both shouted with childish glee. It was an old Joe Johnson gag that had become a private catchphrase.

Kim climbed out of the car, and I drove slowly over Westminster Bridge, round Parliament Square and back over the bridge again. Kim was standing outside the hospital by the time I returned.

'Got it. No trouble at all,' she said triumphantly. 'There were a lot of very noisy drunks having a barney at the reception desk, and I don't think anyone saw me.'

Back home, I put the tape in the hi-fi and Kim poured more malt whiskies. We sat back to listen, Kim with a notebook on her knee. Her shorthand had always been more reliable than mine.

But it didn't seem that notes were going to be necessary. The tape, an ordinary TDK90, appeared to have been made by Sophie for her own, and possibly her clients' enjoyment. Excellent it was too. Tina Turner's 'Private Dancer', Harry Nilsson's 'Without You', Milly Jackson's magnificent 'Loving Arms', Bowie's 'Lady Grinning Soul'. Just the stuff to help a slow reverse massage go with an erotic glow. Then came a song I hadn't heard since my former girlfriend Cathy destroyed my record collection. Tym Church's haunting psychedelic classic 'So Many Miles From Home', an eerie, spaced-out anthem of almost unbearable loneliness. It had been the last track on his first solo album.

'*Oh pleeeeaaasseee help me find my way home,*' sang Tym, over and over again in an off-key cry of terrible hurt, crashing out broken chords on his acoustic guitar.

'Blimey,' said Kim who had never heard it before. 'That guy's either mad or a genius.' The song ended in midphrase with a clearly audible bump. Tym falling off his chair in a fog of Mandrax, presumably. There were a few seconds of silence and then, startlingly, Sophie's voice came over the speakers.

'*Poor old Tym, it always gives me goose bumps that one,*' she said. '*It's Sophie here, and I hope whoever's listening to this enjoyed the songs. There will be some more along in a moment. By then, however, you may not feel like listening. If you ever knew me, you may feel that you never really knew me at all. I'm not sure that I know myself. But the fact is, I'm in need of money, a lot of money, so I've decided to put the bite on some of my punters.*

'*Of course, I don't often know who my punters are. They probably give a false name, or just their Christian name, and I never see or hear from then again. But some of them I do know, and unfortunately you can only betray those you know. So this is a confession of my plans for betrayal. I've got very good black and white photographs of all kinds of interesting things. If you've been to my place recently you may have wondered why the recessed spotlight above the bed didn't seem to be working for a while. Well, there was a camera in the socket and a lead coming down inside the wall, with a switch just behind the bed.*

'So who am I in a position to blackmail? Well, there's poor Tym of course, my darling Tym. I hate the idea of doing it to him, but he's still surprisingly rich, and publicity is the last thing he could bear. Christ, I'm a bitch, aren't I? There was a pause and what sounded like a sob. *'I deserve anything that's coming to me, I really do,'* said Sophie, but after a few seconds of snuffling she continued in the same quiet and controlled voice.

'Then there's David, David Welch, the headmaster of the prep school. And Bill Hutchinson, who everyone's heard of. A surprise that one, I think you'll agree. And the Reverend Hugh McAlistair. And, last but not least, that oily toerag Duncan Adamson.

'So there they are, my line-up of victims. But what's the point of this tape you may be asking? Well, I wanted to leave some record of what I'm up to. And if anything does happen to me, I'd like someone to know what may have been the reason. I'd give it to Henrietta, but she doesn't approve of all this, and the worry would probably kill her. So it will almost certainly be one of my punters who's listening now, if I manage to pass it on at all, and I'm sorry, really sorry to have dragged you into this mess. So what do you do now? Well, there's three options. You can forget all about it. I may well be dead, and you can then destroy the tape.

'Secondly, you could take it to the police, but I'd much rather you didn't. It would cause several fine people a great deal of unnecessary grief. You're probably saying, "She can bloody talk," but I'm trying to be a blackmailer with at least a touch of honour. I'm playing straight. One payment only, a big one admittedly, and the punters I'm putting the bite on will get the the prints and the negatives, and never hear from me again. I'll miss some of them a lot and I hate to think about what they'll think of me. But it's got to be done. But it wouldn't be fair to drag them into what might turn out to be a murder investigation. I'm pretty sure it would send poor Tym back to the bin for a

start. But he can be so weird sometimes I can't entirely rule him out as a potential threat.

'The third choice is the difficult one, and it's the one I'd like you to make. If I have been killed or so badly injured I can't do anything about it myself, I'd like justice to be done. You may not feel I deserve justice, and Christ knows I probably don't, but if you still feel a slight spark of affection for me after hearing this, see what you can find out. Try not to put yourself in danger, try not to upset the innocent ones, and if you do find out what's happened, I leave you to decide what form justice should take. If you can get the police to deal with whoever's had a go at me without dragging in the others, fine. Or you may have your own ideas. It's up to you now. God bless and thanks for listening. I'll leave you with the music now. There's nothing else to say.'

There were a couple of seconds' silence and then Fauré's *Requiem* came on, beautiful and chilling. We sat without speaking for a few minutes, listening to the music.

'Blimey,' said Kim at last. 'The voice of the woman who lost her tongue. Now what do we do?'

Thursday 27 July

The lunatic, the lover and the poet,
Are of imagination all compact
A Midsummer Night's Dream

We'd sat up late, wondering how we should handle
Sophie's disturbing legacy, and collapsed, exhausted, into
bed at 3 a.m. The alarm clock seemed to go off almost as
soon as my head had touched the pillow and after switch-
ing it off I lay there for a few moments feeling spaced out
and mentally blank. Then the memory of Sophie came
flooding back. Last night, the idea of tracking down her
mutilator had seemed not only possible but also rather
exciting. This morning it seemed like an exceptionally
daunting and potentially hazardous undertaking. Perhaps
we should take Sophie's first option: destroy the tape and
forget all about it. I put this to Kim, who was curled up
and pretending the alarm hadn't gone off. She jerked
herself into a sitting position as soon as she got my drift
and told me, forcefully, not to be such a wimp.

'Right,' I said wimpishly. 'I'll go and make the tea.'

We drank it in bed together, Kim breezily determined to
press ahead. 'It's just what I need to take my mind off
things,' she said.

'Yes, but you're supposed to be taking it easy. You can't
get involved in any rough stuff, if there is any. Some of
those guys might turn nasty if we come bearing messages
from Sophie.'

'We'll see,' she said. 'I think constantly worrying about

whether the IVF is going to work is more destructive than forgetting all about it until next week. We'll know one way or another then. And I can certainly do some digging around today into the five men Sophie mentions on the tape. Thursdays are always pretty quiet at the office. I'll make a few calls in the privacy of the boardroom. The main thing is we're going to have to see all five of them, get an idea of what they're like and see if they've got an alibi. We know more or less exactly what time the attack took place – about 3.30 p.m.'

'But as far as I know, Tym Church is a recluse who hasn't been seen for years. Though come to think of it, I may have got a glimpse of him on my first visit to Sophie.' I explained about the keyhole view of the old hippy in the mirrored shades and afghan coat. 'I suppose he probably must live somewhere locally. And God knows how we find the headmaster and the vicar.'

'Leave that to me,' said Kim. 'I'm the brains in this organization.'

'I just hope Sophie doesn't have a change of heart when she realizes what's happened to her,' I said. 'Presumably the police will be trying to interview her today. She may not be able to talk but she'll be able to write down answers to questions and shake or nod her head. If she lets the police know I've got the tape, I'm going to be in all kinds of shit with Sergeant Darbyshire.'

'Do you really think she'd tell him, Will?'

'No, not really. I wonder how she is. Should we try phoning the hospital?'

'They're usually pretty guarded if they don't know who's calling. And they're not likely to give you much information if you tell them who you are, not after yesterday's runner. Why don't you phone your sergeant? It would be another chance to demonstrate your gleaming innocence and concern, and he'll probably have much more detailed information than the hospital will give you over the phone.'

When I got through to the incident room Darbyshire answered the phone himself and sounded touchingly pleased to hear from me.

'Ah, Mr Benson, good night's sleep I hope? And all well with your wife?'

'She took it all amazingly well,' I said.

'Delighted to hear it. And have you thought of anything that might help with the investigation?' So that was why he was being so insufferably affable.

'I'm afraid not. I was just phoning to find out if there was any news on Sophie.'

'It's bad, I'm afraid. She's gone into a coma and they suspect it's a subdural haematoma: the kind of thing boxers get when they take an especially punishing blow to the head. They seem groggy for a while, and everyone thinks they're just a bit punchy after the fight, but then they suddenly go into a coma, sometimes up to twenty-four hours later. And, as you must know, some of them never come out of it.'

I did indeed. No doubt about it, boxing is a disgusting sport and ought to be banned. The only trouble being that I love it and experience a deeply worrying thrill of pleasure when a contender finally crumples under a fusillade of punches. Kim hates me watching it and calls me a blood-thirsty sadist.

'Is there anything they can do?'

'They'll be carrying out tests and scans this morning. Apparently if there's a lot of blood or a partially formed clot building up pressure on the brain they'll cut a hole in her skull to remove it.'

'Is there any chance of Sophie coming out of all this normal? I mean, will she be permanently brain-damaged?'

'It's impossible to tell. She may be fine. She may come out of it in a "persistent vegetative state". Or she may not survive at all.'

'In which case,' I said, 'this would turn into a murder

inquiry. And with me, presumably, as your only suspect to date.'

'We've got to keep you in the frame, though as you'll have guessed by now I think it's more likely that you're the Good Samaritan in all this.'

'Thank you for that,' I said.

'We do however have to make further inquiries about you. One of my detective constables will be calling on, er, Botticelli Publications later today to speak to your employer.'

'Oh Christ!' I said. 'I've only just started there. It's not going to make a good impression, is it?'

'I'd have thought a visit to a prostitute would have earned you Brownie points in an organization like that,' said Darbyshire primly. Not for the first time I felt sullied by my present occupation. I had a lot of time for Darbyshire and didn't like to hear his obvious disapproval coming down the line.

'I can see you'll have to talk to my present boss. Could I also ask you to have a word with the editor of *Theatre World*, where I worked until a few weeks ago. He knows me much better and,' I felt suddenly choked, 'he's been something of a father figure to me.'

'Your own parents being dead, as I recall. Yes, I'll do that, Mr Benson. And I want a strict undertaking from you in return that if anything else occurs to you, however trivial, you'll let us know.'

'Right, absolutely,' I said, and hoped he'd put my strained voice down to gratitude or grief. 'And still no sign of Henrietta or Jim the pimp or whatever he is?' I asked.

'Mr Benson, you're still a suspect in this investigation, not a colleague,' he said severely.

'Yes, of course. Sorry,' I said. 'I'll keep in touch.'

We rang off and I gazed forlornly at Kim, who'd been listening. I told her the bad news about Sophie and added that Darbyshire was going to be incandescent if he found out I'd been holding out on him about the tape.

'I can see that. What do you want to do?'

'I still feel my first duty is to Sophie. And she was absolutely insistent that we shouldn't go to the police even if she were dead. I suggest a compromise. If she does die or is left badly brain-damaged we'll get the tape to the police anonymously. If she turns out to be OK, we'll see what she has to say.'

'And in the meantime?' said Kim.

'We'll find out what we can. As discreetly as possible.'

She gave me a warm kiss of approval. We drank another cup of tea and I decided I'd better get off to work sharpish in the hope of having a word with Mr Wintour before the filth arrived. I remembered how keen he'd been about the good name of Botticelli Publications and staying within the strict letter of the law. I might be coming home in a couple of hours clutching my P45. It would leave us with some hefty debts, but my chief feeling was one of anticipated relief. Now that we'd decided to call it a day with the IVF treatment I wanted a job that let you keep your self-respect. I mentioned this to Kim. She said the sooner I left *Wankers' World*, the happier she'd be.

The Northern Line was shut down because of a suspect package and by the time I'd got a bus to Borough I was late for work yet again. Daphne greeted me with wide eyes and the news that a policeman had left the premises just ten minutes earlier. 'Mr Wintour wants to see you at once,' she said, and I was only surprised she didn't add a schoolgirlish 'ooo-er'. 'What's it all about, Will?' she asked, her fat face quivering with curiosity.

'I'll tell you later,' I promised. 'It's just possible that I might be about to get the sack.'

I walked down the corridor and saw Brian glowering behind his desk, absolutely desperate to know what was going on. I mimed cutting my own throat and walked straight on, not so much apprehensive as curious to know how Wintour would react. After hours with the police the night before, this interview seemed entirely unintimidating. I was genuinely intrigued to know if the boss would be able to retain his amiable urbanity in the face of an employee suspected of mutilating a prostitute.

I knocked on the door and was told to come in. Wintour was busy at his espresso machine wearing another of his terrifying home knits. This one was a baggy, banana yellow cardigan with leather buttons and capacious pockets. He beamed at me as if anticipating a game of chess with an old friend.

'Delighted to see you, do make yourself comfortable,' he said, gesturing to one of the chintz-covered chairs by the log fire. 'Your usual double espresso, with the grappa?' he said, and I nodded. 'Perhaps,' he added, 'in view of the circumstances, a small shot of grappa in the coffee and a large one in a glass.'

'That sounds terrific,' I said. 'As I gather you've heard, I've had quite a night.'

'My dear chap, my dear chap . . .' he said.

I was pleased to see he was having a hefty shot of the grappa himself. 'Did they tell you what this was all about?' I asked.

'A little. The detective constable told me that a prostitute had been mutilated yesterday and that you had taken her to hospital. They wanted confirmation that you worked here, and asked my views on your character. I told them that I had absolutely no complaints about your work and that though I knew your private life was difficult at the moment, you struck me as being someone who was coping with it all very courageously.'

'Thank you,' I said, and meant it. 'Although I'm still on police bail I get the impression that Detective Sergeant Darbyshire, who is leading the investigation, is almost satisfied that I'm innocent. I also get the impression that they've got very few leads. But it was going to see Sophie, the prostitute, which I was worried might affect your regard for me as an employee.'

'Not at all, not at all,' he said. 'It is hardly for someone in my line of business to cast the first stone.'

'Well, I suppose the fact that I work here did have something to do with it,' I said, and explained about sperm samples and the dwindling efficacy of girlie mags as an aid to masturbation. I found myself telling him the whole story, including the dreadful discovery of Sophie and the bad news I'd heard from Darbyshire that morning, in fact everything apart from the tape.

When I'd finished, Wintour recharged our grappa glasses and raised his in a toast of absolution. 'You've behaved with honour,' he said. 'Please accept both my commiserations and my congratulations.'

'I half expected to be picking up my P45.'

'I hope that you'll come to know me better than to expect such shabby behaviour. Let's hope that Sophie makes a full recovery. And that they find the sadistic bastard who did it. Anyway, how are you finding Botty Pubs? Settling in all right?'

'Fine,' I said. 'I'm beginning to get the hang of it, though I can't say my sexual fantasies flow with quite the vim of Linda's. And I'm afraid I'm having very little luck getting the kind of showbiz interview you were hoping for. I've been turned down by Melvyn Bragg, Kenneth Branagh, David Puttnam, Jeremy Beadle and Derek Jacobi so far. And Hugh Grant thought I was taking the piss.'

'Ah well, keep plugging away,' said Wintour. 'I've always had a hunch that' – he named a distinguished director – 'might be the kind of chap who bought our magazines on the sly. You might give him a try.'

'Right,' I said. Phoning up famous people and asking them for an interview was proving to be an unexpected perk of the job once I'd stopped feeling embarrassed about rejection. I always announced initially that I worked for Botticelli Fine Art Publications and the sonorous name lulled them into a false sense of security. When I finally got round to telling them that the interview would actually be appearing in *Luv Bytes* their mixture of incredulity, self-righteousness and injured pride was a thing of beauty and a joy for ever. What my furious interview targets didn't know was that I'd got all their spluttering indignation down on tape, a trick I'd learnt from a former nefarious colleague at *Theatre World*. I had a hunch that the verbatim transcripts of their replies would make an entertaining series which might get *Luv Bytes* a bit of welcome attention beyond the dirty mac brigade. But so far only Linda knew what I was up to, and she was a dab hand at slipping me particularly impertinent questions scribbled down on a bit of paper just as the celebs seemed to be running out of intemperate steam. You haven't really lived until you've asked a furious Noel Edmonds whether he ever worries about the size of his penis.

I declined the offer of yet another coffee and grappa and said I'd better get back to my desk. 'I was on the skive yesterday afternoon, so I'd better make up for lost time,' I said. 'Thanks for being so understanding.' He gave me an almost priestly gesture of dismissal and I went back to editorial. Brian was moody because I hadn't told him what was going on, and didn't even look up when I entered. Linda, to whom I sat opposite, gave me a wink.

'He was in a filthy temper yesterday because you'd taken the afternoon off,' she whispered. Mercifully Brian was out of earshot at the lightbox. 'When he heard from Daphne that the police had been round and you'd been summoned to see Wintour he was almost beside him. If there's one thing Bri can't stand, it's a secret he's not party to. And, come to think of it, I'm pretty curious myself.'

'He was here all afternoon, was he, looking shirty?'

'I'll say. Simmering like a nuclear reactor on the brink of meltdown. He said he was sure you were up to something and holding out on him. What is going on, anyway, you secretive sod?'

'I'd better go and make my peace with him,' I said. 'I'll explain over lunch.

I went over to Brian who was gazing at trannies. At first, childishly, he pretended not to notice I was there.

'Come on, Brian. I'm sorry I did a bunk yesterday afternoon, and I'll explain everything at lunchtime. Can we be friends again?'

At last he looked up from the pictures and gave a sheepish grin.

'Yeah, of course,' he said. 'You're not off down to the nick, then?'

'No, at least not yet. It's rather a long tale. Can it wait till lunch?'

'Yeah,' he said, offering me a bag of aniseed twist and grinning. 'I'll look forward to it. You're not in real trouble, are you? Wintour's not going to chuck you out?'

He seemed genuinely concerned. I thought of Brian, surrounded by all his high-tech computer equipment, with only Linda and the sour Janice Cockett for company, and realized that he probably would be sorry to see me go. After Wintour's earlier sympathy, I began to feel rather fond of Botticelli Publications.

'No, he was really nice,' I said. 'I've not got the sack yet.'

'Just as well,' said Brian. 'Janice is off for a few days. She's not back until Tuesday. So do you think you'll be able to handle the subbing side of things till then? There's a whole heap of *Luv Bytes* copy from freelances we need to get into shape.'

'That will be great,' I said. The idea of checking through other people's copy and writing headlines seemed a doddle compared to churning out sexual fantasies and saucy captions. My powers of invention were flagging badly.

I returned to my desk, and settled down to some spendidly dull articles about aftershaves and sports cars and the *Luv Bytes* restaurant column. Not a throbbing cock, a sopping slit or a massive tit anywhere. Kim phoned at noon to find out how things had gone with Wintour. She didn't seem as pleased as I was, but cheered up when I told her I was having a few days off on the writing front. 'I keep thinking you're writing about us,' she said, 'or us as we used to be. It gives me the creeps.'

'It gives me the creeps sometimes,' I said. 'Still, it was lovely last night. Thanks for that.'

'My pleasure,' she said. 'Now, I don't want to say too much over the phone, Will, but I've had a reasonably productive morning. I think I may have tracked down TC.'

'Blimey, that's good work.'

Though Sophie evidently knew otherwise, Tym Church had to all intents and purposes disappeared off the face of the earth. He was often mentioned in the rock magazines I read, and new bands were constantly citing him as a major influence, but there had been no confirmed information about him for years, still less an interview with the man of mystery himself. On the other hand, rumours, from the plausible to the outrageous, flourished. One of these claimed he'd become a Hare Krishna, another that he was an air traffic controller at Heathrow airport, and one, which struck me as being pretty likely after listening to his later, disturbing work, that he was a long-term inmate in a mental institution. (Though presumably by now he would be dossing down near Waterloo Station on one of the Government's 'care in the community' schemes.)

'So where did you find your missing necklace?' I asked Kim. Discreet, eh? Why the secret services didn't recruit me when I was at Oxford I'll never know.

'You're not to start getting jealous?' said Kim. 'I phoned Colin.' Kim had had a few nights of passion with Colin shortly before seeing the error of her ways and taking up with me. Still, it was four years ago now. He was prospering on a Fleet Street tabloid these days.

'That's cool,' I said. 'I can handle that.'

'I suddenly remembered that his paper did a big "Where Are They Now?" series a few weeks ago. Colin put me on to the bloke that did it, and he was incredibly helpful. Probably because I promised him a blow job.'

'You what?' I squealed.

'Just testing, Will, just testing. Anyway, this chap – Paul Gent, he's called – had, as it happened, tried to run a feature on Church for the series. He'd phoned everyone called Church in the Bury St Edmunds phone directory. It's where Tym comes from, apparently, and where he started his first band.'

'That's right. The Moonstruck. A rhythm and blues outfit who were the first in Britain to go psychedelic.'

'Spare me the Trivial Pursuit stuff,' said Kim. 'And you're not supposed to be saying much, remember.'

'Right. Sorry,' I muttered.

'Anyway, on about the fifteenth call this guy struck lucky. He got through to a woman who claimed she was Tym's Auntie Maisie. She said she hadn't seen him for some time but he phoned every week and never forgot her birthday. Paul thought she sounded a bit gaga but when he asked her if she had Tym's address she came straight out with it.'

'Various questions occur,' I said.

'Right, I'll do my best to put you in the picture without you having to say too much. Well, Paul went round to Tym's place that evening. Apparently he lives in Dolphin Square, that huge block of thirties flats on the Embankment. Number sixteen, Hamilton House, if you've got a pen handy.'

'Got it,' I said.

'Good. There's a concierge's desk at the main entrance to Dolphin Square but you can also get to the flats through the gardens. There's a sign saying Residents Only but no one will stop you if you look as if you know where you're going. Apparently Hamilton House is the third entrance on the left as you go in. So Paul found the flat and rang the bell persistently. There was no answer for ages but eventually a voice told him to piss off. Then Paul said he had a message from Auntie Maisie and Tym let him in at once.'

'Gosh, what a tale. About your necklace, I mean. Just fancy it turning up there. But why . . .?' I couldn't think of any way of sustaining this fiction about Kim's missing jewellery, but mercifully she anticipated me.

'Why haven't we read or heard anything about the great discovery, you mean? Well, Paul seems to be that rare thing, a tabloid journalist of honour. He said Tym was completely out of it, just raving. For about thirty seconds he seemed genuinely interested to hear about his aunt, but when Paul told him she was fine and he was actually a journalist, Tym started spouting garbage and waving his arms in the air. He was so disturbed that Paul felt guilty about uncovering him, and after trying in vain to calm him down he left and promised Tym he'd hear nothing more from him. He's a bit of a fan, like you, and was very reluctant to give me any information until I promised we had Tym's best interests at heart and weren't planning to publish anything. I think you should get round there straight after work tonight.'

'Right,' I said. 'So I'll see you outside the cinema at about six.'

'You what?' said Kim. God, she could be slow sometimes. 'Oh, yeah,' she added after a moment's silence. 'I can see that it might be useful for you to have a good excuse for leaving promptly. Good luck.'

'Sounds like good news,' said Linda when I'd put the phone down.

'Yeah. Kim thought she'd lost the opal necklace her grandmother left her. It's quite valuable and she's been searching everywhere for it. It turns out that one of her kid brothers found it in her jewel box and accidentally broke the string. He's finally got round to confessing all to Kim's mum. He hid all the jewels at the back of the ice box in our fridge.'

'Kids,' said Linda ruefully. 'Who'd have 'em.' We grinned at each other in a moment of warm complicity.

Brian, positively pink with curiosity, insisted on an early lunch at the Pride of the Borough. I was rather dreading telling him about Sophie: if he made any of his cheap cracks on the subject of her injuries, I'd probably hit him. But as the three of us settled down to our drinks and waited for the sinfully delicious All Day English Breakfast to arrive, I realized again I'd done him an injustice. The obscenity and the fake northernisms were a shield he used to cover his loneliness and hurt; ways of preventing people getting too close. It's true that my account of my first visit to Sophie was greeted with prurient curiosity, but both he and Linda listened in stunned silence when I told them about her mutilation.

'Eeeh, the poor lass,' he said in his fake Yorkshire, and for once it seemed touching rather than tiresome. 'You'd think she'd have had some form of protection, some back-up. Those girls must be dreadfully at risk.'

'Fucking men,' said Linda, with unusual bitterness.

'We're not all bastards,' said Brian gently. 'If it hadn't been for Will, God knows what would have happened to Sophie. Have you heard how she is, by the way?'

'In a coma,' I said bleakly. 'The really serious damage wasn't to her tongue but to her brain. She must have hit her head during the struggle and no one realized she was haemorrhaging until later.'

At this point the huge fry-ups arrived. Neither Brian nor Linda seemed particularly taken with theirs but I'm ashamed to admit I ate all of mine with gusto. Sharing the story seemed to reduce some of the horror.

'So what happens now?' said Brian, returning from the bar with the large Scotches he said we were all in need of. 'Have the police got any leads?'

'Not as far as I know.' I wanted to tell them about the tape. It was the kind of tale Brian would lap up, and with his stocky frame he'd be a useful man to have around when interviewing the suspects, if Kim managed to locate them all. But I was pretty sure both he and Linda would insist on my going to the police, and though my resolve sometimes faltered, I was anxious to obey Sophie's orders.

'But the police believe you didn't do it?' asked Brian.

'I hope so, yes. The chap who's leading the investigation seems a genuinely nice bloke.'

'Good,' said Brian. 'I don't fancy visiting you in chokey. You're all right, Will.'

'Love's young dream,' said Linda mischievously, and Brian blushed. Once again I had the nightmarish thought that he might have a crush on me.

'Oh, fuck off, you disgusting old dyke,' replied Brian in a return to familiar bilious form.

'Charmed, I'm sure,' said Linda with a giggle, an exchange that seemed to give them both a curious pleasure.

We played the Kinks and Blur on the jukebox and Brian told some of his dreadful jokes in a game attempt to lighten the mood. But news of Sophie had clearly cast a pall on the proceedings and it seemed the wrong time for a boozy session, so we soon drifted back to the office. The subbing of innocuous copy had a pleasantly calming effect, and by the time we called it a day I felt in the right frame of mind to confront whatever weirdness Tym had to offer.

About 5.30 I told Brian and Linda I was off to the flicks and caught the Tube to Pimlico. Dolphin Square was less than five minutes' walk from Sophie's flat, very handy indeed for Tym. I was tempted to see if anything was going on at the basement massage parlour, but decided it would only arouse suspicion if I was spotted, so I turned left instead of right, and walked into the immaculately maintained Dolphin Square gardens. There was a scent of wallflowers in the warm evening air, a fountain in the shape of a dolphin splashed soothingly and a few pensioners sat on benches on the lawns. It was a calm private world of its own, like a vast quadrangle of an Oxford college. Surrounded by the thick high walls of the flats, the sound of the traffic on the Embankment was just a faint background hum. Whatever mental state he was in, Tym Church had clearly found a peaceful place of refuge.

I found Hamilton House, climbed the stairs to Number 16, and rang the bell. On the third attempt I kept the button pushed for a full minute.

Eventually I heard footsteps and a slurry voice telling me to bugger off. 'That's not the code, that's not the code!' the voice shouted. 'I'm phoning the porters to have you, to have you, to have you . . .' He seemed unable to complete the sentence, and lapsed into silence.

'Tym, I'm really sorry to disturb you. I've got a message from Sophie,' I shouted.

'I don't believe you,' he shouted back. 'The glitterball goblins are coming for me.'

'I'm not a goblin,' I said. 'Sophie's in trouble. She needs your help.'

'Don't forget the streaming screamers, the feeler-wheelers, the teeming dreamers,' yelled Tym.

'I'll try not to,' I said. 'I really have come from Sophie.' There was a long silence, and then the door slowly opened. Tym Church stood there, though even his greatest fans wouldn't have recognized him from the haunting pictures on his album covers. He had been a psychedelic elf in those days, with wild curly hair and faraway eyes. Thin, pretty, and pathetically vulnerable in his Carnaby Street clobber.

The man in front of me was fat and bald as a coot, huddled into a towelling dressing gown covered in splatters of paint. A cigarette smouldered between his nicotine-stained fingers. But the dead, spaced-out look had left his eyes. For a couple of seconds they were alert, aware, troubled. He must have noticed that I'd noticed because suddenly the life seemed to drain out of them and his stare became terrifyingly blank. In the years before Tym disappeared and he was still giving the occasional incoherent interview, journalists had been very fond of describing that stare.

But the real proof that this was Tym was his left hand. Its back, including the fingers, was entirely covered with a tattoo of a malevolent green snake, its terrifying head raised with red eyes, bared fangs and a darting tongue. A blown-up photograph of the tattooed hand had provided the cover of his last solo LP, *Viper Bite*, released almost a quarter of a century earlier. Its songs had sounded like a man going under for the third time, drowning in nightmares that raised the hairs on the back of the listener's neck. You felt guilty about eavesdropping on such mad, relentless suffering.

'I'm truly sorry to disturb you,' I said. 'But I must talk to you about Sophie.' There was another flicker of life in his eyes.

'What's the matter?' he said in a slow, thick voice. 'I tried ringing this morning and got someone I didn't know. So I put, I put . . .' Once again words seemed to fail him.

'You put the phone down?' I said.

'Yeah, the phone,' he said, as if it were a word he was encountering for the first time.

The police must be picking up the calls, I thought. A WPC hoping to make contact with a punter who might know something.

'Give you a sign, wild lines through the mime time,' said Tym, apropos of nothing.

'Quite,' I said. 'Can I come in?'

I thought Tym would probably shut the door in my face and I was taken aback when he nodded and led the way down the hall.

'My head's a bit done in and the last one was diamonds actually,' he mumbled, stopping off at a surprisingly clean, modern kitchen. 'Do you want some of the black stuff? I'm having one.'

I nodded. I had no idea what the black stuff was but it seemed only polite to have whatever Tym was having. I just hoped it wasn't a particularly explosive psychedelic.

He opened a fridge packed to the gunwales with cans of

draught Guinness. He got two pint glasses out of a cupboard, carefully poured the drinks and handed one to me.

'Tell me about Sophie.' The eyes were focused again. I had a hunch that Tym Church wasn't quite as 'heavily spaced' these days as he sometimes pretended. It was an excellent device for keeping the world at bay.

'It's bad news,' I said. 'I was one of her punters. I went along yesterday afternoon and found her tongue had been cut out.'

'Oh Christ,' said Tym. I prayed the news wasn't going to push him over the edge. 'She brought me back to life,' he said simply.

I told him about taking her to the hospital and the coma. Tears rolled down his pudgy cheeks and he began to sob convulsively. I went over and hugged this strange, gentle, portly man, who'd had quite enough horror in his life already.

'She may pull through,' I said. 'It's too early to say. I'm sorry to have to break the news like this.'

'Why would anyone do it?' he sobbed. 'She was a creature of the light.'

'I don't know,' I said wretchedly.

He took a long swig at his Guinness and sobbed some more, and gradually began to regain control of himself. 'I'm sorry about the waterworks,' he said. 'Thank you for looking after her. Let's go and sit down.'

We progressed further down the surprisingly long corridor. The flat appeared to be huge. Through one open door I glimpsed what looked like a fully functioning recording studio. Another, almost bare, paint-splattered room contained an easel and scores of canvases turned towards the wall. There was a dining room full of beautiful antique furniture, while the living room, where we eventually stopped, was an old hippie's fantasy. The curtains were drawn against the summer light, and the place was dimly lit with candles and table lamps draped with Indian scarves. Joss sticks burned and Ravi Shankar was playing on the stereo. Tym went and sprawled on a nest of cushions on the pine floor and I pulled one across the room for myself and sat opposite him.

'My little refuse,' said Tym. 'No, that's not it. I can't get the right words sometimes. What is it when it's warm and safe?'

'A refuge,' I said.

'Yeah, that's right. Sophie was my refuge, too.'

'How long had you known her?' I asked.

'About three years,' he said. 'Ever since I started to get better. I was callipered for ages.'

'Callipered?'

'You know, when you don't have sex.'

'Celibate.'

'Yeah. Sorry. Though I was callipered too. Callipers on the soul. Irons on the brain. You know . . .' He paused for a moment, and seemed to be looking back across a wilderness of years. 'God, poor Sophie. I hope she makes it through all this.'

'So do I,' I said.

He suddenly looked rattled. 'How did you find me? How do you know who the fuck I am? There was a reporter here the other day. You're not one of them?'

'No, I'm not a reporter,' I said. 'I was once, but I'm just a poor old hack who turns out pornography these days. And I haven't come to interview you: I won't write anything about our meeting. I'm just trying to find out what happened to Sophie. I'd only known her a week but she was kind to me too.'

'Right. That's cool,' said Tym. His accent retained traces of his native Suffolk which went oddly with the old rock slang. 'But you still haven't told me how you found me. I'm a legendary recluse, you know. The fucking Garbo of rock and roll. I'm not even Tym Church any more. I'm Leo Jackson to everyone here.'

'When I found Sophie yesterday, she gave me a cassette

with the names of some of her clients on it. Your name was among them. As Tym Church not Leo Jackson.'

'Yeah, of course Sophie knew who I was,' he said, his voice suddenly thickening with grief. 'I told her everything. But she didn't give you this address, did she? She always promised she'd never give me away. She wasn't into betrayal.'

'No, she didn't,' I said. 'When I listened to the tape I thought I'd never find you. But my wife Kim had a brainwave and got in touch with that reporter who tracked you down.' Tym's dark eyes showed signs of panic. 'Don't worry. He's not going to write about you either. He only divulged your address because Kim persuaded him it was desperately serious. So here I am.'

'OK. Listen, I don't go out much. I'm no good on the streets any more. Would you come with me to visit Sophie?'

'There'd be no point, Tym. She's in a coma. She wouldn't know we were there.'

'Yeah, but we would. We could hold her hand and talk to her. It's a ... a ... oh shit, what is it when there's something you ought to do, you know, not because someone's told you or because you feel like it, but because it's right?'

'A duty,' I said, touched. 'It's all a bit complicated. Because I was the last person to see Sophie, and foolishly ran away when the police turned up at the hospital, I'm under suspicion of attacking her.'

'But you didn't, did you?' said Tym. 'I know you didn't. Vibes, you know.'

'Thanks. But there's more to it than that. Sophie didn't want me to tell the police about the tape. If we're spotted down at the hospital the police will wonder what we're doing there, and they'll certainly be curious to know who you are, and just what your relationship with Sophie was. You wouldn't want to be interviewed by the, um, fuzz, would you?'

'No way,' he said with a shudder. 'Sophie was always fazed by them too. But what's the big deal with this tape? What's on it? Why did she give it to you?'

Take it easy now, I told myself. Don't scare him, but don't give too much away either.

'It's hard to say. As you'll realize, Sophie was suffering from shock and incapable of speech when she gave it to me. It might just have been that she didn't want the police to find it and draw her clients into the investigation.'

'There's more to it than that,' he said. 'Why should she make a tape naming punters?'

'I'll come to that in a minute. Did Sophie ever ask you for money, by threatening to tell people who you were and where you lived? Did she ever blackmail you?'

His whole face went into a sudden spasm of pain. He climbed awkwardly to his feet, grabbed the lapels of my jacket and shook me with astonishing force.

'How can you say that?' he yelled. 'I thought you liked Sophie. She's lying in a coma in hospital and you accuse her of blackmail. You must be some scumbag of a reporter, after all.' I thought he was going to hit me but he suddenly looked defeated and sank back on the cushions.

'I'm sorry,' he said. 'You found her, you took her to hospital. You could be making it all up, but I believe you. Though Sophie would never blackmail anyone.'

'Listen, Tym, this is going to be painful. On the tape Sophie admits she was planning to put the bite on her clients for cash. She names five of them, and you're one of them. And she said she was making the tape in case anything happened to her. Presumably she gave me the tape because she thought she'd been attacked by someone she was blackmailing. He was wearing a mask, but she might have had a pretty good hunch who it was if she'd been to bed with him. Cutting out her tongue seems like a horribly symbolic punishment for a blackmailer.'

'So Sophie thought I might be capable of harming her?' said Tym. 'And of course she was right.'

I thought that Tym was about to confess to the crime. My emotion wasn't relief that I'd managed to track down Sophie's torturer, but a feeling of sick heartache.

'Acid does terrible things to you,' he said. 'I spent several years tripping virtually non-stop, and you can see something of what it did to me. Though you can't actually see the half of it. There were a lot of dolly-rockers in the sixties, groupies and hangers-on and people who thought it would be cool to take trips with me, fuck me and fuck me up. Even when I was trying to get my head together the bastards would just spike my tea. And often the trips turned nasty and sometimes, not often, I got violent. Thank Christ I never hurt anyone badly, but I've hit girls, and tied them up, and made them do things they didn't want to do.

'And one time with Sophie, about three months ago, I had a flashback. I suddenly wasn't in bed with her but with one of the groupies. Every detail came back and I seemed to be reliving it. This girl's face started changing, melting in front of my eyes, dripping like wax down the pillow case. I kept getting bits of her molten flesh on my hands. And I was so terrified and strung out I started shaking her and hitting her to try to bring her back to normal. And of course I was doing this to Sophie. And while I was doing it I was remembering what happened next. The other people in the house heard the girl's screams and came in, dragged me off and locked me in a big dark cupboard for hours on end. The trip went on for ever and all the time I was convinced that I'd killed the girl and was going to be left in the dark for the rest of my life. So when Henrietta, the maid, came in, I was convinced she was the one who was going to lock me up, so I let go of Sophie and went for her.'

'Jesus,' I said.

'She had a gun,' said Tym. 'But in that state I wasn't worried about guns. Henrietta aimed it at me, and then Sophie dived off the bed and hurled her to the ground and told us both not to be fucking idiots. Sophie's face was covered with blood. Suddenly I realized where I was, who she was, and that I wasn't tripping. I just broke down and wept.'

His voice was trembling with emotion. Two and a half decades after the original trip, and months after the terrifying flashback, the acid horrors were still as vivid as ever in his mind.

'Sophie was amazing. She went and washed her face, then told Henrietta to leave us alone. She just held me in her arms and dabbed at her bleeding nose with a Kleenex and asked me to tell her what had happened. I babbled on about the terrors. Very patiently she talked me down. She must have told Henrietta to put off all the other punters. I was with her for hours and we got pissed on champagne. And at five o'clock she walked me home.'

'She's incredible,' I said. 'But I've got to ask a few more questions. Try not to get cross. You're absolutely sure she never asked you for money, or mentioned any photographs? Or did you ever give her money, you know, voluntarily, a really large sum rather than the usual payment?'

'No. I used to offer her extra money in the early days, but she'd never take it. I'd give her flowers, and records and champagne – she loved her champagne – but when I bought her a bit of expensive jewellery once, she was embarrassed. She was sweet about it, and touched, but she said I shouldn't ever do it again. I always got the feeling that however kind and understanding she was, at the end of the day she needed to feel that it was just, you know, a business relationship.'

'I know what you mean,' I said. 'I felt it too, though I only went once. She did her job with great generosity and compassion, but made it quite clear she didn't want to talk about herself.'

'It's a big sadness to me, that. She knows everything about me, and I know nothing about her. Where she lives.

106

Whether she's married. If she has children. Even if she's happy or not.'

'So you've no idea why she should turn to blackmail? Why she suddenly seemed to need a load of extra money?'

'None at all. But listen, I've been thinking. Have you any idea when she made this tape?'

'Not a clue. What difference does it make?'

'It's thinking back to that time when I beat her up. I'd been seeing her for years and I never had flashbacks with her. I think there was something different about her that day. She was strung up. And I saw something on her face I'd never seen before. A look of cunning. It was the look I used to see on some of the hangers-on – when I was together enough to notice – the look that said, poor old Tym, he's completely out of it, let's take him for everything we can get.'

'Perhaps that day she was planning to blackmail you,' I said, 'and it was her face, or her manner that sent you over the edge. She wasn't the Sophie you knew any more. Suddenly she reminded you of the bad times she'd helped you forget in the past.'

'That's about it,' he said. 'And when she saw how badly affected I was I think she must have changed her mind. That's how wonderful she is, you see. I beat her up and instead of taking me for all she can get, which she now had a really good reason to do, she comforts me and gets pissed with me, then forgets all about it. I'm sure that's what happened. When we were drinking that champagne she was high as a kite, even though she must have been hurting. I think it was relief that she'd decided to let me off the hook.'

'It's all supposition of course,' I said.

'It's vibes,' said Tym solemnly. 'I'm rarely wrong about vibes.'

'Right. I've got to ask one last question?'

'Yeah. You want to know if I've got a halibut for the time when that fucker was cutting out Sophie's tongue?'

'You mean an alibi.'

'Right. I won't have one. I don't keep much track of time, and I hardly ever leave this place. When did it happen?'

'About half-three yesterday afternoon.'

'That's a bummer. If it had been lunchtime I'd have been covered. I was drinking with Stan, one of the porters who's always been good to me. We were in the bar by the swimming pool. But they called last orders at three, and after six pints of Guinness I came back here and crashed out.'

'So no alibi, then,' I said. 'Not even a halibut.'

'I'm afraid not.'

But while it was possible to imagine Tym lashing out wildly as the old madness seized his brain, I didn't think any amount of mental disturbance would cause him to cut out a woman's tongue with such depraved efficiency. 'You're sure you didn't see her yesterday and have another flashback?'

'No, I've not had any trouble like that recently. I've been feeling a lot stronger. I've even been doing a lot of work.'

'Recording?' I asked excitedly.

'Yes, I've been writing off and on through the years. Sophie was always nagging at me to get back to it, and Alan out of the Moonstruck comes round quite a lot to help me get it together.'

He walked over to the stereo system and put on a cassette. There was a wash of spacey synthesizers and then suddenly Tym's voice was there, older and rougher than on his early records, but as hauntingly vulnerable as ever. It sent shivers down my spine. He was singing a song about Sophie:

> *Tripping down the nightmare stairs,*
> *I see your face explode in stars,*
> *Cold stone and the old crowd gone mad.*
> *I cried out aloud,*

108

For I felt so alone,
So dark in disguise,
Won't you smile on my eyes,
Won't you hush my tired cries,
Tell comforting lies,
Oh, Sophie, dear nurse of my hurt,
Oh, Sophie, old whore of my heart.

The words stopped, to be replaced by moans and whimpers, first of pain and fear, then of passion, before the song climaxed with a guitar solo which seemed to soar up to the stars. Tym sat on his cushions and cried. I went over to him and whispered meaningless words of comfort.

'I don't suppose you could stay the night?' he asked at last. 'I don't think I can face it on my own.'

'I've got a wife,' I said. 'She's been going through a tough time too, and I can't leave her on her own tonight. But would you like to come and stay with us?'

His face lit up. 'I'd love it,' he said.

'I'd better phone her first.'

He nodded, and said I'd find the phone in the hall. Kim answered on the second ring.

'I was just starting to get worried. How's it going?'

'He's a lovely man. He seemed really weird at first but that's mostly an act he puts on to keep the world at bay. He's got no alibi, but I can't believe he did it. But you can judge for yourself. He doesn't want to spend the night on his own so I said he could come round. I hope you don't mind.'

'Of course not,' said Kim. 'I'd love to meet him. There's just one problem. I know it's ridiculously hot for it, but I suddenly fancied a roast beef dinner. An old hippy like that is sure to be a veggie, isn't he?'

'I'll go and ask.'

Tym said he was particularly fond of roast beef and I passed the good news on to Kim. 'I told you he was a good bloke,' I said smugly.

Tym disappeared to pack his bag and asked me if I wanted to look at his paintings. I'd been expecting tormented abstracts, or studies of rats and insects and the other nightmare creatures that populated many of his songs. So the peaceful still lifes, lovingly naturalistic paintings of the English countryside, were a surprise. The biggest canvas was lying against the far wall of the studio. I turned it round and was confronted by a life-size portrait of Sophie, lying naked on her bed, with a glass of champagne in her hand and a teasing, secretive smile on her face. It was a picture that glowed with sex and affection and gratitude.

Tym came in as I was looking at it. 'What do you think?'

'It's beautiful. You've got her to a tee. The sexiness. The kindness. The hint of remoteness.'

'I painted it from memory,' he said. 'She doesn't know I've been doing it. And when she's better,' he added, in the tone of a man desperately trying to persuade himself that she would get better, 'I'm going to give it to her. Do you think she'll like it?'

'She'll love it,' I said.

As we left the flat, Tym put on the huge afghan coat, mirrored sunglasses and leather hat I'd seen him wearing at Sophie's. I remembered the confidential way he'd whispered in her ear, and her later remark that Tym was very kind and very sad.

'Aren't you going to be hot in that coat?' I asked.

'Yeah. But I like getting up in the gear sometimes. It makes me feel safe.'

We picked up a cab in Lupus Street and made the short journey to Rita Road. The flat smelled deliciously of roast beef and after I'd introduced Tym, he gave Kim a great bear hug.

'It's really kind of you to have me round,' he said. 'A lot of wives might object to having horrible has-been hippies around the house.'

'Don't worry,' she said. 'I'm married to one.'

I went out for booze and Tym said he'd help in the kitchen. I came home to find Kim teaching him how to peel a carrot. He'd never done it before.

As we drank some wine before dinner I asked Tym if he wanted to hear Sophie's tape. He shivered and said he couldn't face it, and I was glad. I didn't fancy listening to it again myself. We ate at the pine table in the kitchen and Tym told us briefly about his 'lost' years, spent in a succession of mental hospitals until he'd begun to get better and moved in with his Aunt Maisie. But she'd become frail herself, and Tym got her into sheltered accommodation in Bury before finally finding the courage to move back to London himself. He seemed uneasy talking about the past and, eager to change the subject, asked Kim and I how we'd met. So we told him about *Theatre World* and the loony actress with the crossbow, Harriet Smythe.

'She's doing really well now,' said Kim. 'They had her at a psychiatric day centre for a few weeks and then she came out and went into *Macbeth the Musical*. And she's still living with her agent Mr Simon. A masochist. It must have given him a big kick being whipped by Lady Macbeth.'

'Sophie gets a few like that,' said Tym. 'She's not very keen on it but a few of them are so pathetically desperate and so grateful when she agrees to give them a caning that she goes along with it.'

It was only 9.45 by the time we'd finished dinner but Tym said he felt knackered, so I took him to the spare room.

'It's nice,' he said. 'She'll like it in here.'

'Who will like it?' I asked.

'Your daughter,' he said. 'You're trying to have children, aren't you?'

'We're having test-tube baby treatment,' I said. 'They put two embryos into Kim last week. She calls them Bill and Ben.'

'Not twins, not boys,' said Tym, his big bald head

shining under the overhead light. 'A little girl.' With his beer gut and his inscrutable smile, he suddenly looked like a benign Buddha.

I was deeply moved but decided not to tell Kim about his prediction. The despair we could just about cope with. It was the awful possibility of hope that tore your guts apart.

She was already in bed when I went into our room.

'He really is lovely, isn't he?' she said. 'I couldn't take my eyes off that terrible tattoo at first but you can't mistake the sweetness of his nature. And his courage. He seems like a man who's come through a storm.'

I undressed and cuddled up next to her and told her about our conversation at Dolphin Square and his song about Sophie.

'God, it would be marvellous if he made a comeback,' she said.

'I dread to think what will happen to him if Sophie doesn't pull through,' I said.

'Just keep praying,' said Kim. 'I am.'

I switched on the radio to listen to *The World Tonight*, the habit of a chronic news junkie, which drove Kim mad. 'And later in the programme we'll be talking to Government Minister Duncan Adamson about his controversial new proposals for violent and recidivist criminals,' said the presenter.

Kim and I sat up with a jerk.

'The oily toerag,' said Kim with a grin. 'He was the one person I was really worried about making contact with. Government Ministers are always hedged around with civil servants and minders and it takes ages to set up a meeting even if you're a journalist. Come on, Will. We're off to Broadcasting House.'

I was half-way into my jeans when I remembered Tym. It didn't seem fair to leave him alone in the house so I dressed as fast as I could and went and knocked gently on his door. He was sitting in the lotus position on the floor. He looked up abstractedly as I came in and told him that one of the names on Sophie's list was appearing live on Radio 4.

'Great!' he said as soon as he'd got the message. 'Can I come too?'

'Yes, of course,' I said. 'But will you be OK? Out on the streets. In public.'

'I'll be fine with you and Kim,' he said. 'Let's get the fuck out of here!' He suddenly looked like one of the Famous Five, off on the trail of the wicked German scientist in Puffin Bay.

I gave Tym my own overcoat – I didn't think Adamson would be very impressed by the afghan number – and we trooped out to the car. Kim, breaking all the embryo factory's rules, was running down the road towards her battered Mini, with Tym and I lumbering along behind, when suddenly the warm night air was rent with a blood-curdling cry that must have been heard in every house in Rita Road.

'The *fucking bastards*!' screamed Kim. 'The no-good, cruel sadistic *pricks*!' She aimed a mighty kick at the offside wheel, then screamed again, in physical rather than mental anguish this time. She was only wearing espadrilles. Our resident's parking permit had run out the day before. She'd been clamped.

'No time to lose,' I said. 'We'll just have to pray for a cab.' I hared off down the road. Tym helped Kim to limp at a slower but still impressive pace. I thought fearfully of the embryos, and then realized that mollycoddling had done no good in the past. In a state of sweaty desperation I stood at the crossroads, where you could usually get a cab. Not a yellow light to be seen. Tym and Kim had caught up with me by now, and we stood there, stamping our feet and growling. Finally Tym decided he'd had enough. A Mercedes stopped at the lights and he went and tapped peremptorily on the windscreen. The driver, with an expression of alarm on his face, opened his window. Faced with Tym in his cowboy hat and mirrored sunglasses I'm not sure I'd have done the same.

'I'm a famous rock star,' said Tym. 'Eric Clapton,' he added shamelessly. 'These two are my manager and my secretary. We've got to get to the BBC for a live broadcast in ten minutes and . . .' he paused for a moment as though inspiration had failed him '. . . and my limo's being mobbed by groupies. Can you give us a lift, man?'

To his eternal credit, the driver, a bespectacled fortyish businessman in a pinstripe suit nodded. We climbed in, Tym in the front, Kim and I in the back.

'You're not Eric Clapton,' said the driver as the lights changed, gesturing at Tym's tattooed hand. 'You're Tym Church. It's a privilege to meet you.' All our jaws dropped. 'I went to see the Moonlight when I was 12,' he continued. 'It was my first rock concert and my dad took me. A Sunday benefit for RELEASE at the old Savile Theatre in Shaftesbury Avenue. The Moonlight were topping the bill, and the Incredible String Band and Fairport Convention were playing support. It was one of the greatest nights of my life. My dad had his fingers stuck in his ears all the way through, but even he liked it.'

'Shit,' said Tym. 'I can just about remember it myself. One of the last shows before I started falling apart. We were really good that night.'

'And how are you?' asked the driver.

'I'm cool, now,' said Tym. 'Thanks for asking. Do you mind if we have the radio on? I'd like to chat but this is really urgent.'

'Sure,' said the old Moonlight fan, as if he picked up reclusive rock stars every day. 'Which station?'

'Radio 4,' said Kim. He turned the nob and we heard the oleaginous Adamson in full flow.

'This seems to us to be a radical and entirely sensible solution to the problems of our over-crowded prisons and the increasing menace of riot,' he said in his patronizingly silky voice.

'And you are absolutely serious about this extraordinary scheme?' asked the interviewer incredulously.

'Yes. We know that prison works, but unfortunately we haven't got the resources to build as many new prisons as we need. So we have purchased the uninhabited Isle of O'Craigie, in the Outer Hebrides, and we intend that all recidivist violent offenders and those found guilty of prison riot will serve their sentences there.'

'What will conditions be like on the island?'

'Oh, tough, very tough,' replied Adamson, sounding as if he were announcing the winning numbers at a Conservative Party raffle.

'And what sort of supervision will the men be under?'

'Minimal supervision. They won't be bothered much by the authorities.'

'How minimal?'

'Part of our aim is to encourage self-sufficiency and a sense of responsibility.' Adamson outlined his plans for a semi-agricultural, self-serving community. The interviewer pointed out that social problems might arise, given the violent history of most of the individuals concerned. Adamson responded, saying he didn't think 'the vast majority of the Great British public will be losing too much sleep over them.'

'If you will forgive me saying so, Minister, the whole idea sounds barbaric. It puts one in mind of Devil's Island. Or an adult version of *Lord of the Flies*. Men seem almost sure to die on O'Craigie.'

The Junior Minister for Crime and Punishment continued to waffle about being tough on crime, but our driver obviously couldn't bear to listen any more so he turned the sound down.

'Sometimes,' said Tym, like a retired major from the shires, 'I wonder what this great country of ours is coming to.'

'He's barking mad,' said Kim.

'The terrible thing,' said our driver, 'is that the *Sun*-reading scum will just love this. It will satisfy all their spiteful appetite for revenge. They'll be putting out videos of the prisoners torturing the nonces next. As filmed by the SAS.'

He drew up outside Broadcasting House and we piled out of the car and thanked him.

'Now what?' I asked. 'Do we go into the reception area and nab him on his way out?'

'There'll be security men to put their oar in if they think we're hassling a government Minister. This is going to have to be a doorstep job,' said Kim.

'If he comes out of this door at all,' I said glumly.

'Look, there's a chauffeur-driven car over there. I bet that's his.' Kim pointed to a black Rover parked outside the Langham Hilton. 'The problem is, he'll probably walk straight past us and get into the car.'

'Three of us ought to be able to slow him down a bit. Provided he's not got any muscle with him,' said Tym.

'He's coming!' said Kim. 'And no minders. Just one woman.'

Adamson came out of the door and stopped on the threshold to light a cigar. Even Ministers have to obey the BBC's smoking ban.

'I think that went very well,' he said to his middle-aged and understandably miserable-looking civil servant.

'Yes, very well, Minister,' she said dully.

Tym seized the initiative. He'd taken off his sunglasses and held his cowboy hat deferentially behind his back. He looked almost respectable. He went over to the Minister and clapped him heartily on the back. Adamson almost jumped out of his skin.

'What a brilliant idea about the prison island,' said Tym. 'My friends and I were listening to you on the radio as we drove past Broadcasting House and we felt we had to stop to offer our warmest congratulations.'

I thought Tym was laying it on far too thick but I'd forgotten just how vain most politicians are.

'Yes, I'm rather pleased with it,' said Adamson, taking another drag on his cigar. He was a plump, pampered man, and his brilliantined hair positively gleamed under the street lights.

'I feel we have a lot in common,' said Tym. 'I bring you a massage from Sophie.'

Impossible to tell if Tym was having one of his verbal short-circuits or whether he'd hit on an inspired combination of words to rattle this sleek model of complacency. Adamson actually dropped his cigar, but recovered in time not to pick it up himself. The civil servant did that.

'Your cigar, Minister,' she said.

'Do you think I'm smoking a cigar that's been on the pavement?' he snapped. He produced a cigar case from his pocket and lit up another Havana.

'What is all this nonsense?' he boomed grandiloquently, but his eyes were flashing furtively between Tym, Kim and myself. 'Who are you, anyway?'

'Friends of Sophie,' I said. 'We need to have a little talk.'

He turned to his PA. 'Jeanette,' he said, all emollient now, 'I know I promised you a lift home, since it was so late, but I think I really must talk to these people. They bring news of someone in my constituency I've been very worried about.'

Jeanette seemed reluctant to leave our little al fresco party. She wasn't buying that constituent rubbish and what employee of the egregious Adamson wouldn't enjoy a nice little chat about massages and girls called Sophie.

'It's quite all right, Minister,' she said. 'I'm very happy to wait. Just as long as you like.'

'Just cut along at once and don't make a fuss,' he said spitefully, then obviously realized that Jeanette already had a juicy tit-bit against him, even if she heard no more, so he came over all soapy again.

'You've had a very long day,' he said, producing a tenner from his wallet. 'For the taxi,' he added, before leaping out into the road and hailing one himself. He even held open the door for her. As the taxi whisked her away, Jeanette looked like a small girl denied a going-home present at the end of a children's party.

117

The clock on All Souls Church said it was 10.45. A comfortable fifteen minutes to last orders.

'Do you want to talk in a civilized fashion over a drink, or out here on the pavement?' I asked.

'I don't want to talk at all,' he said, striding across the road to his waiting car. 'A very good evening to you all.'

'There's just the small matter of the pictures,' I said.

'There are no pictures,' he said. 'I don't know what you're talking about.'

'I'm talking about a Pimlico tart called Sophie and the pictures she blackmailed you with. Fascinating viewing. Amazing depth of focus.'

He was getting very close to his car now so I tried a long shot. There was something about Adamson's prurient interest in punishment that seemed to indciate where his predilections lay, and I remembered Tym's comments earlier in the evening. 'Rather appropriate, isn't it?' I said. 'A prisons Minister like you taking such a keen interest in physical correction.' His face showed that I had scored, as it were, a direct hit. All the bluster went out of him in a moment and he stopped dead in his tracks.

'I think you'd better tell your driver he's going to have to wait a little longer,' said Kim. Adamson went and did just that and we escorted him into the dimly lit bar of the Langham Hilton and found a quiet corner table. A waiter came over and asked what he wanted.

'We'd better make it two each,' said Tym. 'Last orders in a moment.' He ordered two pints of Guinness, I ordered two large malts, and Kim just the one double gin and tonic since she wasn't supposed to be drinking at all.

'And for you, sir?' asked the waiter, looking at Adamson. Needless to say, sir wanted a mineral water. He really was a jerk. Who could face a grilling like the one he was in for without a drop of alcohol inside him?

'Well, now we're all nicely settled,' said Kim, 'what comes first on the agenda?'

Adamson was back in blustering mode again but he

merely sounded desperate. 'This is all quite preposterous. What do you mean by dragging me in here and making these disgraceful allegations about prostitutes and photographs?'

'You've shot your bolt, mate,' said Tym. 'It was quite clear just now that you knew exactly what we were on about.'

'And we'll be needing straightforward answers before we even think about letting you have the remaining prints.' This was a bluff on my part. Knowing Sophie, she'd have returned all the prints and negatives, just as she'd said she would. But she must have done something to annoy someone very much indeed in the past few days. And Adamson obviously couldn't discount the possibility that a few of the pictures might still be in circulation.

'When did you last go to Sophie?' asked Tym, who'd got his sunglasses and cowboy hat back on now and seemed to be enjoying himself enormously.

'I don't know what you're talking about,' said Adamson.

'Well, we might just as well drink up and go home,' said Tym casually. 'We can start sending out the pictures tomorrow.'

'*News of the World*,' said Kim. 'The Chief Whip. Madam Speaker.'

'And the PM of course, don't forget the PM,' I said.

Adamson held very tightly to the sides of his leather armchair. 'How much do you bastards want?' he said. 'She promised there would be one payment and that would be the end of it.'

'How much did she take you for?' I asked.

'Thirty grand,' said Adamson.

She really had needed a lot of money.

'When did you last see her?' repeated Tym.

'I only went once. About three months ago. It wasn't a success. We had our wires crossed. We didn't share the same, er, interests.'

'Gotcha!' said Tym triumphantly. 'Oh yes, Sophie told

me all about you. Turned up and said you were interested in caning. And Sophie felt sorry for you because you began to snivel when she said she wasn't in that line of business. So you let your pants down and she gave you six of the best, but that was just for starters, wasn't it? What you really like is dishing it out and Sophie wasn't going to have any of that, so there was an almighty struggle on the bed. Luckily she's pretty good at looking after herself and before long she had you pinned down and screaming for mercy. Really screaming for mercy because she'd got her fist round your balls and kept twisting 'em.'

'All in the photos,' I lied. 'I saw the full set the other day.'

Adamson had gone very white indeed. 'She returned the negatives and swore there weren't any others. How come you've got them?' If he hadn't been such a creep it might have been possible to feel sorry for him.

'We're asking the questions,' said Kim. 'What we need to know from you is what you were doing at three-thirty yesterday afternoon.'

'What's that got to do with anything?'

'Just tell us what you were doing.'

A look of sly triumph spread over his face.

'If you'd read the papers or watched the television news you'd know very well what I was doing. I was opening the new, privatized maximum security prison on the Isle of Wight.' He fumbled in his briefcase and brought out a copy of the *Daily Mail*.

MINISTER PROMISES STRICT DISCIPLINE AT THE HIGH-TECH SIN BIN said the headline, with a photograph of our man brandishing a pair of handcuffs outside one of the cells. He could never resist the cheap publicity stunt.

'There's no mention of the time here,' said Tym gallantly.

'Unfortunately for you there were scores of reporters and photographers present who will confirm that I was at the Isle of Wight from three to five p.m.,' he said.

'We'll be checking that,' said Kim, but it was clear his

alibi would hold up, or he wouldn't have been looking so pleased with himself.

'Rather convenient that you should have such a solid alibi for the time in question,' I said.

'I don't know what's supposed to have happened at the time in question,' he said.

'Sophie was attacked and had her tongue cut out. She also suffered a serious head injury. She's in a coma and it's still not known whether she'll recover.'

Adamson made a big mistake at this moment. He smirked. Just for a second there was no mistaking his mean, smug pleasure in Sophie's fate. Unfortunately for him, Tym spotted it. He walked very calmly to the Minister, who was sitting at the other side of the table, knelt beside his chair as if about to confide a secret, and grabbed Adamson very hard by the balls. In our quiet corner no one else in the bar could possibly guess what was going on.

'I'd be very quiet if I was you, or I'll be a great deal nastier,' whispered Tym. 'You don't like this, do you? Sophie told me you didn't. Most people who enjoy inflicting pain are cowards. I've been there myself, you see. In fact, I'm enjoying myself now.'

'Let go, please let go,' whimpered the Minister as Tym tightened his grip. Adamson looked as though he was about to be sick.

'Now, will you please apologize for grinning so horribly when you heard what had happened to Sophie?'

'I'm sorry,' croaked Adamson. 'I'm truly sorry. Please let me go.'

Tym seemed reluctant to loosen his grip. There was sweat on his forehead, and his face was contorted with rage.

'Did you arrange to have Sophie mutilated?'

'I didn't. I had nothing whatever to do with it. I swear. On my life.' His last words were a whispered screech of agony. This had gone on long enough.

'Stop it, Tym,' I said. 'You don't want to come down to his level.'

Tym stood up, shaking, his face white. 'I'm sorry,' he said. 'I think I'd better find the gents. I'm not feeling at all well.' Kim stood up and went and held his hand.

'Come on, Tym,' she said gently. 'It's all right. You just got upset. Let's go and find the loos.' She put her arm round his waist and steered him towards the lobby.

'I'm sorry about that,' I said. 'Physical intimidation wasn't part of the plan. It's just that Tym was very fond of Sophie.'

'He's a fucking psychopath,' said the Junior Minister, cupping his crotch in his hands. 'I'm going to have you all for this. I'm phoning the police now. As you must realize, I've got a lot of friends in the Met.' He climbed unsteadily to his feet.

'I shouldn't do that if I were you,' I said. 'You seem to forget that we still have the photographs.'

He sat down again. 'Just who are you anyway? Sophie's ponce?'

'Just tell me in some detail about your relationship with Sophie, and any reasons you can think of why I should believe you didn't arrange to have her so brutally attacked.'

He sighed, and looked longingly at the drinks on the table. I nobly passed over my second glass of malt.

He took a grateful swig, then spluttered as though he wasn't used to raw spirit. But some of the colour came back to his smooth, plump cheeks.

'You know from the paper that I didn't do it myself. And you can hardly believe that someone in my position would take the risk of hiring thugs.'

'I could believe anything of you,' I said.

'But I had no reason to attack her. I thought it was all over. Any further involvement with the wretched woman, even at a remove, would just increase the risk of my being found out. Hiring heavies would have laid me open to blackmail for a second time.'

'How did the blackmail work?'

'I went to Sophie about three months ago as I said. I knew it was a risk, but even politicians have their little peccadilloes.'

'What I can't understand is why you went to Sophie. Why didn't you go to one of those girls who claim they like to be caned?'

'I couldn't take the risk of going to an unknown girl. A colleague gave me Sophie's number. He said he'd been going to her for years and she was one hundred per cent discreet. I didn't tell him that my interests tended to the exotic. I just hoped that the woman would fall in with my plans.'

'Who was he?' I asked.

'You don't expect me to answer that? I'm not going to land a friend in the shit.'

'Fair enough. But when you were blackmailed did you go to this friend and complain that Sophie didn't live up to his recommendation? Did you ask if he'd been blackmailed too?'

'Although distinguished, my friend is not well known to the public. Whereas I,' even now he couldn't resist his little gloat, 'am known to millions. I didn't want to burden him with my problems.'

A top civil servant, probably, I thought. Someone Sophie didn't know enough about for blackmail. And perhaps someone who would have felt no compunction about putting the skids under Adamson if he realized the Junior Minister was about to become a serious liability. Perhaps the Minister himself nursed the faintest suspicion that his friend might have set him up.

'So you went to Sophie, and you had your little misunderstanding, and presumably you went home with your tail between your legs.'

'I wouldn't say that. I marched straight out with my head held high,' he said smugly.

'You didn't apologize, didn't offer any payment?' I said.

'Why should I? I had been disgracefully treated.'

'You tried to force a prostitute into doing something she didn't want to do. Luckily for her, she was physically stronger. I would have thought a certain magnanimity on your part might have been prudent, if nothing else.'

'Why should I be magnanimous to a bitch like that?' he asked.

'Because if you had been magnanimous, she might not have behaved like a "bitch",' I said, remembering Sophie's charity when Tym had suddenly turned on her. 'But that's a lesson people like you never learn. Anyway, what happened next?'

'Two days later I got the photographs. No message, just the photos. She'd shown no sign of recognizing me when we met, but she obviously had and she'd also got hold of my London address and phone number. She rang late that night, and said I was to post £30,000 in used twenties through the door of the Belgrave Road flat, between ten at night and eight in the morning, within a week. Otherwise the photographs would be sent to the Prime Minister, the national press and my wife.'

'Who presumably has no idea of your unusual sexual predilections?'

'Good God, no,' he said, appalled at the very idea. 'I mean, I love her. Anyway,' he spluttered, clearly regretting this admission of emotion, 'I got the money from my bank, and shoved it through the letterbox in two foolscap envelopes. I received the photographs and the negatives two days later and I heard nothing more until you bastards came along. So tell me, why should I have chosen to attack her now?'

'Because revenge is a dish best tasted cold,' I said. But I believed Adamson, chiefly on account of his smirk on hearing of Sophie's fate. Someone who had arranged to have her tongue cut out would have masked his feelings better than that. Adamson's horrid smile had been a spontaneous expression of surprise and perverse pleasure.

'I still don't know who you are?' he said again, as I let the silence lengthen. 'What happens next? I don't have as much ready cash as you might imagine.'

The idea of blackmailing him and giving the proceeds to the Howard League for Penal Reform was an attractive one, but vile though he was, he'd probably suffered enough. And while his account seemed plausible, there was still no proof that he hadn't been involved. It was far too early to let him off the hook. And if he was innocent, and learnt that we didn't actually have the photographs, he might just go to the police. I didn't like to think how Sergeant Darbyshire would react to that.

'I'm not in the business of blackmail, and nor are my friends. Like you, I'm one of Sophie's clients. I found her shortly after she was attacked. She gave me copies of the photographs. I'm trying to find out who took such spectacular revenge on her.'

'Why not hand them over to the police?' asked Adamson, who appeared to be a man of very little intelligence.

'Yes, you'd love officers of the Met poring over pictures of you thrashing about with Sophie with your trousers down, wouldn't you?'

He looked aghast. 'I see what you mean. But you do believe me now, don't you?'

'I'm agnostic on the matter.'

'But you will let me have the photographs?' he said. 'How do I know I can trust you not to circulate them?'

'You don't,' I said brutally, remembering once again his pleasure in Sophie's downfall. It may have proved his innocence but it also put him beyond the pale. 'You'll just have to sweat it out and see what happens.'

Kim and Tym were weaving their way across the room. Tym looked very pale, Kim anxious. The raddled old singer went over to the Minister, who flinched at his approach.

'I'm sorry about that,' he said. 'You may be a cunt but it was quite unforgettable.'

'I think you mean unforgivable,' said Kim. 'Though I expect Mr Adamson found it unforgettable as well.'

'Yeah,' said Tym, peering like an injured animal into Adamson's unreadable eyes.

'Why don't you just piss off?' said Adamson.

'Right,' said Tym. 'The screams were dying on the roller-coaster ride, neck-tie glide, so unkind,' he added. When Tym started babbling, I'd quickly come to learn, he felt threatened.

'I think it's time to go home.' I said. 'Mr Adamson has kindly offered us a lift.'

'I've done no such—' began Adamson.

'Oh, but I think you have,' I said sweetly. 'Those photographs.' It would, I thought, be very easy to become addicted to blackmail.

As we walked over to the car, I told the Minister he was to say nothing to anybody about our little chat.

'Fuck you,' he said. But I knew he'd keep his mouth shut. So long as he thought we had the photos, he had far too much to lose.

We'd reached the Ministerial Rover now, and the uniformed driver was standing attentively beside it.

'I promised these three a lift home,' said Adamson. 'They're on the production team of *The World Tonight*.'

The driver looked at our scruffy clothes and lingered on Tym's tattoo. Pigs, his expression seemed to say, might fly.

'Very well, Minister,' was all he actually said. 'Where to?'

'Vauxhall,' said Kim.

'Would you like me to drop you home first, Minister?' asked the driver.

'No,' snapped Adamson testily. He couldn't risk our talking in front of the chauffeur.

So we sat in silence until we crossed the Thames and then I got the driver to drop us a few streets away from

Rita Road. Better all round if Adamson didn't know where we lived.

'Thanks for the lift,' said Kim, who was holding Tym's tattooed hand in both of hers.

'And I am really tormentedly sorry,' said the singer.

'Just get out,' barked Adamson.

'Nice,' said Kim. We climbed out and watched the car doing an awkward three-point turn. Kim waved as it finally pulled away, but Adamson was staring straight head and never looked back. Once we'd reached home Tym began to shiver as soon as we were over the threshold.

'Scotch?' said Kim brightly.

'We finished the bottle the other night.'

'I've got one hidden away,' said Kim. 'For emergencies like this.' She went away to fetch it and I sat on the sofa with the obviously anguished Tym.

'It's OK,' I said. 'He deserved it.'

'I hate violence,' he said. 'I hate what's inside me.'

'You were just furious because he smiled so vilely when he heard about Sophie. Your anger does you credit.'

'He's innocent though, isn't he?' said Tym as Kim returned with a bottle of Talisker, three glasses and a jug of water.

'I think he probably is.'

We sat and drank and Tym continued to look edgy.

'I don't suppose . . .' he began at last, but he seemed unable to finish the sentence.

'We'll come and sit with you when you're in bed,' said Kim, apparently reading his mind. 'Until you're asleep.'

He grinned. 'Cheers. Just this once. Lovely,' and lumbered off to the bathroom.

'He was really sick in the gents at the Langham,' said Kim when he'd gone. 'I could hear him retching his heart out even though I was standing outside in the corridor.'

'It's the violence. Not only the violence done to Sophie, but the violence he feels in himself.' I told her how he had once attacked Sophie himself.

'Poor man,' said Kim. 'It's like that line on old maps. Here be Dragons.'

'Yeah, psychedelic dragons locked inside his head which he can't quite get rid of, however hard he tries.'

I lit a candle to ward off the terrors of the dark, and Kim poured Tym a glass of milk to settle his stomach. We knocked at the door of his room, a bit like parents, I suddenly thought, with a troubled adolescent son.

Tym was lying flat on his back, the sheets pulled up to his neck, gazing blankly at the ceiling. He sat up to drink his milk, and I turned out the light and placed the candle by his bed.

'Golden glow,' he said, lying down again.

'That's right, golden glow,' said Kim, picking up his tattooed hand and stroking it gently. 'There's nothing to worry about here,' she said, as if soothing a frightened child. 'We're both here, and we'll be here when you wake up in the morning.'

She began, very gently, to sing Richard and Linda Thompson's 'I Want To See The Bright Lights Tonight'. She'd once sung it to me, on our first proper date, and we'd always regarded it as our tune. Sometimes prone to dismaying bouts of jealousy, I didn't mind her sharing it with him. I hummed along quietly myself, and gazed at Kim in the candlelight. After a few minutes the song was also accompanied by gentle snores from Tym. We tiptoed silently out of his room and into our own bed.

Friday 28 July – Sunday 30 July

Lighten our darkness, we beseech thee, O Lord;
and by thy great mercy defend us from all perils
and dangers of this night.
Evening Prayer, Third Collect

It was a pig of a weekend, one way and another. Friday morning began sombrely when I phoned Sergeant Darbyshire for a progress report on Sophie. Sophie had been operated on the previous afternoon. A piece of her skull, two inches long and one and a half inches wide, had been sawn out in order to remove the clot and release the pressure. She was now in a carefully maintained coma in intensive care, but still hanging in there with at least a chance of a full recovery.

'When will they try to bring her round?' I asked.

'Tuesday morning at the earliest,' he said.

Darbyshire asked again if I'd thought of anything else that might have a bearing on the case, and I said 'No, what about you? Any new information you feel able to impart?'

'We've spoken to a few punters. Most were willing to help when they learnt what had happened to Sophie.'

'She was a genuinely nice woman,' I said. 'Is a genuinely nice woman,' I corrected myself.

'That seems to be the unanimous verdict. No one had a bad word to say about her. They all knew Henrietta, who was described with considerably less rapture, and most of them had heard of big-bosomed Jenny, though none of them had actually been with her. No one, apart from yourself, had ever heard of Jim, nor had the impression of a ponce hanging around the place. It's a waiting game for us. A lead to Henrietta seems to be our best hope. Unfortunately Henrietta seems to have gone to earth. And naturally the landlord of the flat, whom we've managed to trace, claims he had no idea the place was being used as a knocking shop. Unfortunately I believe him.'

'And no one has mentioned blackmail?' I asked.

'No. But if you think about it, if Sophie had blackmailed anyone, none of her victims would be likely to turn up again as a punter afterwards.'

'No hint of a possible political connection?' I asked and immediately cursed my own stupidity.

'Why do you ask that?' said Darbyshire sharply. 'I'm warning you, Mr Benson, if I find out you've been holding out on me . . .' There wasn't a trace of humour in his voice.

'It just struck me that, um, Sophie's place is only a few minutes from the Houses of Parliament. And you know how the press love a nice juicy parliamentary sex scandal. If Sophie was intent on blackmailing anyone, and personally I doubt it, a well-known politician would seem to be a God-given target.' My voice seemed to be quavering alarmingly, but if he noticed, Darbyshire wasn't letting on.

'It's a possibility, I give you that,' he said emolliently. 'But then anything seems possible at the moment. I hope we'll get some new leads today. The *Sun*'s gone big on it. They've even printed the incident-room number and a promise from us about complete confidentiality. Did Henrietta look like a *Sun* reader to you?'

'*Daily Mail* through and through,' I replied.

'Damn,' said Darbyshire. 'They've not printed anything yet. I'll have to try and think of a new angle for them.'

An alarming thought occurred. 'God, my name isn't mentioned in any of the reports as someone out on police bail, is it?' I thought of my much-loved aunt in Thames Ditton who'd brought me up after my parents' death. I hadn't even found the nerve to tell her what Botticelli Publications actually published.

'I've managed to keep your name out of it,' replied Darbyshire. 'And the fact that you work for porn magazines, which the tabloids would naturally love. I will, however, have no hesitation about leaking your name, occupation and address if I suspect you're being less than frank with me. And I might just hint to the hacks that it's possible you have more to do with the case than we've been able to prove so far. Have you ever been at the centre of a tabloid feeding frenzy, Mr Benson?'

'Not directly, no,' I said, remembering the tabloid trial of Joe Johnson with a shudder. 'There's no reason for me to be less than frank with you,' I added. 'I liked Sophie, remember, and I want the bastard caught as much as you do.' My protest sounded worryingly shrill.

'All right, Mr Benson. Keep your hair on and just phone me if you have any ideas.'

'Right,' I said. 'Thanks.' My hand was trembling as I put down the phone. Darbyshire was evidently a far more ruthless operator than I'd previously given him credit for.

'What was all that about?' asked Kim.

Tym looked physically ill when he heard about Sophie's skull and wandered off into the kitchen.

I told Kim about Darbyshire's threat to leak my name to the tabloids.

'Shit,' she said.

'My biggest worry is what Henrietta will say if they find her. She knew Sophie was involved in blackmail. What we don't know is whether she knew about the existence of the tape, or worse still, whether she suspects Sophie's passed it on to me.'

'My hunch is that as long as Henrietta thinks Sophie is alive, she'll keep quiet, even if the police do track her down. She'll realize that any mention of blackmail will get Sophie into deep trouble if and when she recovers.'

'You're right,' I said. 'Still, it's no fun at all having Darbyshire getting heavy down the phone with you.'

'Do you want to hand over the tape, then?' asked Kim.

'We can't,' I whispered, gesturing towards the kitchen. 'Think what a police investigation would do to Tym. And Sophie specifically instructed us not to go to the police.'

'We could destroy it,' said Kim. 'She said we could do that.'

'Yeah. But if Henrietta does know about the tape and tells the police, I'll be in even worse trouble if they discover I've trashed it. But there's another aspect to all this. Because we're depriving the police of vital information, we've got a moral duty to follow up the leads ourselves. We can't just let Sophie's attacker get away with it.'

'I hoped you'd say that,' said Kim. 'I'll do some research into the other three names on the tape today.'

'Right,' I said, and we went and joined Tym in the kitchen. He looked red-eyed and snuffly but managed a brave smile.

'Would you mind if I hung around a bit longer?' he asked shyly. 'I could make myself useful. Get your car uncramped for instance.'

'Unclamped,' I said, and he nodded eagerly.

Kim explained what a terrible job it was. First of all he'd have to deal with the officious busy-bodies at the town hall parking permit office, then he'd have to brave the subterranean hell of the car pound and clamping office at Hyde Park Corner. It wasn't, I added, a task for someone who didn't like being out on the streets.

'I need to do it,' he said. 'As a thank you for taking care of me and as a kind of pilgrimage for Sophie. Like lighting a candle for her, somehow.'

'Are you sure?' said Kim.

He nodded, so she gave him all the necessary documents, but he insisted on paying himself. 'Believe it or not, I'm still quite loaded,' he said. 'My records still sell a surprising amount worldwide, especially the first one with the Moonlight. It is a bit of a classic, after all, and since I wrote all the songs the royalties are good.' He said this without a trace of arrogance and it was good to discover there was still a bit of self-worth in that confused bald head.

'Well, thanks,' said Kim, and the two of us set off for the Tube. I bought the *Sun* at the newsagent's. Sophie had made the lead on page eleven, under the headline MYSTERY HOOKER'S TRAGIC TONGUE JOB. The mutilation was described with unpleasant relish, along with the fact that Sophie was in a coma, and that the police had no idea what her surname was or where her associates were. Darbyshire was quoted as saying it was vital that her brutal attacker was tracked down as soon as possible, and he particularly wanted to hear from the woman believed to be the massage parlour's maid, Henrietta. As well as the incident-room number (PHONE NOW IF YOU EVER VISITED VICE-GIRL SOPHIE IN HER BASEMENT DEN OF SHAME) there was a paragraph about the man who had discovered Sophie being released on bail after helping the police with their inquiries. No mention of the fact that I'd taken her to the hospital of course. Darbyshire was right. The tabloids would just love to get their claws into me.

'Try not to worry,' said Kim as we separated to board our different trains. I wished her luck with her investigations.

I hoped no one would have seen the *Sun* piece at work, but the men in dispatch wasted no time in showing it to me when I arrived, and Brian had thoughtfully cut it out and stuck it on to my computer terminal. I had to endure a good deal of ribbing over the lunchtime pints, and shortly before I was about to call it a day and go home, I pressed the wrong button on my computer and lost the whole of the video review column I'd been subbing. It took Brian an hour to find it again in the electronic stew, and he insisted I buy him a pint to make amends. The pint turned into four, and it was ten by the time I got home feeling half-pissed, exhausted and more than a little sorry for myself.

Kim and Tym were watching Clint Eastwood on the telly, and had eaten the rest of the roast beef which I'd been looking forward to all the way home. I had to make do with baked beans on toast.

'How did your researches go?' I asked Kim when I'd got my miserly supper. She told me to shut up until the movie was over. It seemed to go on for ever, and a film about a psychopathic cop was just what I didn't need.

The credits rolled at last, and Kim went and got the malt whisky, which cheered me up.

'How did you get on with the clamp?' I asked Tym.

'It was fine,' he said. 'Picked up the permit with no problem and then got a taxi to that amazing underground car park. I think there might be a song there. Exhaust fumes, half-light, vague paranoia and endless tunnels. Just my scene.' He looked a genuinely happy man.

Kim called the meeting to order. 'Right,' she said. 'Well, as you both know there were five names on Sophie's list of blackmail candidates. Tym here, who Sophie called her darling Tym and who we believe is innocent despite his lack of an alibi.'

Tym looked rattled at this and Kim blew him a kiss and told him not to worry. 'Then there was Adamson, the hateful Government Minister who does have an alibi. I checked with the Home Affairs correspondent of the *Telegraph*. Adamson was on the Isle of Wight when he said he was. There's no way he could have been in the Belgrave Road at the time in question, and we've agreed hired thugs are unlikely.'

I nodded.

'Which leaves three more: Bill Hutchinson, the famous actor, for whom I hope I've got something planned on Monday night – I won't know for sure till Monday; David Welch, the prep-school headmaster; and the Reverend

Hugh McAlistair. I've arranged to see them both this weekend.'

I was impressed. 'How on earth did you trace them?'

'It was so easy I'd almost rather not say. Spoils the mystique. But McAlistair was in *Crockford's Clerical Directory*, which lists every Anglican clergyman. It might have been more difficult if he belonged to some non-conformist group.'

'And the dominie?'

'Independent Schools Information Service,' said Kim, blushing. 'In the phone book. I just told them I'd heard David Welch's school very highly recommended but had lost the number. They came up with it at once.'

'Easy when you know how. But very efficient, Kim. Well done.'

'You patronizing creep,' she grinned. 'Anyway, I thought the best way to see McAlistair was simply to turn up at one of his services. He's taking two on Sunday, Holy Communion at 8 a.m. and Evening Prayer at 6 p.m. Except he doesn't call it Evening Prayer. He calls it his Sunday Sundowner Service.'

'Oh Christ, how ghastly,' I said.

'Our Lord's sentiments too, I'm sure,' said Kim. 'McAlistair's parish is in Suffolk, a few miles from Aldeburgh. My plan is that we drive there on Sunday and attend the evening service. We'll be able to get the cut of his jib while he takes it. And better still, he's one of those vicars who invites the entire congregation to refreshments in the Church Hall afterwards. His wife told me when I phoned the rectory inquiring about service times.'

'What about the headmaster?'

'Another cinch,' said Kim, 'though I'm afraid it might be better if you stayed behind on this one, Tym. I just said we were prospective parents, exploring possible schools for our young twins, William and Benjamin.' Her last words hung uneasily in the air. 'Anyway, we're booked in for an interview at 11.30. The school's in a village called Five

Beeches, near Alton in Hampshire. Thanks to Tym we'll be able to drive down tomorrow. Do you mind staying here, Tym? Or you can come with us and wait in the car. You don't exactly look like a respectable uncle.'

'I'll stay here,' he said. 'I want to work on this underground car-park song anyway. And I'll go shopping and cook supper for tomorrow night.'

'For a clapped-out old rock star, you're all right,' said Kim fondly. Tym grinned and looked like an obese twelve-year-old. We had a last drink and went to bed.

I'd just drifted off to sleep when the phone started ringing. 'Shit,' said Kim. I told her I'd get it.

'Is that Will Benson?' said the male voice at the other end.

'Yeah,' I said sleepily.

'And do you work for a firm called Botticelli Publications?'

'Yes, what of it? What do you want?' But the line immediately went dead. It was a warm night but I shivered. I had the uneasy conviction that I'd just given an enterprising reporter exactly the break he needed. I felt exposed, like a nervous deer in a woodland clearing as the hunter, invisible in the undergrowth, takes careful aim through his telescopic sight.

'Who was it?' mumbled Kim when I climbed back into bed.

'Wrong number,' I lied, and she grunted and went back to sleep. It was a long time before I joined her in the land of nod.

The next morning Kim and I put on our smartest clothes, said goodbye to Tym and walked down Rita Road to the Mini. It was clamped again.

'I don't believe it,' wailed Kim, kicking the cruel metallic monster, very gingerly this time. 'I gave Tym my car keys and he said he'd stuck the permit on to the window as soon as the car was unclamped.'

'He didn't stick it hard enough,' I said, peering through

the window. The distinctive green permit was lying on the floor amid the usual detritus of sweet papers, Coke cans and rotting apple cores.

'The bastards,' said Kim bleakly. 'They could have seen it too if they'd bothered to look. Now what?'

'Taxi to Waterloo and catch a train. We can phone Welch from the station if it looks as though we're going to be late.'

We found a cab without trouble and discovered there was a train that stopped at Five Beeches leaving in a quarter of an hour. We'd arrive with ten minutes to spare before our interview.

I bought all the papers and was relieved to find there were no follow-ups on the Sophie case. Not even anything in the *Mail*, which wouldn't please Darbyshire. I decided not to burden Kim with my anxiety about the midnight phone call and gazed out of the window. It began to rain, gently at first, but by the time we arrived at Five Beeches it was coming down in buckets. There were no cabs in the forecourt, and no likelihood of any arriving, the station master informed us with gloomy satisfaction.

'Is it far to Sheridan House, the prep school?' asked Kim.

The station master pointed across the road to a sloping field. At the top of the rise, a large Edwardian house was visible on the other side of the hedge.

'That's it there,' he said. 'It's well over a mile by road to the front entrance, but it's just five minutes across the field.' We stared glumly at the rain and realized we had no option. We were due to see Welch in exactly five minutes. The station master kindly offered Kim a small ladies' umbrella that was languishing in the lost property box.

'It's the only one I've got,' he said, 'but it will keep at least one of you dry.'

We thanked him, crossed the road, and climbed over a stile into the field. There were large black and white cows in it and I eyed them nervously.

'Do you think it's safe?' I asked. 'Aren't most cows mad these days?'

'Don't be wet,' said Kim, then giggled inanely when she saw I was drenched.

We climbed the slope, which was steeper than it looked, and the indistinct path got muddier and muddier as the rain sheeted down. By the time we'd got half-way up our shoes were caked in clinging mud, and I was drenched from head to foot. Then I slipped and fell arse first into a cowpat. Kim, snug beneath her brolly, found this terrifically entertaining, though she did at least have the grace to wipe my trouser seat clean as best she could with handfuls of grass. 'I hate the fucking countryside,' I puffed as we reached the top of the field at last.

Another stile gave access to the school grounds, and we skirted a well-maintained cricket pitch on our way to the endearingly eccentric pile of red-brick Gothic. Muddy, bedraggled and, in my case, smelly, we weren't going to make an ideal first impression as prospective parents.

I rang the bell, and it was opened by a middle-aged woman in an electric wheelchair. 'Mr and Mrs Benson?' she said, with a smile that flickered only slightly as she got an eyeful of the state we were in. 'I assumed you'd be coming by car.'

We muttered about car-clamps and trains and cow-filled fields as we tried to remove the worse of the mud from our shoes on a scraper in the porch. Mrs Welch then showed us into a large, tiled cloakroom. I rubbed my drenched hair with a towel and Kim then had another assault on the cow shit on my bum. To judge by the state of the towel when she'd finished, there had been an awful lot of it.

'What shall I do with the towel?' she giggled nervously when she'd finished. 'It looks absolutely disgusting.'

'Chuck it out of the window,' I said, catching her giggly mood myself, and Kim did just that.

Mrs Welch was waiting for us outside, and we followed

her humming chair across the large expanse of well-polished parquet floor. She opened a door and led us into the headmaster's study. David Welch was sitting at his desk, smoking a pipe. He was older than I'd expected, in his early sixties, and he didn't look like a man one would enjoy either deceiving or upsetting. His face was stamped with authority, but his eyes held a suggestion of deeply buried hurt.

'Mr and Mrs Benson, darling,' said his wife. 'I'll go and make you all coffee.' Mrs Welch put her wheelchair into reverse and whizzed away backwards with a smile on her face. The effect was oddly comic, and feeling faintly hysterical, I found it hard to stifle another fit of the giggles.

'Now, you've come about, er . . .' began Welch, hunting for a note on his desk.

'The twins,' said Kim.

'Our daughter,' I said simultaneously. Tym's insistence that we were going to have a girl had obviously taken root.

'There appears to be some confusion,' said Welch. 'I'm afraid we don't take girls here.'

Kim gave me a baleful glare and to my intense shame I found I was blushing. I was beginning to feel like a naughty prep-school boy myself, in grave danger of receiving six of the best from the head beak. Welch finally found the note he was looking for.

'My wife said you had twin boys. William and Benjamin. Or I suppose you might call them Bill and Ben. I fear you could be exposing your sons to considerable ridicule with names like that. Little boys can be very cruel sometimes.'

Welch suddenly, and thoroughly disconcertingly, came out with a flibble-ubbledub-bebop that sounded exactly like the Flower Pot Men, followed by a shrill cry of 'little weed'.

'Do children still watch the *Flower Pot Men*?' asked Kim.

'Very popular on video,' said Welch. 'The young ones here love them.'

'Fascinating,' said Kim.

'Not quite as fascinating as prospective parents who don't know whether they've got twin boys or a little girl. I think you've got some explaining to do.'

'We've been rumbled,' said Kim, adding, *sotto voce* but all too audibly, 'you twit' at the end of the sentence.

It dawned on me that Kim and I had come pathetically unprepared for this interview with Welch. Tym had been so sad and honest, Adamson so vile and slick, that it had been a doddle to raise the matter of Sophie. Here was a man who looked about as likely to visit a Pimlico prositute as the Pope.

The silence grew and grew, and as Welch waited, and twitched his nostrils, I became uneasily aware of just how strongly I was smelling of cowpat. If it hadn't been for Kim sitting next to me with an expectant look on her face I think I'd have tried to escape through the French windows.

'Well, Mr Benson,' said Welch at last. 'Just what have I rumbled?'

'Um, er, um,' I said.

'Come on, Will,' said Kim. 'Spit it out.'

'Why don't you spit it out,' I said cravenly.

'Because this is chap's talk,' she said smugly. I could have throttled her.

'It's rather awkward,' I faltered at last. 'But, we've come about a tart called Sophie.'

Welch stood up, his face blanched with fury.

'I think you'd better leave at once,' he said.

It was naturally at this moment that Mrs Welch made her entrance, whizzing across the room with a tray on her lap containing three steaming mugs of coffee. It was a treble Scotch I felt in need of but it looked as if we weren't even going to get the coffee.

'I'm sorry, Margaret,' said Welch. 'It turns out that Mr and Mrs Benson will be leaving almost immediately and the coffee won't be necessary. I'd appreciate a few moments alone with them.'

Mrs Welch executed a nifty three-point turn and was out like a shot.

'There's just one thing I'd like to get straight,' said Kim. 'As far as you are aware, are there any other prep-school headmasters called David Welch?'

'No there are not,' snapped the headmaster.

'So your anger just now,' said Kim, always steadier under fire than I was, 'wasn't because you were appalled at the very suggestion that you might know a prostitute, but because you did know Sophie ... and had come, very possibly, to resent her.'

'You know very well why I have come to resent ...' he obviously couldn't bring himself to say her name and paused for a moment before adding 'that woman', like Edward Heath referring to Mrs Thatcher. 'And I'm telling you now that I'm not paying another penny. She promised it would be a once-and-for-all payment, and in any case I have no reserves left.'

'We've not come to blackmail you,' said Kim.

'I give you our solemn word on that,' I added.

The relief on Welch's face was palpable. He took a couple of deep breaths, sat down again, and lit his pipe.

'Do you mind?' I asked, indicating my own tin of much nastier tobacco.

He shook his head and I rolled a ludicrously amateurish ciggie with trembling fingers. There had been something awesome about Welch's brief moment of consuming anger. I took a grateful lungful and said there was one further question I needed to ask before we explained ourselves.

'Fire away,' he said.

'What were you doing on Wednesday, at about 3.30 in the afternoon?' I said.

He looked at his diary. 'I was here at the school, in my study in fact. Talking to a couple of prospective parents.'

'Do you have their number?' I said. 'Can we phone them?'

'Do you seriously expect me to allow two strangers

linked with a blackmailing prostitute to phone prospective parents?' he said irritably.

'It's desperately important,' said Kim. 'For you as well as for us. I think I can manage it tactfully and we'll explain all if your alibi holds up.'

'What do you mean, alibi?' said Welch, with a spurt of his earlier anger. 'What do I need an alibi for? I must say you two have an infernal cheek.'

'It won't take a moment,' said Kim. 'And I promise I'll be discreet. I can't tell you how important it is.'

He thought for a moment, and Kim looked appealingly at him, and Welch reluctantly divulged their name and number and pushed the phone across his desk.

'Is that Mrs Weston?' said Kim, after a few moments. 'It's the school secretary at Sheridan House. I'm afraid I've double booked the headmaster and I'll have to rearrange your appointment with him next Wednesday.'

We could hear a few squawks at the other end.

'Oh, I am sorry,' said Kim. 'How silly of me. I've got the wrong Wednesday in the diary. Of course you came this week. Could you just confirm the time of the interview to put my mind completely at rest? Three o'clock, excellent, I'm so sorry to have troubled you. I hope you liked the look of the school, inefficient secretaries aside?' There was more squawking. 'Oh good, I'm delighted, I'll tell the headmaster. Thank you so much. Goodbye.'

Kim put the phone down and smiled at Welch. 'You've just got yourself a new pupil,' she said. 'And a rock-solid alibi. Congratulations.

'I must say you handled that rather neatly,' said the HM. 'Now perhaps you'll tell me what all this is about?'

If ever a man deserved a full explanation it was Welch. 'I take it you're not a *Sun* reader?' I asked, and he shook his head. So I told him the full story, from my own first visit to Sophie and the reason for it. He looked absolutely appalled when he heard about the tongue and the subsequent coma.

'My God,' he shuddered. 'I've cursed her a good deal in recent weeks but I'd never have wished that on her.' I remembered Adamson's poisonous little smirk and felt like clapping Welch on the back.

'How much did she take you for?'

'Fifteen thousand,' he said. 'It was a struggle. This old building is in constant need of maintenance and our school roll is falling. The recession hasn't helped and boarding seems to be going out of fashion anyway.'

I was longing to know how Welch had come into contact with Sophie. But since he was obviously in the clear, it seemed impertinent to inquire. Kim however suffered from no such restraint.

'Are you going to give us all the lurid details, then?' she asked cheerfully. 'You don't have to but it might be helpful.'

'I thought you'd never ask,' he said, with a wintry smile, then remembered Sophie's condition. 'It obviously suits me that the police aren't involved in this. But considering the gravity of the crime, shouldn't they have all the information available to them?'

'Sophie thought something might happen to her when she embarked on her blackmailing. That's why she made the tape. And she made it absolutely clear that, whatever happened, she didn't want the police involved. If she dies, I may have to think again,' I said.

'Fair enough. But you ought to be careful. Whoever did this has already shown they can be exceptionally vicious.'

'Point very much taken,' I said.

'And you've no idea why she started to blackmail people?' asked Welch.

'None at all. It seems completely out of character.'

'I agree. I liked her very much myself. At first. You can choose to believe this or not, but she was the first prostitute I'd ever been to. As you can see my wife is badly disabled. Hunting accident a couple of years ago, and the, er, personal side of our marriage hadn't really existed since.

Anyway, I was in London for a conference, saw all the cards in the phone boxes and succumbed.'

'When was that?'

'About three months ago.'

'Exactly the same time as Tym had his bad vibes and she put the bite on Duncan Adamson,' I said to Kim.

'Not that monstrous Minister?' asked Welch with a look of malicious pleasure.

'Absolutely,' I said. 'I'm afraid I can't bring myself to honour that creep's right to confidentiality. Thirty thousand smackers he had to pay.'

'Life does have its lighter moments amid the encircling gloom,' said Welch. 'No chance of him being the villain of the piece, I suppose? The prospect of him spending a good few years banged up in one of his own stinking prisons is irresistible.'

'He seems to have an excellent alibi,' said Kim.

'Ah well, you can't win them all. Anyway, to get back to my own experience with Sophie. The card was actually for a 44DD brunette.' He looked apologetically at Kim. 'I'm sorry if this is offending you,' he added. 'I'm afraid these are murky waters.'

'Don't worry about me,' said Kim. 'Will hoped he was going to get the busty one too.'

'Anyway, I was very happy with Sophie. Afterwards she opened a split of champagne and we got talking, and I found myself telling her about my wife and life at the school.'

'She inspired confidences,' I said.

'She did indeed. But I never gave her my name or said where the school was. She must have gone through my wallet and found one of my cards when I went to the bathroom for a few moments.'

'And how long was it until you found out she was going to blackmail you?' I asked.

'I got the photos first, just three days later. Desperately rattling as you can imagine. Mercifully she'd written

144

"strictly confidential" on the envelope. The real school secretary,' he said, favouring Kim with a conspiratorial grin, 'isn't quite as broad-minded as you are. She would have had a fit.'

'Then a couple of days later, by which time I was in a terrible funk, she rang. She said she hated having to do it but she was in desperate need of money. And I must say she did sound sincerely upset. Nevertheless she still insisted I send £15,000 in cash by Datapost to the Pimlico address. Otherwise my wife, the chairman of our governors, whose name she had somehow got hold of, and the *News of the World* would be sent the pictures. I started remonstrating with her but she said she knew she was behaving like a bitch but she had no choice in the matter, and put the phone down.'

'So you sent the money?'

'Yes. I also told my wife.'

'Good for you,' said Kim. 'Fatty here owned up too. Mind you, he took his time about it, and he had very little choice.'

I squirmed uncomfortably and Welch gave me a sympathetic grimace.

'Confession actually helped a lot,' he said. 'Cleared the air. We found, in fact, that there were still things we could do to please each other. We'd just been too foolishly embarrassed to talk about it properly before. My real worry was the governors and the press. The school couldn't have survived a scandal like that. But Sophie sent me the incriminating photos and the negatives by return of post, and swore I'd never hear from her again. And until you turned up, my wife and I both thought it was something we could put behind us.'

'You still can,' I said. 'I very much hope that it will be possible to alert the police to whoever's guilty without dragging anyone else into the investigation. I'm just sorry to have given you such an unpleasant surprise.'

He handed me his card. 'Do phone if I can be of any

further help. And I would be very glad to hear what you find out. And for any news there may be of Sophie – good or ill.'

We got up to go and Welch showed us to the front door.

'Where's your car?' he asked, surveying the empty drive.

'We came by train and walked across the field,' said Kim. 'And in case you're wondering, the funny smell's coming from Will. He fell into a cowpat on the way up.'

Welch tried to look sympathetic and ended up laughing.

'I tried to clean him up with a towel in the cloakroom,' added Kim, in an entirely unnecessary burst of honesty. 'I'm afraid it was such a revolting mess that I threw it out of the window.'

'I'd almost certainly have done the same myself,' said Welch gallantly. 'Let me run you to the station. There's a London train in ten minutes.'

He left us in the forecourt of the station and made me promise to let him know how things went. We waved cheerfully as he drove off, and went on to the platform where the station master told us with every appearance of pleasure that the 12.15 had been cancelled because of staff shortages and there wasn't another train for over an hour.

'There's a pub down the road, though,' he added. 'Not a very nice one.'

It was still raining, so we asked if we could hang on to his umbrella a bit longer and tottered off down the road. After all the initial tension and embarrassment with Welch, I felt in need of a stiff drink.

'Sorry about my gaffe,' I said.

'It was probably just as well,' said Kim charitably. 'It got us down to the nitty-gritty very quickly and he wasn't the sort of man you'd want to string along.'

The pub was worse than not very nice. It smelt of stale beer and damp dog, and was entirely deserted apart from ourselves, the landlord and the dog, a dropsical Labrador. Our less than genial host looked like a heavyweight boxer gone to seed and poured our drinks with ill grace. When I asked him if there was any food available, he looked as though I had personally insulted him.

'Might be some pie in the back,' he mumbled at last, and shuffled off to look for it. Kim's gin and tonic came without ice or lemon, and my pint tasted rancid, though not quite rancid enough to complain about unless you were spoiling for a fight. I got it down me as quickly as I could, and ordered a double Scotch when our host returned with the food. It was a revoltingly pink pork pie, with stale crust and a grey-blue slice of hard-boiled egg in the middle.

'*Bon appétit*,' said Kim bravely, but neither of us managed more than three mouthfuls. There was a peculiarly sweet and deeply unpleasant aftertaste to the substance masquerading as pork.

'Let's get out of here,' said Kim. 'I'd rather sit on the station platform and watch the rain.'

I went up to the bar. 'Nothing wrong with the pie, was there?' the landlord asked menacingly.

'It was revolting,' I said calmly.

'Ah, I thought it might be,' he said, ringing up £5.00 for food on the till.

'You're not thinking of charging us for it, are you?'

He leant over the bar and put his large red face uncomfortably closed to mine.

'I can't serve it again now you've taken bites out of it, can I? That will be eleven pounds ninety, with the drinks.'

'No wonder you do such a roaring trade,' I said. But I paid and left feeling I'd got considerably the worse of the exchange. I wasn't to find out how much worse till later.

We walked back through the dreary, sodden and apparently completely deserted village and sat on a bench on the platform. Just before the train arrived, an enormously tall man in a Barbour raced into the station, glanced momentarily at Kim and me, then ran to the end of the platform where there was no protection from the rain.

'Do I smell that bad?' I asked Kim.

She looked thoughtful and said nothing, then the train arrived and we climbed in.

Once we'd set off, Kim took a decko around the almost empty compartment and came back and sat down again.

'I think that giant might have been following us,' she said. 'I saw him board the train at Waterloo.'

'Shit,' I said, and told her about the midnight telephone call. 'Perhaps some hack's got wind of the fact that it was me who found Sophie. Even worse, Darbyshire could have put him on to me because he thinks I'm holding out on him.'

'There's a silver lining to all this,' said Kim. 'If any newspaper gives the impression you were actually involved in attacking Sophie, we can sue for libel.'

'Gee, that makes me feel a whole lot better.'

But it wasn't long before both Kim and I began to feel a great deal worse. Thanks to endless, unexplained delays, the train took two and a half hours to reach Waterloo, and by the time we got there both of us were feeling feverish and sick. Kim actually was sick on the platform, and I was so preoccupied in helping her to a cab and trying not to throw up myself that I forgot to look around for the giant. When we'd finally got into a taxi I glanced out of the window and saw him standing on the pavement, watching as the cab drew away. He must have been at least six feet six inches tall, and he was chunky with it. Disconcertingly, his pink chubby face seemed to belong to a boy of fourteen.

Neither of us felt well enough to discuss the matter. The next twelve hours were a succession of nightmarish trips to the lavatory, often with one of us waiting impatiently outside while the other suffered within. The pork pie had taken a spectacular revenge. As Kim said, if we'd eaten the whole portion we might well have been dead. Tym was an angel of mercy, mopping brows, bringing glasses of water and even finding time to get the car unclamped again. Between our trips to the loo, Kim and I told him piecemeal about our expedition, and the worrying presence of the giant. Tym walked up and down Rita Road several times but said he could see no sign of anyone keeping watch on the house. By midnight, the poisonous pie seemed to have done its worst, and Kim and I felt well enough to drink weak tea and nibble dry toast. We collaped into bed, slept soundly until eleven, and woke up feeling restored in the morning.

I went out for the papers, and checked again to see if the giant was lurking in any of the parked cars but there was no sign of him. A couple of the linens had short paragraphs saying the prostitute known only as Sophie was still critical but stable at St Thomas's Hospital, with further appeals from the police for anyone with information to come forward.

Tym helped Kim cook the chicken he'd bought the previous day and we had a leisurely Sunday lunch. Too leisurely in fact. As Tym and I finished the second bottle of Château Musar (Kim having nobly volunteered to do the driving), we suddenly realized that it was almost three and we were in grave danger of not getting to the church on time.

We piled into the Mini and headed east. As usual the traffic was a sluggish crawl down the bleak wastes of the Mile End Road, and when we finally hit the A12 we were greeted with cones and contraflows and an exceptionally slow crawl for almost three miles. 'These fucking cones are taking over the whole country,' yelled Kim in frustration.

Eventually we reached a clear stretch of dual carriage-way, and Kim put her foot down and the Mini rattled up to its maximum speed of 65 m.p.h. We stopped for petrol after by-passing Ipswich, and a few minutes later Kim sprang another of her bombshells as we headed up the A12. 'I think we're being followed,' she said. 'I first noticed that black Golf, three cars behind us, when we were crossing Vauxhall Bridge, and it reappeared about ten miles back.'

'How do you know it's the same car? Black Golfs are very common,' I said.

'Its registration number is PGB something or other. I noticed it because they were the initials of my favourite English mistress at school. Also, and I think you'll agree this clinches it, when the car came rather close at the roundabout a couple of minutes ago, I realized the driver was absolutely enormous, his head's actually touching the roof.'

'Shit,' I said. 'Another depressing thought occurs. Supposing he isn't a journalist, but a plainclothes policeman. That midnight call might just have been to put us on the wrong scent. If Darbyshire thinks I'm holding out on him, he'll be very anxious to find out who I'm visiting. If he knows we've seen a headmaster, and a vicar, both respectable people, he might well put two and two together and come up with a possible blackmail scam. Who knows, we might even have been under observation when we cornered Adamson.'

'We've got to lose the Golf,' said Tym.

'Yeah, but how?' wailed Kim. 'I can hardly outspeed him in this pile of scrap metal.'

I excavated the road-map from the rubbish on the floor. 'A couple of miles on, there's a road on the right that looks very bendy. If you suddenly accelerate we might lose sight of him for a few minutes and find a narrow country lane to disappear down. We can zig-zag across country, using minor roads only, to McAlistair's church.

'Right,' said Kim. 'Hold tight for a fast ride.'

She turned off to the right without signalling, causing the car immediately behind us to blare its horn furiously, but the Golf was alert enough to follow us. It was a narrow road with exceptionally sharp and deceptive bends. Kim took them, with considerable risk and even greater flair, like a rally driver roaring along at 50 m.p.h. in third gear. The Mini's engine screamed in protest. As we rounded what felt like the twentieth stomach-churning bend, Kim spotted

150

a country lane to our left, slammed on the brakes and turned blindly into it. Once we were out of sight of the main road, I got out of the car and doubled back as discreetly as possible to check whether the black Golf went past. I kept close to the hedgerow, and took what cover I could behind a hawthorn tree. After about a minute the Golf shot past at speed, and I was just heaving a sigh of relief when it reversed slowly back into view. The giant, just a silhouette behind the window, seemed to peer up the lane for a couple of seconds. I stood absolutely still and prayed that he wouldn't decide to explore further. 'Keep going straight on, you bastard,' I muttered under my breath, and he finally revved the engine and did just that.

I raced back to the car, told the others the news, and Kim reversed the Mini down the track, and doubled back along the bendy road at a marginally less heartstopping speed than previously.

I've never been much good at map reading, indeed my incompetence in that department has led to some of our more memorable rows, but the adrenalin pumping round my body after the chase must have helped, because I managed successfully to guide Kim to McAlistair's parish via myriad country roads.

We arrived with only five minutes to spare before Evensong, and parked near the entrance to the graveyard. The spectacular fifteenth-century perpendicular wool-church, almost as fine as the one at Blythburgh, stood in splendid isolation almost a mile from the nearest village. The great flint-faced building looked impressive enough from the outside but, like the Tardis, it seemed far bigger within; an extraordinary celebration of space and light. The soaring height of the delicate columns, the superb hammer-beamed roof and the delicate tracery of the enormous clear glass windows created a feeling of awed wonder.

Regrettably, McAlistair had done his best to rob the place of its majesty and mystery. A few plain wooden pews remained at the back of the nave, but it was clear we were meant to sit in a side chapel, on orange plastic seats arranged in a semi-circle around an altar that looked like a table from Habitat. The magnificently carved main altar in the sanctuary was plainly too grand and too remote for our Hugh. Indeed, the Reverend seemed to be deeply apologetic about the grandeur of his church, for the 'worship space' was surrounded by felt-covered screens adorned with sick-making posters bearing such legends as 'Smile if you've prayed today' and 'Sing out loud for Jesus' beneath pictures of smily happy faces, most of them cute, gap-toothed children of impeccable multi-cultural variety.

One began to understand the vicar's evident unease about the size of his church when you saw how many people turned up for the service. By the time Tym, Kim and I had taken our seats, the rest of the congregation consisted of three old ladies and a harassed mother with a mardy child in tow. Two minutes later four teenagers sloped in, two of them ominously carrying acoustic guitars. And that was the lot.

As the clock chimed six McAlistair himself wandered in. He was in his early forties I guessed, and his maker hadn't been kind to him. His fair hair was scanty, and what few long strands of it survived were arranged in a disastrous baldy style over the crown of his head. His ears and Adam's apple were grotesquely protuberant, his mouth weak, while his eyes put one in mind of a terrified rabbit, frozen in the beams of oncoming headlights. His brow was beaded with sweat and beneath his cassock he was wearing open-toed sandals and tartan socks.

'I would like to bid you all a very, very warm welcome,' he said in a voice in which bogus enthusiasm was effectively swamped by tremulous embarrassment. 'How sp-sp-sp-sp-splendid it is,' he stuttered, like a car failing to start on a freezing morning, 'to see some visitors here for our Sunday Sundowner, which I always like to think of as a hap-hap-hap-hap-happy family gathering, in which we can give thanks for the week that has gone past and look forward, together, with serenity and faith, to the week to c-c-c-c-come.'

I looked around at the boot-faced old biddies and the pustular teenagers. If this was a family, it was a dysfunctional one. And no one seemed more dysfunctional than poor, scraggy Hugh. This was a pity in many ways. Looking at his horrid misarrangement of the church, noticing that we were going to be using the most anodyne of all the 'alternative' services, and shuddering in dread at the prospect of the teenagers and their guitars, I was all nicely worked up to start hating him very much indeed. Here, in a beautiful church on a sleepy summer evening, when we ought to have been mumbling the hallowed, resonant words of the Book of Common Prayer, was surely a microcosm of all that was wrong, weak and contemptible about the Church of England. If religion were a kind of food, then the Church of England now seems intent on serving up the kind of tepid junk you find in a motorway service station.

Hugh's nervousness, stammering and sweaty anxiety seemed to get worse rather than better as we recited the flat words of the service and listened to a truly terrible 'song of praise' written by 'four extremely talented young members of our parish', the gist of which consisted of the repeated assertion that not only was Christ their saviour but he was also 'God's true raver, better than a tablet of pure E, Jesus supplies real ecstasy.'

This dire ditty was delivered with much blushing and abashed staring at the floor before all four succumbed to the giggles after one of their number farted in mid-verse and they scurried back to their seats covered in shame and confusion.

McAlistair gallantly pretended not to have noticed this fiasco and it became horribly apparent that he was going to deliver a sermon. It was, he said, a great mistake to think that God could only be praised in the words of 'dusty old hymns'. And while he could make no claim to being as 'with it' as Robert, Michelle, Bryony and Julian, he had himself, as a young teenager, been very fond of the Beatles. But he had been a Nowhere Man in those days, because he hadn't invited Christ into his life. And then, with the encouragement of a friendly beak at school, he had knelt down one day and asked for Help. At that moment, when death seemed preferable to the embarrassment of sitting in that beautiful, abused church, the Rev Hugh began tunelessly to warble an unaccompanied rendition of the opening verse of 'Help'.

Eventually we were allowed to sing a proper hymn, 'Jerusalem', to the accompaniment of a battered upright piano played by one of the old biddies, and then the vicar gave the blessing, and invited us all to 'Sundowners' in the church community centre. This turned out to be a hideous octangular building in yellow brick, erected twenty feet from the body of the church and ruining the view of the south façade.

The lady with the child had sneaked out during 'Jerusalem' and greeted the rest of us as we ambled into the hall with McAlistair bringing up the rear. The teenagers had wisely done a bunk, and the boy, who looked about seven, appeared to be taking a leak in the corner of the room.

'I'm Mrs Vicar,' she began unpromisingly. 'So nice to—' but we were never to learn what was so nice, as Mrs Vicar had noticed her micturating son out of the corner of her eye, and rushed over to scoop him up and deposit him in the graveyard.

'Sorry about that,' she said when she returned. 'Hugh, dear, could you find a cloth?' With true Christian humility, the vicar went uncomplainingly into the kitchen area and returned with a bowl of water and a cloth. He got down on his knees on the frayed carpet and began to mop up the mess.

Meanwhile Mrs Vicar was dispensing the sundowners. These consisted of a choice of tea, coffee or orange squash. 'I thought sundowners were supposed to be alcoholic cocktails,' said Kim, who was clearly in a filthy mood after the service and sounded like a petulant teenager herself. 'I was looking forward,' she added in a loud voice to ensure that the pensioners didn't miss a word, 'to what I believe is popularly known as a Long Slow Comfortable Screw Against the Wall'. There was a long and pregnant silence, and then mercifully Kim came to her senses. 'I'm sorry,' she said, 'that was unforgivable of me. An orange juice would be lovely.'

The vicar had finished his task and hove into view with a fatuous smile on his face and a dripping hand proffered in greeting. Knowing what he'd just been mopping up, this wasn't exactly an attractive proposition, but Kim, perhaps in penance, shook it warmly, and Tym and I felt obliged to follow suit.

'A lovely service,' said Kim, now in grave danger of overdoing things.

'You're too too too too k-k-k-k-kind,' he said.'We c-c-c-c-an't seem to get many of the locals in. Indeed, numbers have been falling off very discouragingly since we arrived here three years ago.'

'Have you thought of going back to the Book of Common Prayer, and a proper organ, and perhaps the odd smell and bell?' said Tym, who seemed to be surprisingly well versed in high Anglicanism.

'But all that's so off-off-off-putting and fuddy-d-d-duddy and irrelevant,' said the vicar.

'How relevant is a congregation of nine, plus three visitors?' asked Tym with an edge of anger. 'I'm sorry,' he said in more emollient terms. 'It's not for me to criticize, a long-lapsed communicant and former choirboy. But I know faith needs a bit of mystery about it. You're depriving people of whatever rhymes with luminous,' he said.

'The numinous,' proffered Kim helpfully.

'Well, it's certainly worth thinking about,' said the vicar unhappily.

I looked at Kim and Tym. 'Would you mind if I spoke to the vicar alone?' I said. They shook their heads.

'No, I think you should,' said Kim. 'My husband, Will,' she explained, 'has been having doubts about the problem of suffering. Perhaps it would be better if you went to talk outside.'

'Of course. Delighted. Only too glad to help. Always a bit of a p-p-p-poser, the old prob of suff.' And of course you'd know, I thought.

We went outside and sat on a bench. The vicar's son was doing something unspeakable with a stick and a dead hedgehog, and we both pretended not to notice.

'I'm afraid this is going to come as a bit of a shock,' I said. 'I've come to ask you a few questions about Sophie.'

'Oh Cripes,' he said. 'Double cripes.'

'You know her, then?'

'Yes. As a f-f-f-friend and also in what one might call the Biblical sense.' He swallowed, and his painfully large Adam's apple bobbed up and down in his scrawny neck. 'I really must do something about that son of mine,' he said. The son was now waving several feet of hedgehog's intestines in the air on the end of his stick. The vicar removed the stick from his son to anguished howls, picked up the remains of the hedgehog with it and threw the whole lot across a hedge into the adjoining field. Young Damian, as he seemed to be called, was dispatched back into the hall with the strict instruction to tell mummy that his hands needed washing.

'He's not really called Damian, is he?' I asked.

'No, it's a nickname the teachers and pupils seem to have given him at school. He won't answer to anything else now. Can't understand it. His real name's James.'

'You haven't ever seen a film called *The Omen*, I suppose?'

'No. Am I missing anything good?' he asked eagerly.

'No, no,' I said. 'I should give it a miss if I were you. How did you meet Sophie?'

'I say, you're not one of those frightful tabloid journalists doing a naughty vicar story, are you?' He was rattled, but not as rattled as he would be if he'd read about Sophie's terrible fate in the press.

'No I'm not. I give you my word on that,' I promised.

'Phew, what a relief. Well, I met Sophie at a meeting of the General Synod.'

'You what?' I said incredulously.

'Well, not actually at a Synod meeting. That wouldn't have been Sophie's cup of tea at all. But while I was in London for a meeting. I was staying in a rather awful hotel in the Belgrave Road and was feeling desperately lonely, when I saw a card in a phone box. So with my heart in my mouth, I rang the number and made an appointment. And I went. And I'm afraid I enjoyed it very much. She's ever so nice I think.'

'Yes, she is,' I said. 'I hope.' I didn't like to think of her making a misery of McAlistair's life. Welch had been bad enough but he was strong enough to stand it. Taking money off Hugh would be like taking sweets off blind children.

'And when was this. About three months ago?'

'No, a couple of years ago. I have to pop up to London quite regularly, for meetings at Church House and to research my book on the early Christian martyrs. I usually find time to pay a visit to Sophie. In fact, to be honest, I always find time for a visit to Sophie. Sometimes indeed for two visits to Sophie.' He smiled conspiratorially. It was strange. He had seemed so uncertain of himself in the church, so meek and miserable with his wife and the parishioners, but when he talked about Sophie, obviously exceptionally dangerous territory for a vicar, he seemed confident, indeed happy; as if a light had been switched on. Even his stutter disappeared.

'If you'll forgive my saying so, isn't going to Sophie rather against the rules?'

'Well, yes, of course it is,' he said. 'And I experienced

terrible agonies of guilt at first. But the fact is I feel better after a visit to Sophie, more loving, more confident and better able to fulfil my duties at home, which is often difficult, and in the parish, which as you'll have seen, isn't exactly a hotbed of religious fervour. I have prayed long and hard over this, and though you may think, Well, he would say that, wouldn't he?, I've come to believe that God may have meant me to see that sign in the phone booth.'

'There are those who suggest that Christ and Mary Magdalene may have . . .' I suggested diffidently.

'Yes, there are. It's a terrible heresy but one to which I sometimes find myself clinging. That God incarnate should have known and enjoyed carnal relations, as it were. I have no trouble in accepting that Christ is wholly divine. It is sometimes harder to perceive him as being fully human.'

'I take your point,' I said. 'But I wouldn't go scurrying off to tell your bishop about it if I were you.'

'No. Crikey. Certainly not,' he said.

'You can choose not to answer this question. But does your wife know about Sophie?'

'Good grief no.' Suddenly he looked ill with anxiety. 'You've not come here to tell her, have you?'

'Absolutely not.'

'Sexual intercourse has never played a prominent part in our marriage,' he said sadly. 'None at all since James was born. She has always actively disliked it.'

'I'm sorry,' I said.

'It is a sadness. No doubt she has her sadnesses about me. That I am such an ineffective parish priest for one.'

'The next few questions might be painful, I'm afraid. But I have a good reason for asking them.'

'Fire away.'

'Did Sophie ever blackmail you? Probably about three months ago. Did she send you any pictures of you and her in, er, compromising positions?'

158

For the first time this sad, trusting man showed real signs of anger.

'Certainly not. Sophie would never do anything like that.'

'I'm afraid she has,' I said. 'To a politician and a prep-school headmaster to my certain knowledge.'

'It's inconceivable,' he said, though his tone of voice suggested that he was possibly beginning to have the faintest flicker of doubt.

'You're not certain,' I said. 'Tell me, what were you thinking just then?'

'A few months ago, three months ago as you suggested, we were drinking champagne. It's one of the treats of a visit to Sophie. And she started asking me about James's trust fund, which I'd once mentioned while telling her about my marriage. She must get frightfully bored of people telling her about their marriages but she never shows it.'

'I know,' I said. 'I'm a former client myself. Go on.'

'Well, Deirdre's parents violently disapproved of her marriage to me. They are wealthy upper-middle-class agnostics who find the whole idea of religion faintly embarrassing. They disliked the fact that their daughter became a devout Christian at school, and they disliked it even more when she took up with me. I was never a handsome or an impressive man, a right weed in fact, and it was clear both Mother and Father despised me. At that time I was the curate of Holy Trinity in Guildford. Deirdre was a regular communicant and we'd fallen in love. Chastely, of course, but deeply.

'Well, I went to her father and asked for Deirdre's hand. He was the kind of man who still expected that kind of thing. And he told me that if Deirdre was damn fool enough to marry me neither he nor his wife would ever speak to her again.'

'Sounds like a Victorian melodrama,' I said.

'It was. Anyway, we were married three months later.

Her parents didn't come to the wedding of course, didn't even send a card, and though we both occasionally proffered the olive branch, it was ignored. But then, after twelve years of marriage, James was born.'

'Sounds like an immaculate conception if what you were saying earlier is true.'

'Deirdre would permit sexual intercourse for the purposes of procreation. By then we'd both given up hope, but we went on trying, spasmodically, when Dee could face it.'

The more I saw and heard of Deirdre, the less I liked her. A pious, frigid little prig who bossed her husband something rotten. It was undoubtedly Mrs Vicar who wore the trousers.

'We told Deirdre's parents she was pregnant, and what you might call an armed truce began. We met for the first time in more than a decade, and when James was born we saw each other quite regularly. They fawned on James, relented towards Deirdre and regarded me as something the dog had brought in. Still, I'm used to that,' he said with a wry smile.

'The parents insisted on setting up a trust fund for James. It will provide for a private education, a generous allowance at university and a worryingly large lump sum when James is twenty-one. A potentially corrupting lump sum, one might almost say. Deirdre's father took me to one side and said that just because his daughter had been foolish enough to marry an impoverished, spavined little curate there was no reason why his grandson should suffer. That "curate" hurt. I had my own parish by then, a tough inner city parish in Birmingham.

'Over the months and years I'd told Sophie all this, and three months ago she asked me if, in an emergency, I could gain access to any of the money in James's fund. I told her there wasn't a chance. The whole thing's so hedged about with lawyers and authorized signatures that it would be easier for me to rob a bank.'

160

'"So you've only got your measly vicar's pay, then?" she said. "That's peanuts, isn't it?"'

'"Peanuts,"' I said.

'And she told me to forget she'd ever said anything and offered me an FPS on the house. Actually she seemed relieved I hadn't got any money. And when I saw her a few weeks ago, nothing was said about our earlier conversation, though she seemed a little sad and abstracted at times.'

'It all seems to fit,' I said. 'Sophie was looking for big money about three months ago and she resorted to blackmail to get it. But she hated doing it. And she seems to have let off the people she liked best.' Or, I added to myself, pitied most.

'But what proof do you have that she was blackmailing anyone?'

'How do you think I found you?' I said. 'Sophie made a tape of the people she had targeted, and she handed it to me. When I found her . . .' there was no gentle way of putting this, 'with her tongue cut out.'

The vicar got to his feet, took a few staggering paces behind an elaborate box tomb and threw up whatever Deirdre had given him for lunch. He came back wiping his mouth with a handkerchief. 'When did this happen?' he asked in an appalled tone of voice.

'Last Wednesday,' I said and told him the full gory story.

'I must go to her. But how can I? What can I tell Deirdre? I'm not due to go to London for another fortnight.'

'I'd much rather you didn't go to her. It's not going to do Sophie any good at the moment. And the hospital authorities might tell the police you've been. Sophie didn't want the police involved and I'm going to be in all kinds of trouble if they find out I've got this tape. And I don't suppose you would enjoy a police interrogation very much either.'

'No, you're right. But poor Sophie. Poor Sophie.'

'This is going to seem a terrible cheek. But just for the

sake of keeping things tidy, do you have an alibi for last Wednesday afternoon?'

'But you can't possible think—'

'I believe you. But I'm down to my last suspect now. I don't want to start getting doubts in the middle of the night.'

He got out his diary. 'No, I'm afraid not,' he said. 'I made some house visits in the morning and took the rest of the day off. Bird-spotting in Walberswick. Deirdre gave me a packed lunch and I didn't come home till seven. Hardly saw a soul all day. Certainly no one I knew. But you do believe me?' he pleaded.

'I believe you,' I said, but a tiny corner of my brain was thinking that he would have had ample time to drive up to London, attend to Sophie, and be home in time for supper. But why now, three months after Sophie's black-mailing appeared to have ceased? And in any case, his whole story rang true. It was impossible to believe this nervous man could be so persuasive a liar, still less that he should be capable of such violence.

We stared across the fields in silence for a minute or two, thinking our own thoughts, and then Deirdre appeared at the door of the community hall.

'Hugh, I'm sorry to interrupt, but Damian's started having a temper tantrum and I can't stop him screaming.'

'I'll come in a moment,' he yelled back tetchily. 'Can't you see I'm busy?' Deirdre visibly bridled at this unfamiliar brusqueness and retreated huffily back inside to the sound of a blood-curdling scream from within.

'I must go in a moment,' he said. 'If he gets really hysterical he can go on all night.'

He awkwardly pulled a bit of paper out of a trouser pocket beneath his surplice, and scribbled a phone number. 'Keep me posted. And will you join me in praying for Sophie?'

'Yes, of course,' I said.

'Your pretext for our private chat seems to have had

more than a grain of truth in it,' he said sadly. 'One way or another we seem to have given the problem of suffering a pretty comprehensive airing.'

I nodded. 'Are you going to send James away to school?'

'I long to,' he admitted. 'He needs a discipline we are well beyond giving him. But Deirdre's dead against it.'

'I should try putting your foot down more often,' I said. 'It seemed to work just now. And you might find this place helps her to change her mind.' I handed him David Welch's card.

'The headmaster you were talking about?'

'Yeah. But keep it to yourself. Though I'm sure he wouldn't mind a private chat on the subject if you feel a need to talk. And here's my number too,' I added, writing it on the back of Welch's card.

'Thank you,' he said. 'I think I might need to talk. It's all been a dreadful shock.'

He was just about to get another one. There was a huge crash of breaking crockery from inside the hall, and then the James/Damian creature shot out like a bullet, screaming with devilish glee. Deirdre followed in hot pursuit, and Tym and Kim and the old boots appeared at the doorway with broad smiles on their faces. For a moment it looked as though Mrs Vicar was going to catch her son, but she took a terrific tumble after tripping over a broken cross. Damian, and it was by now hard to think of him as James, turned, saw her plight, flicked her a malevolent V-sign and nipped through a gap in the hedge.

'Hugh, for once in your life can't you do something to help?' screamed Deirdre spitefully.

'Whoops, I'd better go,' he said. The vicar had considerable difficulty in getting through the hole in the hedge. Deirdre was through it like a ferret up a drainpipe. We watched, in wonder, as first Damian, then McAlistair and finally Mrs Vicar disappeared into the woods on the other side of the field.

*

Tym and Kim fell asleep once we'd reached the A12, and I drove along fretting about the identity of the giant. An enterprising reporter trying to get some dirt on me seemed preferable to being tailed by one of Darbyshire's men.

Thank to endless delays coming into London we didn't get home until after 11. I parked, and we patrolled the street to see if we were under observation, but there was no sign of either the black Golf or the tall man. I closed the front door gratefully behind us, and Kim poured out large malts. They were so nice that we all had another one, and the booze was just beginning to soothe away the rough edges of the day when the doorbell rang, persistently. Kim, who was making chicken sandwiches in the kitchen, called out that she'd get it, and I heard her gasp when she saw who was there.

'Well, Mr Adamson,' she said. 'This is an unexpected treat. You must have got that nice driver of yours to follow us.'

Adamson, doing a good impression of a rabid Rottweiler, marched into our sitting room, closely followed by Kim.

'That thug belongs behind bars,' said the Minister, pointing at Tym.

'But you seem to think that about almost everyone you disagree with,' said Kim sweetly.

'I haven't come here to argue or explain,' he said. 'I want those photos and I want them now.'

'But—' began Kim, and I feared she was going to blow the gaffe.

'We haven't got the pictures here,' I said quickly. 'They're somewhere safe. Under lock and key.'

The Minister actually growled. He was, I realized, almost beside himself with rage and fear. The prospect of political ruin must be terrible to a man of such puffed-up vanity. After an evident struggle Adamson seemed to gain control of himself.

'Let me spell this out very plainly,' he said. 'I mean to

have those photographs. And I can make things very unpleasant for you if you don't hand them over.'

'And how would you go about that?' Kim asked.

'As I've already suggested, I have excellent contacts within the police and the security services. You might find it inconvenient, to say the least, if the drug squad were to raid this house and find say, half a kilo of pure heroin.'

I gulped. 'I think the Minister's got a point, I really do. The trouble is we can't get hold of the pictures tonight. Would tomorrow do?'

He nodded curtly.

'Do you want to come here for them?' I asked.

He shook his head with distaste. 'You will come to my house,' he said, giving a swanky address near St James's Park, 'at 9.30 p.m. You will leave that . . . thing behind,' he said, pointing at Tym.

'Will you be alone?' I asked. 'Aren't you under twenty-four-hour protection? And what about your wife? She might find it a bit odd, two scruffy strangers calling round.'

'I will be alone. Though I can naturally ask for Special Branch protection whenever I need it,' he explained smugly. 'And my wife is staying in the constituency this week.'

'Well, see you tomorrow evening, then,' I said.

'You will seriously regret it should you fail to turn up.' He wandered over to the shelves which contained our CD collection and the hi-fi. 'Do you enjoy your music?' he asked.

'Very much,' I smiled sweetly.

'What the fuck's it got to do with you?' said Kim, giving me the furious look of a woman who has just realized she is married to a wimp.

'Just this,' said the Minister, picking up our really quite expensive stacked stereo system and hurling the whole lot on to the tiled hearth. 'I'm afraid you won't be listening to it for a while.'

Tym stood up with a scowl on his face. Kim looked at

me with contempt. 'Are you just going to let him get away with it?'

'Sit down, Tym,' I said. 'And be quiet, Kim. I don't think you realize quite how serious our position is. Mr Adamson undoubtedly has powerful friends.'

The Minister smirked. He was a great one for smirks. 'I'm glad at least one of you has seen sense,' he said. 'I look forward to seeing you tomorrow.'

'Yes, of course,' I said, and saw him to the door. 'Goodnight, Minister.'

Tym looked confused and Kim scornful when I returned to the sitting room and surveyed the wrecked stereo. 'We should be able to claim for it on the contents insurance,' I said.

'Is that all you've got to say?' asked Kim furiously.

'It's usually a good idea to let bullies think they've got the upper hand for a while,' I said. 'It lulls them into a false sense of confidence.'

'But what are we going to do?'

I went over to the sideboard, found the malt whisky, and refreshed all our glasses. 'I'll tell you,' I said. 'But first a toast. To Her Majesty's Junior Minister for Crime and Punishment.'

'To Her Majesty's Junior Minister for Crime and Punishment,' they echoed in puzzled voices.

'Right,' I said. 'Here's the plan.'

Monday 31 July

Look here upon this picture, and on this.
Hamlet

We gathered in the Dolphin Square cocktail bar, 8 for 8.30 p.m., as arranged over several telephone calls during the day. Tym was there to greet us as our host. He'd surprised Kim and me that morning by thanking us for putting him up and saying he was going to walk back home to start recording his Hyde Park car-pound song.

'I suppose twenty-five years is quite a long gap between albums,' he said with a grin. 'But this new one's going to be my masterpiece.' His eyes were shining as we arrived, and he looked terrific in his black velvet evening dress with a scarlet cummerbund and bow tie. I made the introductions.

'Tym, this is Brian, the production editor at Botticelli Publications. And this is Daphne, our receptionist.' All thirteen stone of Daphne was swathed in what seemed like several square kilometres of black tulle, artfully arranged to expose her breathtaking cleavage and surprisingly shapely ankles to maximum advantage.

'I've got the other costume in my bag, Will,' she said cheerfully, as she squeezed herself into one of the wicker chairs and began her assault on the peanuts. I'd phoned Bri the previous evening, told him about Sophie's tape and our adventures over the past few days, and invited him to help us in the final round.

'I'd be reet pleased if there's owt I can do to help,' he'd

167

said. I told him my plan. 'Gradely, very gradely indeed. 'Appen I'll get on with it now.'

Tym poured out glasses of champagne and Kim arrived next, straight from work but dressed to kill in her chap's dinner jacket, dress shirt and tight black satin trousers. She greeted Brian with generous warmth considering how often he'd led me astray in the past, and gushed over Daphne's outfit. The two seemed to hit it off immediately. I looked anxiously at my watch, sweating uncomfortably in my own too-tight dinner jacket. It was quarter to nine, and two of our key players hadn't arrived.

'Don't worry,' said Brian. 'They're both one hundred per cent reliable.' And at that moment they waltzed in. We'd all made an effort to look smart for the evening, but these two gleamed with a star quality that made everyone else seem dowdy. The man was well over six feet tall, Ray-banned, impressively pony-tailed and dressed in an amazing midnight-blue silk suit. His partner, with her great mane of dark hair, somehow gave the impression that she wasn't so much wearing her studded leather jacket, leather mini-skirt and low-cut white T-shirt as on the point of taking them all off. Which, of course, she usually was.

'Hello, Bri,' she said in a homely Essex accent. 'How are you doing, mate?'

Brian made the introduction. 'This is Miriam,' he said with almost paternal pride. 'Three times winner of Botti-celli Publications' annual poll for the model our readers would most like to have sex with.' Miriam smiled demurely and looked becomingly modest about this dazzling accolade. 'Load of old cobblers, really,' she giggled.

'And this is Mr Vince Baxter, Britain's top glamour photographer.' Vince raised a hand in greeting. I noticed that two of his fingers were missing.

'Vince used to be in the army until he got blown up by a landmine in Northern Ireland,' said Brian. 'He was an unarmed combat instructor, which might prove handy later on.'

Tym poured champagne for our sublime new partners in crime and refilled everyone else's glass. 'Bottoms up,' he giggled, like an over-excited schoolboy. 'Bottoms up,' we roared back at him.

Forty-five minutes later Kim and I stood on the steps of the beautiful Georgian town house near St James's Park. I kissed her on the cheek and she squeezed my hand. 'Here we go, then,' I said. There was a heart-stopping wait and then the Minister opened the door.

'On time, I see,' he said, looking with relief at the large brown envelope in my hand. 'I thought you'd come round to my way of thinking. You'd better come in.'

At this Kim put her fingers to her mouth and blew a deafening wolf whistle, a trick I'd tried to learn, in vain, ever since I was a child. The doors of the two taxis parked outside opened, and the gang came storming up the steps to the door. Vince was first and at the sight of his athletic steps and tall frame, the Minister vainly tried to slam the door in all our faces. I got my foot in it and Vince immediately forced it open. Within a second he had the Minister up against the wall of his own hall with his arm twisted painfully behind his back.

'If you don't struggle I won't feel obliged to hurt you,' he said calmly. Brian came next, carrying Vince's aluminium camera suitcase, followed by the others.

'Nice to see you again, Minister,' said Tym, locking the door behind him and pocketing the key.

'Right, chaps and Kim search the house quickly, girls get changed,' ordered Vince briskly. 'If there's anyone else around shout out immediately and I'll come and deal with them.' He led the Minister into the first room that opened off the hall. 'See you back here as soon as possible,' he told the rest of us.

Daphne and Miriam disappeared down the corridor and Brian said he'd check the basement. Tym took the rest of the ground floor with Kim and I searched the two upper floors. It was a perfect house, immaculately furnished and decorated, and I spent thirty seconds gazing covetously at Adamson's wonderful wood-panelled study with its Turkish carpets, huge antique table, and sonorously ticking regulator clock.

We returned to the drawing room on the ground floor and reported that there was no one else around. The Minister was pacing the room, trying to look furious but actually looking deeply apprehensive. 'This is outrageous,' he kept spluttering. 'Quite outrageous.' I noticed however that he didn't seem to be making any effort to pick up the phone on its gold-leaf encrusted occasional table to call his friends in Special Branch. Daphne was already dressed in her St Trinian's outfit and brandishing a cane, while Miriam was fully covered in a dowdy towelling dressing gown.

'Right,' said Vince, who had a natural authority about him that commanded respect rather than resentment, 'I want this to be short and sharp and as painless as possible. Nor do I want it to turn into a ritual of sadistic humiliation, so everyone is to leave the room except the girls.'

Brian groaned out loud with disappointment. 'Oh, Vince,' he wailed, like a child who'd dropped his ice cream cornet. 'I've been looking forward to this all day.'

'Out,' said Vince firmly. 'Someone keep watch on the front-door steps and ring the bell three times if anyone looks like interrupting us.'

We filed out of the room.

'Oh, Will,' Vince suddenly called. 'We'll be needing you as well.' I caught Kim's eye and she looked shifty. She'd been in the same cab as Vince and the girls while I'd travelled with Tym and Brian.

'What's all this about?' I hissed.

'You're about to find out,' she said. Except she could hardly speak because she was giggling so much.

'If this means what I think it means—' I began, but Vince told me to shut up and close the door.

'Right,' said Vince. 'I'm not using any fancy lights, just a flash, because it will make the pictures look as though they've been snatched in clandestine circumstances and add to the drama. Minister, I'd like you to strip, please, and bend over the sofa. Daphne, you pretend to be giving him six of the best.'

'I have no intention of doing any such thing,' said Adamson.

Vince walked over to the Minister, put his arm companionably round his shoulder and whispered in his ear. The colour drained from Adamson's face and he began to take off his shirt and tie with almost indecent haste. Within fifteen minutes Vince had got all the shots he needed. Indeed, rather more than he needed in my view. First he took a sequence of Daphne pretending to cane the Minister. She did land one absolute sizzler on his backside and was swiftly rebuked by Vince. 'I've got a brother in one of his 'effing boot camps,' she explained.

'This is no time for personal vengeance,' said Vince. 'We've got a job to do, OK.'

Vince followed the corporal punishment shots with snaps of the Minister ogling Miriam as she disported herself in a number of delightful and at times frankly improbable positions on and around a *chaise-longue* wearing a rapidly diminishing collection of black silk lingerie. By the time Miriam had finished this routine Adamson was in a state of considerable, and in the circumstances, almost heroic arousal, and Tym got shots as Miriam fondled him while Daphne, now divested of the upper half of her costume, gently rubbed one of her enormous breasts against his cheek. For a few moments the Minister looked genuinely happy, as if he'd forgotten that all this entertainment was both compulsory and being documented for posterity.

'No paper would use a photo of an erect penis,' said Vince. 'But it will give the boys on the picture desk a giggle, and these shots will crop very nicely at waist level.' The Minister's manhood shrunk visibly as he spoke.

171

'Right, Will, get your kit off,' ordered Vince.

'I say, that's not absolutely necessary, is it?' I whimpered.

'Get your kit off, Will,' repeated Vince, to cheers and whistles from the girls. I stripped off, feeling horribly ashamed of all my acres of pale white naked flesh. I stood there, helplessly, my hands modestly clasped in front of me, when Vince suddenly grabbed both my arms from behind and I found that I'd been handcuffed.

'Right, Will, on your knees in front of the Minister, head bowed, as if you were giving him a blow job.'

'Oh, come on, dash it all, I can't, I really can't,' I blustered.

'No need to get too close. You can remain a good six inches away from the Honourable Member's honourable member and the camera angles will tell a very different story,' said Vince. 'Kim said he'd been theatening you with the old planted drugs routine. If he tries it you'll be able to produce these pictures in court. They should be useful when you suggest that the Minister might have been taking a personal interest in your affairs.'

I closed my eyes and knelt and thought of England, and after a few seconds Vince said I could get up again. He undid the cuffs and the girls put on their dressing gowns and went back to the kitchen to change. The Minister, still naked, knelt forward on the sofa and buried his face in his hands.

'What happens now?' he said at last.

'You get dressed, you write me a cheque for nine hundred and fifty pounds, which is exactly what I paid for the hi-fi, and you do nothing else whatsoever,' I said, squeezing myself into the trousers of my dinner-jacket.

'But what about the pictures, you'd already got pictures. What do you need more for?'

'Your big mistake was coming round and making threats,' I said. 'We had no pictures. If Sophie said she'd let you have the prints and negatives back that's just what she'd have done. And if you'd stopped to think about it, you would have realized she couldn't possibly have got all the shots I described with a single camera, in the middle of a violent tussle.'

He groaned.

'Making threats was very silly. The slate could have been wiped clean by now. But with you demanding photographs we hadn't got, and threatening dire consequences if we failed to deliver, we had no alternative but to get some, fast. As our insurance policy. I'd put some clothes on if I were you.'

Adamson, about the same height as me and just as plump, shambled to his feet, and started getting dressed.

'If you publish those pictures, I'll explain just how you obtained them, you shits.'

'It wouldn't really do you any good,' I said. 'I haven't told you this before but we've got a tape made by Sophie listing the people she was planning to blackmail. It's got your name on it, which wouldn't do you any good at all with the police if they were to get hold of it. You must have heard they've been asking people who knew her to come forward.'

He groaned again.

'And however culpable the circumstances in which the photographs were taken, no tabloid newspaper could resist publishing them. Your career could never recover from the ridicule, never mind the scandal.'

'Especially since we'd send the ones of you smiling,' said Vince. 'The camera never lies, as they say. There were just a few moments back there when you were enjoying yourself.'

'But we have no intention of sending the photographs to anyone,' I added. 'I was tempted to say that keeping them secret was conditional on you dropping your plans for that absurd prison-island, but that would be blackmail too. You're free to pursue whatever potty scheme you like, just so long as you keep quiet about poor Sophie and leave all the people who have been here tonight alone.'

'Why should I believe you?' he said.

'No reason at all. Only time will tell. But if it means anything at all to a politician as devious as yourself, I give you my word that those photographs and the negatives will be lodged in a solicitor's safe, sight unseen, and you won't hear about them again provided we have no trouble from you.'

'So I've just got to trust you?' he bleated.

'I can see that trust is a difficult concept for a politician to grasp. But it will be much better for your peace of mind if you do trust me.'

'Well, we'd better be off,' said Vince. 'I don't suppose you'll want to say goodbye to the others. If I was you, I'd have a few stiff drinks and forget all about it.'

The fluent, slimy Minister was for once almost lost for words. But not quite. I offered him my hand but he ignored it. 'You cunt,' he snarled.

'And a very good night to you, too,' I said, and we left the room and shut the door behind us. The others were waiting in the hall.

'Did you enjoy the handcuffs?' asked Brian.

'How did you know about them?' I hissed.

'I'm afraid,' said Kim, 'that we took it in turns to look through the keyhole.'

'You bastards,' I said, then giggled. 'One way and another it was quite a show, I should think.'

'We could have sold tickets at a hundred quid a time,' said Tym, unlocking the door and letting us all out. He closed it, very gently behind him. Our cabs were still waiting, as instructed, and we piled into them. I glanced up and down the street but I was reasonably confident the giant wasn't on our trail.

I told the driver to take us to the Alhambra Theatre. We were off to confront the last punter on Sophie's tape, and the butterflies were fluttering wildly in my stomach.

'You're certain he'll be there?' I asked Kim, who was travelling with me and Tym this time.

'Nothing is certain in this sublunary world,' she replied infuriatingly. 'But the PR man Danny Timson was ninety-nine per cent sure that he would be.'

'Right,' I said. 'Fingers crossed and let's just hope he hasn't got too many leather-clad boot boys with him.'

The cabs dropped us outside the Alhambra where the 1500th performance of Andrew Lloyd Webber's *Macbeth the Musical* was drawing to a close.

'The party doesn't get underway for half an hour or so,' said Kim, consulting the invitations. 'We've got time for a drink.' We joined the others and crammed ourselves into an impossibly over-crowded pub. The idea of getting served in this throng made me feel weak and I worried that Tym would be fazed by the crowd. But Vince volunteered to get them in and Tym said he'd help. They approached the bar with the determination of men going into battle.

Brian had bought an *Evening Standard* and showed me the front-page splash. FURY GROWS OVER ISLAND PRISON SCHEME it screamed. It wasn't just the Opposition and the prison unions that were gunning for Adamson, said the report, but also many of his Government colleagues, who were appalled by what was seen as yet another 'public relations fiasco'. It was only a matter of time, predicted the paper's political editor, before the Minister 'resigned' to spend more time with his family.

'It hasn't been his day, really, has it?' said Kim.

'He'll survive somehow or other,' I said gloomily.

'You realize,' said Brian thoughtfully, 'that we could make an absolute fortune with those pictures. There couldn't be a better time to flog them than in the middle of this row. All we'd have to do is hand them over to Max Clifford, enjoy the fun and get rich.'

'Get thee behind me, Satan,' I said, though exactly the same thought had crossed my mind.

Vince and Tym returned with two bottles of miraculously cold champagne, and we drank a second toast to the beleaguered Junior Minister for Crime and Punishment. Vince, Miriam and Daphne had only a sketchy idea of what we were up to, so after swearing them to secrecy, Kim and I told them the tale to date.

'So you see,' said Kim, 'unless Sophie was attacked by someone we know nothing about at all, it looks as though Bill Hutchinson's our man. He's our last chance.'

'But he's gay, isn't he?' said Daphne. 'I was ever so disappointed when he announced it. I'd always fancied him something rotten.'

Bill Hutchinson was indeed gay, loudly and vengefully gay. Until just a few months earlier he'd seemed an entirely amiable thirtysomething actor with a meaty role as a harassed GP in a popular soap. The character he played was gay, and at a time when the programme's ratings seemed to be slipping, Hutchinson had come out, noisily and tearfully, on a TV chat show.

'But aren't you often seen in nightclubs with an enviable succession of attractive women?' his interviewer had asked.

'A diversionary measure of which I now feel thoroughly ashamed,' Bill had replied. He now believed it was time for all gay men and women to stand up and be counted.

Fine and courageous stuff if you felt the need to parade your sexuality in public, though for the life of me I couldn't see why anyone should, and Hutchinson had been applauded by many. But he had promptly become the most tedious kind of gay activist. He'd joined an organization called Act Queer. It had originally been founded by a group of actors who argued that gay roles in theatre, film and television should only be played by gays. Having straights playing gays, they argued, was as offensive as having white actors blacking up to play ethnic minorities. A contentious but possibly justifiable proposition.

But Act Queer had then extended its range. They'd

begun to insist that at least 15 per cent of the cast of any film, play or television show should be played by gays, and had set up a register of gay actors to help casting directors achieve the quota. Many had been only too happy to put their names down. But others had no intention of declaring themselves one way or the other, yet nevertheless found their names on the register. Several actors had threatened to sue for libel but the cases still hadn't come to court. And one actor, with a wife and family, had shot himself after Act Queer had outed him.

Now, in alliance with a couple of other militant homosexual organizations, Act Queer was intent on outing other figures in the public eye – bishops, politicians, high-ranking soldiers, headteachers, judges and even prominent journalists – and Hutchinson seemed to be a particularly busy member of the homosexual bully-boys. Sophie couldn't have chosen a more deserving target for blackmail. On news footage of demonstrations, he seemed to be warped with fanaticism, his face twisted with spite. He would have had a huge amount to lose if Sophie had managed to get pictures of him with her, and I wasn't looking forward to our interview one bit.

Vince refilled our glasses. 'How do we know he's going to be at the do tonight?'

'He played Macduff when the show first opened. All the past cast members have been invited,' said Kim.

We crossed the road to the Alhambra, and went down the stairs to the Cinderella Bar, which was packed with luvvies shouting at the tops of their voices and pouring gallons of champagne down their throats. My old domain, I thought sadly, and suddenly *Theatre World* seemed like an Eden from which I'd been banished by the stain of infertility.

Vince and Miriam spotted a beautiful model turned fifth-rate (but hugely profitable) actress they knew, and Daphne and a visibly star-struck Brian went with them to be introduced. I asked Tym if he was OK and he nodded happily, swigged his champagne and suddenly spotted a musician he said he recognized from years back. 'Do you mind if I go and talk to him?' he asked. 'It would be great if I could get him to help on the new album.'

'On your way,' Kim told him fondly, and squeezed my hand as we watched him fight his way through the crowd. 'Like a child growing up and leaving the family home,' she said with a sniff and a smile. 'And all in the space of a few days. I'm going to miss him when he's gone.'

We trawled the room together in search of Hutchinson. There were, as always, people to avoid. Andrew Lloyd Webber for one, who had been less than chuffed by *Theatre World*'s cool review of the show ('CURSE OF MACBETH AS LLOYD WEBBER FLOPS' we had confidently and erroneously predicted). Then there was the insufferably patronizing impresario Raymond Hawkes, who would delight in hearing about my new line of employment ('In the gutter at last, Mr Benson, where you belong').

But there were some notably good eggs there too – including the saintly trio of Donald Sinden, Bob Monkhouse and Tim Rice – and after a lot of chat and far too much champagne, we'd finally made it right round the huge circular bar without catching a glimpse of Bill Hutchinson.

At that point Daphne lurched into view, tottering daintily. 'I've spotted him' she announced, pink-faced and triumphant. 'He's sitting all on his own in a corner, but with so many people standing up he's virtually invisible. I only found him 'cos I was looking for somewhere quiet to take out my contact lens.'

She pointed to an obscure alcove and Kim and I pushed our way through the heaving crush of theatricals. He looked rather forlorn in his corner, sitting at a small table covered with other people's discarded glasses.

'Bill Hutchinson?' I said.

He looked up and gave a curiously shy smile. 'Don't tell me you're prepared to speak to the pariah?' he said. 'I've lost count of the number of times I've been cut dead tonight. So I'm just sitting here, drinking my way through a bottle I collared from a waiter, trying to get up the Dutch courage I need to fight my way back through the crowd and go home.'

This wasn't the Bill Hutchinson we'd seen on the news clips of late. He was ironic, dignified and instantly likeable.

'We need to talk,' I said. 'Somewhere a little quieter and more private than this.'

'Great,' he said. 'It won't be so bad getting across the room with the two of you. Who are you, anyway?'

'I'm Will Benson,' I said. 'I used to work for *Theatre World* but don't any more. And this is my wife Kim. She's still chief sub there.'

'Right, let's go,' he said, picking up his half-full bottle and another unopened one he had secreted beneath his feet. 'I didn't think one bottle was going to be enough,' he explained.

People turned their backs on Hutchinson as we made our way through the room and words like rat and scum were muttered. One doughty old actress, a memorable Lady Bracknell a few years earlier, attempted to throw her glass of champagne in his face. Unfortunately she missed and hit mine, but perhaps I was tarred by association anyway. She certainly didn't apologize.

'Phew,' I said, mopping my face with a hankie as we made it into the corridor outside. 'I wouldn't like to be in your shoes twenty-four hours a day.'

Bill led the way upstairs, down another corridor and opened a door.

'The royal box,' he said. 'We're unlikely to be troubled here.' It was gloomy, almost dark, the only light coming from the stage, where a few technicians were adjusting the set. But there were gilded chairs, a table to sit around and, best of all, an ashtray. Princess Margaret, for the use of, presumably. I rolled an Old Disgusting and Hutchinson asked if he could have one too. 'Thanks,' he said, taking a deep drag and coughing violently. 'I needed that.'

'If you don't mind my saying so,' said Kim, pouring champagne, 'you're supposed to be a shit and yet you quite obviously aren't.'

'Ah, you noticed that, did you?' he said with a grin. 'God, I've been longing to talk to someone, and come to think of it, a representative of *Theatre World* suits me very well indeed. I think I've got a bit of a scoop for you.'

'I haven't got my notebook,' said Kim. 'And I'm too pissed to take down shorthand anyway.'

'It'll keep,' he said.

'Right,' said Kim, gratefully taking another swig of champagne.

'Well, the first thing you need to know is I'm not exclusively gay. I'm cheerfully bi, though mostly I go for the ladies these days. But Act Queer was approached by a vindictive former boyfriend who told them about our relationship, and because I was playing a gay character on televison and had always refused to comment on my sexuality, which, as the bishop said, is something of a grey area, I was targeted for outing.

'I got a letter from Act Queer, and though there was a lot of cant about what a brave and wonderful thing my coming out would be, what a beacon of hope for oppressed gays everywhere, there was no mistaking the implicit threat that things could get very nasty for me if I didn't comply.

'I was furious, though not especially upset. But I've got a couple of friends whose lives have been made a misery by Act Queer, and I decided it was time to do something about it. So I told the producers of *Group Practice* that I wanted to come out. The devious men in suits were delighted because it would give the ratings a boost, and fixed me up with the chat show.'

'So all the tears and emotion were false,' said Kim. 'I was genuinely moved.'

'It's called acting,' said Hutchinson. 'I'm a much better actor than I'm often given credit for. Anyway, after the chat show, I contacted Act Queer, said I felt hugely relieved about coming out and would like to offer my services to the organization. And they greeted me like the prodigal son.'

'But what was your aim?'

'Infiltration and subversion,' he said with a hint of irony. 'I've dug up a lot of dirt. How they get their information, the kind of pressure they put on people. I've got photocopies of the letters they sent to the actor who shot himself, for instance, revealing their cruel cat-and-mouse games with him and his heartbreaking, panic-stricken appeals to be let off the hook.

'And you may have noticed, despite the strong words and the evil-looking demos, that there hasn't actually been much naming of names in the past few months. While pretending to be the most radical and spiteful member of the organization, I've actually been telling them to hold their fire until they can come up with some really big names. They've agreed, and in the meantime I hope to publish everything I've found out. With luck everyone will be so disgusted with Act Queer even the gutter press will ignore them.'

'Blimey,' said Kim. 'I take my hat off to you. And are you really going to give this story to *Theatre World*? You could make a fortune with it elsewhere.'

'I wouldn't want to make money out of those scum. And if I give it to *Theatre World*, it's a quick way of getting all the other papers to take an interest. They won't feel like spoiling the story because it doesn't come from a direct rival. Anyway, I've a soft spot for the paper. I've been a subscriber since I was ten.'

'We'll need to move fast if it's to appear this week. We go to press on Tuesdays.'

'I'd like to leave it another week actually. I'm just about to get the cherry on top of the cake.'

'What's that?'

'A photograph and a sworn statement from Terry Heer-

181

ing's former girlfriend,' he said, naming the leader of Act Queer. 'He confessed all one drunken night in the pub, how he'd lost his virginity to a girl called Rowena Gwilym in the rec at Leatherhead when he was a teenager. She was a local girl and Gwilym is quite an uncommon name, so I tracked down her parents simply by looking in the phone book. They put me on to their daughter, who absolutely hates what Heering's doing and says she has some very juicy stories to tell. She's married now, but more than happy to talk. I'm meeting her for lunch. We're going to "in" our Terry.'

'Cor!' said Kim, her eyes lighting up at the prospect of the scoop to come, before suddenly staring embarrassedly at the floor. 'This is a bit awkward, isn't it, Will?'

'It is a bit,' I said, but having met Hutchinson and heard his tale, I couldn't believe he'd done it. But, as the man said, he was a very good actor. I opened the second bottle and refilled our glasses.

'Have you seen the papers in the past few days?' I asked.

'No. I got sick of reading about my new and nasty self and decided to have a rest from them.'

'And does the name Sophie mean anything to you?' I asked.

'What, Sophie, the Pimlico tart?' he said cheerfully. 'I'll say. She's been my salvation these past few weeks. The only person apart from my agent who knows what I've been up to. You're not easily offended, are you?' he added looking at Kim.

She shook her head.

'Well, there's me and Sophie,' he said, producing a photograph from his wallet. They were lying on their backs, naked, and holding glasses of champagne. Hutchinson was cupping one of Sophie's breasts with his free hand, and I noticed that Sophie had an arm down the side of the bed, presumably reaching for the trigger which set off the camera. I felt a sharp tug of grief for her. She seemed so alive in that picture. Alive I thought, looking intently at her face, but also troubled.

'Try not to get cross,' I said. 'I've got to ask you this. Did Sophie ever try to blackmail you. With a picture like this?'

'Yes, the silly twat did. But I told her not to be so daft.'

'Tell us about it,' said Kim.

'What's this all about?' Hutchinson asked, suddenly suspicious. 'Why the big interest in Sophie and whether I've seen the papers?'

'I promise we have her best interests at heart,' I said. 'And yours, too, come to that. I'll explain everything if you'll just trust us for a few minutes and answer our questions as accurately as you can. When did you first meet Sophie?'

'About four months ago,' he said, apparently mollified. 'Act Queer had made their first unwelcome advances and I was already thinking up my scheme. I realized I'd need to be a bit discreet on the sex front, couldn't be seen in any public places with the ladies, and when I saw Sophie's card I went to see her. We got on really well and she pretended she hadn't a clue who I was, which can be a relief sometimes when you're in the public eye. I used to go at least once a week. Anyway, after I'd done that chat show, she seemed really strung up the next time I visited her. I asked her what the matter was and she said she was terribly sorry but she was going to have to ask me for thirty thousand. She'd seen me on the telly, she'd got pictures of us together, and she'd send them to the press unless I paid up.

'I could tell she was upset, so I asked her why she was doing it. She wouldn't tell me. She just wept. So I gave her a cuddle and we had a glass of champagne and when she'd calmed down she asked me why I'd made such an unnecessary exhibition of myself on the chat show. So I told her all about it. And she said I was to forget she'd ever said anything and wished me luck in queering Act Queer's pitch, as she put it.

183

'I was still worried though. If Sophie could threaten me she could threaten others. I begged her to give it up but she said the money was desperately needed and she was only targeting people who could afford to stump up and were strong enough to stand up to it emotionally.'

'That's true,' I said, and told him about the vicar and Tym.

'But what's your interest in all this?'

'One last question,' I said. 'Can you tell us what you were doing at 3.30 p.m. last Wednesday?'

He thought for a moment, then smiled. 'Spending a chastening couple of hours with my agent. He's fed up with getting complaints about my behaviour from his other clients, and he's even more fed up because I haven't had an offer of work since I joined forces with Act Queer. He respects what I'm trying to do, but he's missing his percentage. The BBC has already told him they're planning to write me out of the next series of *Group Practice*. Most of the cast are refusing to work with me. And quite right too, really.'

'Who's your agent?'

'Andrew Simon.'

'But we know him. He's Harriet Smythe's agent, isn't he?'

'Rather more than that now. They got married last year.'

'And he never sent us an invite,' said Kim.

'He's here actually. He gallantly agreed to stick with me at the party and then melted into the background when things got nasty.'

'He has a way of disappearing when he's wanted. It was a gastronomic tour of France last time.'

'But he's honest,' said Kim. 'And he did turn up in Blackpool when we needed him.'

'Do you mind going to find him?' I said to Kim. 'I'll break the news to Bill here.'

Kim went off to look for Mr Simon. I told Bill the story of the last few days.

'But why didn't you tell me earlier?' Bill asked angrily.

'Because I thought you'd done it,' I said. 'And you're still under suspicion until Simon gives you the all-clear.'

Kim arrived with Simon in tow, blinking owlishly behind his specs.

'Harriet wasn't at all pleased to see me,' said Kim with a grin. 'Especially when I told her how upset we were that we hadn't been invited to the wedding.'

'Yes, I'm sorry about that. I put your name on the list, and Harriet crossed it off. She was very angry indeed.'

'With satisfactory results, I hope?' asked Kim.

'Very satisfactory indeed, thank you,' he smiled. 'Now, lovely though it is to see all three of you, I really must be getting back to the party. Sir Andrew seems to be on the point of offering Harriet the lead in his next musical.'

'What were you doing at 3.30 last Wednesday afternoon?' Kim and I chorused together.

'Haven't a clue,' said Simon, consulting his diary. 'Ah yes,' he said, 'I was talking to this silly sod here. Are you going to pack it in soon, Bill?'

'I'll be hustling for work on Thursday week,' said the actor. 'After *Theatre World*'s come out.'

'Another scoop for Mr and Mrs Benson?' Simon asked politely.

'Just Mrs Benson this time,' I said. 'I might help her with the spelling.'

Kim stuck her tongue out, and Simon wandered affably back to Sir Andrew. I shook Hutchinson by the hand.

'You were our last shot but I'm delighted it's not you,' I said. 'Though fuck knows what we do now.'

'Let's go home' said Kim. 'I'm fed up with this champagne. It always gives me an acid tummy and there's more of that nice malt whisky at Rita Road. Not that I'm supposed to be drinking, but sod it.'

'Would you like to come?' I asked Hutchinson. 'It would be an honour to give you a drink.'

'I'd like that very much,' he said.

There was still a terrific crush in the Cinderella Bar, indeed the party was only just beginning to warm up, but we found Tym talking to his musician near the door.

'The others have all gone,' said Tym. 'Vince took them off to a nightclub. They send their love.'

The musician said he'd better get back to his wife and Tym said he'd be in touch. 'He's going to produce my album,' he added for our benefit. 'Can I spend the night at your place?'

'Of course,' said Kim fondly. We staggered out into the night. Whisky was the last thing we needed and we were all determined to have it. 'Sorry, I should have introduced you,' I said as we stood in Oxford Street, waiting for a cab. 'Tym, this is Bill, a fine actor and a brave man. And Bill, this is Tym, the great lost legend of British pop. Both of you true friends to Sophie.'

They shook hands warmly and a cab turned up just to complete the happy scene. We bucketed home on a wave of champagne and tumbled into the sitting room. There was a single green light flashing on the answering machine, and I switched it to play.

'Mr Benson, it's Sergeant Darbyshire here. 9 p.m., Monday evening. Bad news I'm afraid. Miss Brignall, Sophie Brignall, died at St Thomas's Hospital this afternoon. I'd like you to come round as soon as you get this message. I'll be at the station all night.' The message ended and I briskly shut off an earlier message from Kim's mum. So that was her surname, I thought numbly. Unusual. And then Tym started to scream.

Tuesday 1 August

Death Don't Have No Mercy
Song by Revd Gary Davis; a mainstay of the
Grateful Dead repertoire

The Deadheads had taken over the Docklands Light Railway. There were hundreds of them, spilling out of the Tube, tripping gaily past the old London Wall and riding the escalators up to the DLR concourse, where the jobsworths in their sky-blue uniforms were having great problems in controlling the throng. 'Please wait patiently. There will be another train to the Arena in three minutes,' said a desperate voice over the PA system, at which scores of Deadheads chanted back the line from 'Casey Jones': 'Driving the train, high on cocaine.' I'd been expecting an army of gnarled old hippies but the heads were alarmingly young; surprisingly few, apart from Brian and me, were over thirty. Almost all of them were American, spending the summer touring Europe in the wake of their wizened idols. At last Brian and I succeeded in squeezing ourselves on to a train. The smell of patchouli oil was overpowering and I suddenly felt faint and sick.

'I need a drink,' I said as the train lurched forward. 'We've got an hour till the show starts. Do you fancy getting out a couple of stations early and going to an exceptionally ratty pub I know. It's an easy walk from there to the Arena,'

'Sure,' said Brian kindly. 'It must have been a hell of a few hours for you.'

'Not so hot,' I said. 'But I couldn't possibly miss coming to the Dead with you.'

The train stopped at South Quay (later bombed by the IRA), and we fought our way through the crush of Deadheads. I pointed out the *Theatre World* office as we passed it, and led him off the red-brick road of the enterprise zone into the darker heart of the Isle of Dogs. And there, at the end of Manila Street, was the dear old Perseverance. At this time of great stress, it felt good to be back in familiar haunts. Larry, the morose barman, raised a languid hand in greeting.

'I thought you'd deserted us for the fleshpots,' he said. 'Lots of flesh if what Kim tells me is true.'

'Yeah, no shortage of flesh, one way or the other.' Dead, some of it, I thought, and blinked back scalding tears.

I ordered two pints of Holsten and two large whisky chasers, and Brian and I settled ourselves into a dark, corner table.

'Doesn't half niff in here,' said Brian.

'Always did,' I replied. 'You get used to it after a couple of years.'

'How do you feel? OK?' he asked.

I knocked back half my Holsten in one voracious swig and took a gulp of Scotch.

'Yeah,' I said. 'I'm feeling better now.'

The night before, I'd left Tym in the tender loving care of Kim, with Bill Hutchinson gamely volunteering to stay on to make cups of tea and offer a second shoulder to cry on. The actor was clearly shocked and grieving himself but he was making a good job of disguising it. Tym wasn't screaming by the time I closed the door of Rita Road behind me, just rocking backwards and forwards in his chair and whimpering. If anyone could get Tym through this crisis with his precarious sanity intact it was Kim.

I said a prayer for him, and another for Kim and a third for the soul of Sophie as I stood on the corner waiting forlornly for a cab. I wondered if they'd found Henrietta and, if they had, whether she'd told them about Sophie's tape. If she had I could expect a less than cordial welcome at Belgravia nick.

The place seemed calm and Darbyshire himself came to the desk and led me to the interview room. 'I'm sorry to drag you out at this time of night,' he said in a reassuringly friendly manner. 'The brass are getting a bit interested now it's a murder rather than just a grievous wounding case. They've put a chief inspector in charge but they're letting me get on with most of it. And we've got hold of the maid Henrietta at last. She's here now. She's described you in some detail as the man who went out of his way to help Sophie. A formal identification will put you in the clear, unless the two of you are acting in collusion and there's no grounds for thinking that, especially when you've seen the state she's in.'

'Has she given you any new leads?' I asked.

'Not a thing. Even though he was wearing a mask she's pretty sure the attacker wasn't one of Sophie's regulars. She'd have recognized most of them just by their size, manner and bearing, she says. And she's convinced none of the regulars would have done it anyway. They went back years some of them. It looks like a random psycho off the street, which makes our job very difficult.'

'How did you find her?'

'The hospital was getting regular calls about Sophie's condition from a woman with a posh voice. Like Princess Margaret, as you said, so we guessed who it was. But Henrietta always used phone boxes and by the time we'd traced the call and got someone there she'd invariably disappeared. But this afternoon the nurse kept her talking for a bit longer, and said matters were critical. Sophie had already died by then, very suddenly and without warning, as is often the way with these head injuries. Thankfully the hospital isn't allowed to give information like that over the phone, or we'd probably have lost Henrietta for good. The nurse somehow kept Henrietta talking until we got a car there.'

'And she's taking it badly?'

'Very badly. Did you realize Henrietta and Sophie were lovers? They lived together, in a thirties semi in East Sheen of all places.'

'Jesus. I didn't know that, and I'd never have guessed. Did she give any kind of description of the attacker?'

'Nothing of any real use. Shortish, stoutish, a bit like you in fact,' smiled Darbyshire. 'Wearing jeans and a pale blue shirt and carrying a tartan duffel-bag. There's not that much to go on when someone's wearing an Elvis Presley mask and surgical gloves.'

The surgical gloves were new to me and I shuddered. 'Has she come up with anything about the man we thought might be the ponce, Jim, wasn't it? And Sophie's partner, the 44DD brunette?'

'More dead ends,' said Darbyshire gloomily. 'Jim turns out to be one of the barmen in the pub round the corner. He was a punter who became a friend. They'd occasionally phone him if they had trouble with drunks. Certainly not a pimp and very upset when I insisted he might be. He was definitely working behind the bar at the time the attack took place, we've checked that thoroughly. And he was absolutely distraught when he heard Sophie was dead. He hadn't seen the papers and Henrietta hadn't made contact with him. He seemed a hard kind of guy, not the sort you'd want to pick a fight with, but I don't think it's an exaggeration to say that he genuinely loved Sophie.'

'She was a very lovable woman. And presumably Jim's got no fresh leads either.'

'Not a thing, I'm afraid.'

'And big-bosomed Jenny?'

'If Henrietta's to be believed, and I think she is, Jenny was only ever a part-timer, and she moved back to Edinburgh six months ago. But they found that the 44DD brunette card attracted a lot of calls so they kept using it.'

'They were very honest about explaining that the 44DD girl wasn't on duty though,' I said, remembering my own experience and the headmaster's. 'Come to think of it, I never actually saw Sophie's card.'

Darbyshire opened his wallet and, a bit like a punter letting someone else on to a good thing, passed one over. *Sophie: Good Humoured Tart With a Heart. No Hurry. No Hassle. No Kinks.*

'Honest as always,' I said. 'The perfect epitaph, really.'

'There have been moments in the last few days when I've wished I'd been one of her punters myself,' said Darbyshire. 'And I never said that. Come on, we'd better go and see Henrietta.'

She was sitting in an interview room dressed in her hideous puce tracksuit. Her face was puffy and her eyes suggested a woman who had been staring into an abyss of misery for far too long. Darbyshire kept the formalities to a minimum. He got Henrietta to identify me as the man who had discovered Sophie after she was attacked, and also as a client who had called the week previously. The WPC present took a note and left.

'Right, you can go now, Mr Benson. The police bail stands for the time being, but don't worry about it. It's useful to know that we'll have you around as a witness.' But at that moment someone Darbyshire addressed as Chief Inspector stuck his head round the door and asked if he could have a quick word. Darbyshire looked anxious about leaving us alone, but neither of us were suspects and the call of his superior clearly brooked no refusal. 'I won't be a moment,' he said, and disappeared into the corridor.

I went over and gave Henrietta's shapeless baggy bulk a squeeze. 'I'm so sorry,' I said. 'She was a lovely woman.'

Henrietta sniffed. 'You haven't let on about the tape, have you?'

'No. And from what Sergeant Darbyshire says, you haven't mentioned Sophie's little sideline either.'

'No. She'd be furious if I dragged her clients into it, I've got to be loyal to her memory. That's why I couldn't contact the police if there was a chance of her pulling through.'

'I've been to see everyone on the tape,' I told Henrietta. 'I'm sure they're all innocent. Apart from anything else, I've just learnt from Darbyshire that the attacker was the same shape as me. All the others were either taller or thinner. Apart from Duncan Adamson, who had a rock-solid alibi.'

'The soft cow only got round to blackmailing two of them in the end,' said Henrietta fondly. 'She made that tape before she started, just in case anything happened. She knew I wasn't up to handling it. I thought she was running a risk with that sick politician. But apart from the schoolmaster, who she felt guilty as hell about, he was the only one she could finally bring herself to blackmail.'

'So I gather.'

'How's poor Tym?' she asked. 'He was always Sophie's favourite, even though the daft prick attacked her once. Has he heard?'

'Yeah,' I said. 'He's pretty upset. My wife's looking after him. Listen, I've got to ask, Henrietta. Why was Sophie involved in blackmail? I know she only went ahead with two of them but the whole idea seems so unlike her. And she said on the tape that you disapproved.'

'I disapproved because there was a risk attached. Because I hadn't got the heart she had,' sobbed Henrietta. I feared she was going to collapse completely but she wiped her eyes and pressed doggedly on. 'There was another punter. Who had a twelve-year-old son with leukaemia. The health authority thought his chances of recovery were so small they wouldn't pay for further treatment. So Sophie raised the cash for the final round of chemotherapy. £75,000. She gave the father the money, out of the blue, when he called one evening. Not that they ever did anything in those last months. Just talked.'

'But I've spoken to everyone,' I said. 'She only raised £45,000.'

'The rest was her money. Her savings. Our savings, though I can't say that because I didn't have to earn it like she did.'

'But why didn't she tell anyone the reason? They might have contributed voluntarily.'

'Because she felt that what she was doing was morally wrong, however good the motive. And if she'd told them the truth it would have been a different kind of blackmail, emotional blackmail, and there would always be the implicit threat that she'd grass on them if they didn't stump up. She said she'd rather the people she put the squeeze on regarded her with healthy contempt than as "some bloody Esther Rantzen on the game". Her words, not mine.'

'And the boy?'

'The boy died. Six weeks ago. And now I've got to tell his dad that Sophie's dead too.'

'And you've really no idea who Sophie's attacker might have been?'

'None at all. Though there's one thought that keeps nagging at the back of my mind. The Friday before last I had a day off with a bad cold and Sophie insisted on working. I hated her doing it when I wasn't there, but she insisted. We needed the money and she said she could always phone Jim. Anyway, she told me that night that she'd had some punter, a new one, who put her in mind of Big Tool Mike, as we called him, one of her regulars. Not the face so much, but the body. Short, plump and a lot of body hair. Even his nails were bitten to the quick like Mike's used to be. The thing is, you see, Mike's dead. Heart attack a couple of years ago. And Sophie said it was really eerie watching this other guy strip because he looked so similar. She'd felt quite freaked out by it. But then he'd taken his knickers off. And she couldn't help herself. It was the relief after feeling so spooked, I suppose. She laughed. You can imagine why Big Tool Mike got his nickname. But this guy was minute, a tiny little winkle. And she said just

193

for a moment he'd looked at her with absolute hatred and she was sure he was going to belt her one. And being Sophie, she said she'd have understood it if he had. She used to get furious with me for putting that video on. Part of her job, she always said, was making the inadequate feel adequate.'

I remembered the kind 'not the usual trouble, then' with which she'd comforted me in my distress and felt a sharp pang for the departed Sophie.

'Anyway. He didn't hit her. He took his clothes into the bathroom, got dressed and let himself out. Sophie was full of remorse.'

'And did Sophie's attacker look like, um, Big Tool Mike?'

'About the same height and build.'

'So you think he might have come back?'

'It's a possibility. And there was just one other thing. Sophie said his breath smelled funny. She noticed it when she let him in. Nothing unpleasant. But a strong smell, medicinal almost. She said it took her back to her childhood, but she couldn't place it.'

The grief and the sheer futility of ever finding Sophie's killer suddenly seemed to overcome Henrietta, and she began sobbing inconsolably. I went and stood behind her and held her shoulders while she wept.

'I can't go on without her,' she said. 'She was all I had.'

Darbyshire returned eventually and called the WPC to comfort poor Henrietta. I gave the wretched woman a last hug and left the room with the sergeant. Once again he escorted me to the side door and as he lit his pipe I told him about the Big Tool Mike lookalike, and the medicinal smell.

'You remember that last cab ride with Sophie? How she wrote the word "cough" on a cash dispenser slip. She might have been trying to write the word cough medicine or cough sweet, only she was trembling so much she dropped the pen before she'd finished.'

'Great,' he said wearily. 'We're looking for a short fat

man with a small willie who looks a bit like someone we've never heard of who died two years ago. And he might have had a bit of a cough. We can hardly fail to crack the case with information like that to go on.'

'There's something else you ought to know. Henrietta's got a gun. She's just told me,' I lied. 'They kept it in case things turned nasty. And much good it did them when it came to the crunch. I think it would be a good idea to find it. Or keep an eye on her. She's desperately upset and I think she might be suicidal.'

'Right,' he said. 'There was no trace of a gun at the Belgrave Road flat so she must have taken it with her when she disappeared. I'm sending her home with that WPC. She might be able to wangle it out of her, with a bit of luck.'

'Well, goodnight, then,' I said. 'Good luck.' Darbyshire said he could arrange a car to take me home but I said I'd rather walk. It was a fine, warm night and I needed to clear my head and think and grieve. I'd not gone 100 yards down Buckingham Palace Road when a black Golf drew up alongside me. 'Can we talk?' called the large, baby-faced youth inside.

'I was wondering when you'd turn up,' I said, pointing at a bench outside the Victoria Library. 'I'll give you ten minutes.'

He climbed out of the car and joined me.

'Chris Powell,' he said. *'Victoria and Pimlico Times.'* Despite his size, he hardly looked old enough to drive a car. 'I've just started, straight out of college,' he confessed. 'I was hoping you'd be my first scoop.'

I thought of the hours of sweaty anxiety he'd caused when I'd feared I was being pursued by a hard-nosed tabloid hack or, even worse, one of Darbyshire's men in plain clothes. You had to hand it to young Mr Powell though. He'd sacrificed his weekend to the chase, and followed us with considerable ingenuity.

'I'm sure it will be the first of many exclusives carrying

your byline,' I said, and offered him my hand. 'Will Benson, but you know that. How did you get on to me?'

He explained that he'd been briefed about Sophie on one of the paper's routine calls to Belgravia nick and DC Fox had said that in exchange for what he called a 'large gold watch or two' he might be able to supply some background information. Powell had drunk more Scotch than he cared to remember with the junior detective, and by the end of the evening he'd got my name and the fact that I worked for a soft-porn outfit called Botticelli Publications drunkenly but legibly inscribed in his notebook. 'Unfortunately,' he said. 'I was so pissed when I wrote down your address that I couldn't read it back. I was too embarrassed to contact Fox again, who's a patronizing shit if you want the honest truth, so I had to phone all the W. Bensons in SW8. Hence that midnight call.'

'And what were you hoping to gain by following my every move?'

'Well, it would obviously be fairly sensational if I'd found you going to another massage parlour,' he said. 'But I was just trying to build up as much background information as I could. Not that I got much. What were you doing in Hampshire? And in Suffolk? And who's the weird bald guy?'

'Just a friend,' I said blandly. 'We went to Hampshire to look at a school and to Suffolk to visit a church. It's got nothing to do with Sophie.' As indeed it hadn't. Not any more.

Powell said he'd had to cover a Westminster Council meeting earlier that evening, and hadn't got to Rita Road till ten. He'd patiently waited till we returned and was trying to pluck up courage to ring the bell and confront me when I'd left the house again and come to the police station.

He looked a bit desperate. 'Can you tell me what the fuck's going on? We go to press tomorrow and I haven't got a clue what to write.'

So I told him Sophie was dead, and explained why I'd gone to her in the first place, and what had happened on my second visit. I couldn't tell him about the tape of course, or the punters she named on it, but I did mention that she'd been 'active in raising funds for leukaemia sufferers' and tried to convey something of her warmth, kindness and generosity of spirit. 'And though the police won't tell you this, I think it's safe to say they are no closer to solving the case now than they were the day it happened. It looks like a random sicko off the street.'

He got it all down in his notebook, and then, rather charmingly, asked me how much he could use. I toyed with the idea of asking him to keep my name out of the paper, but the story would fall apart without it and he'd worked hard for his scoop. Besides, I suddenly realized, I would be proud to have my name linked with Sophie's.

'You can use it all. Just give her a good send-off, that's all. She deserves it.'

He was touchingly grateful and offered me a lift home, but I still felt in need of a walk. By the time I got home it was 2 a.m. Bill Hutchinson was crashed out on the sofa, Tym was fast asleep in the spare room and Kim was sitting up in bed waiting for me. I told her what had happened at the police station, and about my meeting with Chris Powell, and asked her about Tym.

'He's going to be all right, I think,' she said. 'He calmed right down soon after you'd gone, and said in his heart of hearts he'd been expecting it. When he'd tried thinking of the future and of Sophie all he got was a mist. You know what he's like.'

'Yes,' I said.

'I was a bit worried about tomorrow. It's our busy day at work and there's everything else too. But he said he wanted to go home tomorrow. He said he'd howl a bit in his sound-proofed studio and then get down to work. He says he owes it to Sophie. And he wants us to go round at the weekend to hear what he's got down. He says it will spur him on.'

'Great. And how are you feeling?' I said.

'OK. Apprehensive.'

'Yeah, me too. I'm meant to be going to the Grateful Dead tomorrow night with Brian. I'll cancel if you like.'

'No, go. You'll kick yourself if you miss it. And I might want some time on my own tomorrow evening anyway.'

'Right,' I said, and we went to bed. My mind seemed to race all night long but Kim slept soundly and there was a kind of comfort in her gentle snores. Tym brought us tea in bed at 7 a.m., exactly the time Kim had to get up for her early start at the printer's. He thanked us, and promised he'd be OK. We'd see him on Saturday, we said, and he gave us a last, brave peace sign and left us to our tea.

Kim scurried off to work, and by the time I crawled out of bed an hour later, Bill Hutchinson was making coffee in the kitchen. He said he felt rough. I agreed rough was the word. We sat in companionable silence for a time and drank Nescafé and listened to the birds singing.

'Everything OK last night?' he asked.

'I suppose so,' I said. 'Henrietta was in a state. And Sophie wasn't really a blackmailer.' I told him about the boy with leukaemia.

'Typical of her not to mention that,' he said. 'A kind of grace. God, I'm going to miss her.'

'I should have told Tym before he left.'

'There was no need. Not yet anyway. He knows she was decent through and through. You could tell.'

'Another kind of grace,' I said. 'Perfect trust.'

I got ready for work and Bill asked if he could stay on in the flat and write some notes for Kim on the Act Queer story. He said he'd let himself out and get in touch as soon as he'd met the former girlfriend. 'Great,' I said, fetching him some paper. 'Thanks for everything.'

When I arrived at work I told Brian the blunt news about Sophie's death, but didn't go into details and asked him not to tell the others. I couldn't face another long round of explanations. Nor had I felt up to writing that morning's required sexual fantasy. I was half-way through it – a scenario involving an over-sexed housewife, her pathetically small-dicked husband and the hugely endowed father-in-law who regularly serviced her when his son was out at work – when I felt a great stab of grief and suddenly burst into tears at my desk. They'd all been very nice, and no one asked any questions so I guessed Brian must have told them what had happened while I went to the gents to wash my face. Linda had sweetly said she would take on my short story as well as her own work that day and Janice Cockett, back from her brief holiday, had given me a nice dull piece on windsurfing to sub.

And now, here I was with Brian, sitting in the smelly Docklands pub and telling him about my time at the Belgravia nick. I'd got to the bit about the boy with leukaemia when I began to cough. I'd been smoking like a man with a death-wish all day, and the Old Disgusting was finally wreaking its revenge. I sipped at the beer, then at the whisky, but still couldn't get rid of the infuriating tickle at the back of my throat. And then Brian burrowed in his trouser pocket and produced a grubby bag of aniseed twist and the coughing stopped. Just like that.

I must have looked aghast for a fraction of a second, before realizing that was the last thing I should look. So I started coughing again and took an aniseed twist from Brian's bag and sucked greedily.

'What was the matter just then? You looked as though you'd seen a ghost,' he said. And I suppose I had. The ghost of Sophie bleeding in the back of a cab as I sat opposite the man who had killed her.

'It was just that coughing fit. A bit scary when it goes on and on like that and you think you'll never stop.'

Thank Christ, I thought, I'd started coughing before I got to Henrietta's remarks about the strong-smelling breath of Sophie's attacker. Utterly distinctive, aniseed twist, though hard to place if you haven't smelt it for years. Faintly medicinal and irrevocably connected with childhood. And aniseed twist and cough candy had always been different words for virtually the same product. Except aniseed twist came loose with a dusting of sugar and cough candy was usually wrapped in cellophane. Sophie must have favoured the latter as a child.

'Delicious this aniseed twist,' I said. 'I thought you'd packed it in because of your teeth. Makes a nice change from edible knickers.'

'Special occasion this,' smiled Brian. 'And I'm trying not to chew.' Presumably a visit to a prostitute merited as a special occasion too.

I told Brian about Darbyshire's gloom about solving the case and my fear that Henrietta might do away with herself, and all the time I was trying to think. Brian had been pruriently fascinated about what had happened when I'd gone to produce my sperm sample two weeks earlier. He knew I was keeping something from him when I'd phoned from the pub, and knowing Brian's devious little ways he'd have gone through my wallet at the earliest opportunity. I always kept it in my jacket, which I hung over the back of my chair throughout the working day. And there he'd have found the card. And perhaps a couple of days later, sick of his CDs, his pile of magazines and his disgusting flat, he'd decided to pay her a visit himself. But when? Sophie usually called it a day at about 6 p.m., and went back to safe suburban East Sheen with Henrietta. Henrietta had been off at the end of the week before last. And Brian, I remembered with a lurch of the stomach, had knocked off at five o'clock that Friday because he said he had some dry cleaning to pick up before going away for the weekend. Linda and I had wondered where he was going.

'What's she like, this Henrietta?' Brian asked.

I was finding it quite a strain talking and thinking at the same time. 'An extraordinary woman,' I said, and started on the Princess Margaret accent and my first conversation on the phone with her more than two weeks earlier. No, you wouldn't know much about her, I thought viciously, because she wasn't there on your first visit and on your second you wasted no time in smashing her face and hitting her knee with a truncheon. But had he? Had he? When I'd arrived at the office that Thursday morning after the attack, Linda had said Brian had been in the office all afternoon, angrily wondering where I'd gone. I felt relief flood over me. It was the fatigue, I thought. I was seeing labyrinthine conspiracies where there was actually only a bag of aniseed twist. But there was no harm in checking. Linda and Brian did sometimes seem to be as thick as thieves. Wednesday had been Janice Cockett's last day in the office before her long weekend. And the last thing one could imagine was the despised Mrs 'Cock-up' covering up for Brian, her tormentor.

'Do you mind if I make a quick call?' I asked Brian. 'I just want to see if Kim's OK.'

'Sure,' he said. 'Another Holsten and a whisky chaser?'

If ever I needed to keep a clear head it was tonight.

'Just a pint of Holsten. I'm knackered and I don't want to sleep through the Dead.'

I went to the phone which, luckily for my purposes, was over at the other side of the bar, and dialled Janice's direct line. She'd announced, self-righteously, that she'd have to work late because we'd fallen behind schedule in her absence. It was 7.20 and I hoped to God she was still chastely labouring with the raunchy prose.

She picked up the phone on the second ring. 'Botticelli Publications,' she said, with manifest distaste.

'Janice, it's me, Will Benson,' I said. 'This is urgent.'

'Yes, Will,' she said with unusual warmth. 'What's the matter?'

'Last Wednesday, before your break – when I didn't come back to the office – did Brian come back that afternoon?'

'No, he didn't, and I was very peeved because I was going to sort out what needed doing while I was—' She suddenly stopped for a moment. 'Hell's bells,' she said, a phrase she reserved for particularly acute moments of crisis. 'Was that the afternoon your prostitute was attacked?' She was appalled, but she was also excited, one might almost say hopeful.

'Yes, it was,' I said. 'You are alone there, aren't you?'

'Quite alone. Listen, Will, I was relieved you called. Be careful with Brian tonight. I think he's planning something, and knowing Brian it will be something nasty. He and Linda were giggling in the corridor this afternoon when I went to the ladies. I heard your name and then something that sounded like "well-spiked", and then they saw me and shut up. Doesn't sound very pleasant, does it?'

'No, it doesn't,' I said. 'But forewarned is forearmed. Thanks, Janice, you've been really helpful.'

'Will, shouldn't you contact the police?'

'I've got nothing to give them except suspicion. Nothing that will hold up. I've got to find out more. And I'll be careful. See you tomorrow.'

She wished me luck and rang off. I thought about phoning Kim, but it wasn't fair to worry her. My only evidence was the aniseed twist and a dud alibi. I was convinced now that Brian had done it, that he'd followed me as I left the Pride of the Borough that Wednesday, saw me go into the Pimlico pub and realized he had at least a pint's worth of time to take his revenge on the woman he believed had mocked him. By cutting out her tongue so she could laugh no more. But what a risk he'd taken. He could have attacked Sophie any time. Why choose the very afternoon I seemed certain to go there? A few thoughts presented themselves. None of them reassuring.

I sauntered back to our dark corner. Brian had bought me my pint and was thirstily drinking his.

'Get it down you, mate' he grinned. 'We ought to be off in a few minutes.'

I sat down, and as I did so I knocked over my drink.

'You clumsy fucker,' said Brian, with a spitting fury out of all proportion to the incident. Anyone would have thought I'd poured the whole lot into his lap but it had just fallen harmlessly on to the already filthy carpet. I remembered Tym's tales of acid-spiked cups of tea. It was likely to be acid, I thought. What else but LSD at a Dead concert? Brian evidently had a regular supplier of cannabis. He'd probably placed a side order for a few tabs. Taking a trip with Brian as your less than friendly tour guide didn't bear thinking about. I was going to watch what I was drinking that night. Though with a bit of luck he'd have exhausted his stock by now.

'Sorry, Brian,' I said, pretending not to notice his outburst of bad temper. 'I'll get another. Anything else for you?'

Brian was out of his chair, clearly itching to buy the next drinks himself. 'No, let me, let me, it's my round,' he said with almost manic fervour. So it looked as though he'd got at least something in reserve. Shame. Or perhaps not.

'Sit down, Brian,' I said firmly. 'I'm getting them myself. What do you want?'

'A pint,' he said sulkily.

At the bar I asked Larry to put four shots of vodka in Brian's Holsten if he could manage it without Brian noticing.

'It's a despicable trick, that,' said Larry.

'He's a despicable person,' I said.

Larry did the business, very niftily, below the bar. He wasn't a man to turn down an extra fiver. We finished our drinks and walked in the shadow of looming high-tech office buildings towards the Docklands Arena. Outside, the Deadheads were doing their best to turn back the clock to the Summer of Love. There were hundreds of them selling tie-dye T-shirts, home-made jewellery and repulsive-smelling veggie burgers. Forlorn individuals stood around chanting that they needed a miracle (Deadspeak for a free ticket), and the few policemen on duty seemed happy to ignore the smell of dope. Brian had no time to stand and stare. He hustled me inside the arena, and made straight for the bar. I asked for a bottle of mineral water, and he couldn't hide his scowl. I'd noticed that the mineral water came in plastic bottles with the cap screwed on. No chance of any funny business there. We went to find our seats; excellent ones in the middle and near the front. Brian, still simmering with barely containable rage, rolled a joint and passed it over to me. I took a couple of cautious drags and then a couple more. Mercifully it wasn't nearly as strong as the last time I'd smoked with Brian. When the band shuffled on, only ten minutes late, the whole audience rose to its feet and stayed that way for the rest of the show, performing the trance-like jiggle that passes for dancing among the band's *aficionados*. And within a few minutes of the opening number, 'Jack Straw', I was amazed to find that my anxiety was giving way to euphoria. It's easy to knock the Dead, but they do wonderful things to your head. Sure, they are faintly ridiculous old hippies, sure, Jerry Garcia's voice was shot to shreds, but as they launched into the spacy delirium of 'Dark Star' and Garcia began to let rip with his chiming, exploratory guitar, I was so caught up in the music I forgot all about Sophie, Henrietta and even Brian who was standing right next to me.

After seventy-five minutes, Bob Weir announced that the band were going to take a twenty-minute break, and Brian began sprinting towards the bar like Linford Christie, though bearing Sophie's unwise laughter in mind, that isn't perhaps the most felicitous of comparisons. I puffed along behind him, and we arrived well ahead of the crush. This time Brian didn't even bother to ask what I wanted and I stood just behind him and watched. He ordered two pints of lager and two whisky chasers. The lagers were served first, and as the barman turned his back towards the spirit optics, Brian dipped his hand in his pocket and held it, briefly, over one of the pints. It was all very deftly done, and if I hadn't been expecting it, I'd never have noticed. I went up to Brian and he passed me my two drinks, before picking up his own. 'Get those down you and none of that mineral water crap,' he said cheerfully. Because we were among the first out, we were able to stand by a ledge, which was handy when you had two drinks on the go.

Brian lifted his pint. 'Here's to Captain Trips,' he said.

I raised my glass of whisky. 'I think the Dead deserve to be toasted in Scotch,' I said.

Brian put his pint down on the ledge, picked up his whisky, and tried to force his face into a smile. 'To the Dead,' he said.

'To the Dead,' I echoed, and we both took a swig. I immediately slapped Brian with matey firmness on the back and pointed excitedly down the now crowded concourse.

'Good God,' I said. 'It looks as though Jerry has come to mingle with his fans.'

'Where? Where?' shouted Brian, turning his back to the shelf.

'Just over there, near the hot-dog stand. In the black T-shirt.'

'I can't see him,' said Brian, as I switched the pints.

'I'm sure it was him,' I said. 'Oh no,' I added after a couple of seconds of anxious scanning. 'Nothing like him when you take a closer look.'

Brian picked up his pint, grumpily, and told me, with tiresome predictability, that 'all that wanking' was damaging my eyesight. But at that moment I could have kissed him. It was, after all, my glass he was holding in his bitten-to-the-quick fingers.

'Race you?' I said cheerfully.

'You're on,' said Brian, for whom such an offer must have seemed like a wonderful stroke of luck.

We both got them down in one.

'I'll go and get us another,' I said, and Brian, thinking his task was done, nodded happily.

'Gradely.'

It took me ages to get the drinks, and by the time I returned to Brian it was time to go back to our seats. You weren't allowed to take glasses inside the auditorium, so we got those down us in double-quick time too. I just hoped Brian didn't throw up before the drugs began to kick in.

But Brian seemed in the pink as we took a slash and returned to the auditorium. Three minutes later the Dead were back on stage. I don't think either of us took much notice of the second half. I kept glancing at Brian and he kept glancing at me, and sometimes our eyes met and we both swivelled our eyes back to the stage again. There's a much dreaded moment in every Grateful Dead concert when the rest of the band file off leaving the two percussionists to a tedious drum routine, which is followed by several agonizing minutes of quite unnecessary feedback. As the screeching reached an almost unbearably loud and dissonant crescendo, Brian began to exhibit serious symptoms of distress, waving his arms in the air and screaming that he was on the end of a burning pier.

I needed to act fast. From my own limited experience of LSD as a student, I knew that a bad trip could become so overwhelming that you lost all notion of reality. The drug created its own alternative world which eclipsed the one you'd left behind. I had little doubt that Brian had administered me, and therefore himself, a terrific dose. What's more, LSD and alcohol don't mix, and Brian had by now drunk a good deal more than he realized. If I wanted any questions answered I was going to have to ask them before the trip went totally out of control. I dragged Brian by the arm and he followed like a little lamb, whimpering as he went. 'It's a bad trip,' I explained, as we negotiated our way between the chairs and the dancers, who nodded in brief sympathy and went straight back into their own little worlds of movement and music. The one place where you could experience a bad trip and raise only the faintest flicker of interest was a Grateful Dead concert. My only worry was that a St John Ambulanceman might see the state Brian was in and offer Valium and sympathy. I wanted the bastard to suffer.

'If you don't want me to hurt you very badly indeed,' I hissed in his ear as we made it out into the concourse that led to the main exit, 'you're going to walk outside without making a sound.' I nervously let go of his arm and to my relief Brian just kept walking, his eyes gazing straight ahead. No one stopped us, and we made it out into the deep warm dusk. 'Where are the stars, where are the fucking stars?' screamed Brian, gazing up at the cloudy sky as though their non-appearance was a personal snub. 'Where's the fucking moon?' And then the little shit began to run as if the hounds of hell were after him.

After all the tiresome swimming and only recently abandoned moderation with the booze and fags, I was fitter than usual, whereas Brian seemed to exist only on booze, dope and junk food. But he was still faster than me as he pounded down the road that led to the southern tip of the Isle of Dogs. There was scarcely a soul abroad as we passed the mean council houses, the recreation ground and the Asda Superstore. I wondered whether Brian had any idea where he was going. And was he running from me or from the horrors inside his head? I put on a spurt and narrowed the gap between us as the road bent round to the left towards Island Gardens, the terminus of the DLR, hard by the foot tunnel which allows pedestrian access under the Thames to Greenwich. Surely, I thought, he couldn't be contemplating going down there? It was a claustrophobic and threatening place at the best of times, even when you were in your right mind and walking through the thousand-foot tunnel in the reassuring company of other harassed commuters. At this time of night and with acid sloshing around the brain, it would be a nightmare.

But that was just where Brian was going. Perhaps his mother had brought him here as a child after a visit to the Cutty Sark in Greenwich. With its massive lifts and dripping echoes, this great hollow snake beneath the Thames is a place to excite and possibly disturb the imagination of any small child. The lifts, with their flickering video screens and uniformed staff, were shut at this time of night, but Brian seemed to know just where he was going and hoofed it down the spiral staircase, two steps at a time. I went more cautiously, and reached the bottom some 30 yards behind him. From one end of the tunnel you can't see the other. And in the middle, there seems to be neither entrance nor exit, just an apparently interminable perspective of white tiles and harsh light. The stale air reeks of old piss and it's like being stuck in the middle of a monstrous urinal.

We were just reaching the midway point when Brian suddenly stopped running. He turned round to look at me, seized his chest and slumped to the floor. Oh Christ, I thought, the drugs and the unprecedented exertion had brought on a heart attack. I hurried over to him and prodded him gently with my foot. He was still breathing, sucking in great violent lungfuls and exhaling them with a worrying wheezing noise. I knelt down beside him and put my hand on his chest, and he suddenly sprang back to life, rolling on top of me until he was astride my stomach with his legs holding me in a tight grip. This was no time for fair play. His eyes were somewhere else and his mouth was twisted into a grimace that seemed to combine pain with the prospect of pleasure. He could beat my brains out any time he liked, just by grabbing the lapels of my jacket and banging my head up and down on the concrete floor. I reached into my jacket pocket which was splayed out to my side, grabbed the Swiss Army Knife that I always kept there as a lucky charm, and yelled, 'Behind You!' It was the second time that night I'd played the trick but Brian's brain was mercifully too scrambled to notice. He glanced suddenly over his shoulder, and in that moment, with practised hands, I opened the smallest, sharpest blade and stabbed him, hard, in the upper thigh.

He screamed. I quickly withdrew the blade, and he screamed even louder. It sounded unearthly and terrifying in the echoing, deserted tunnel. Then he curled up into a ball with his hands over his head and moaned. 'The slugs are coming,' he said. 'They're coming down the walls.' I realized I had to get him out of there as soon as possible. Someone would be along soon. I yanked him up by his collar, still holding the knife in my free hand, and sat him up against the wall. He kept on repeating the word slugs. Juicy slugs, black slugs, albino slugs. While he muttered I went through his pockets. There was a small empty pill bottle with a few drops of liquid at the bottom; a cellophane sachet of white powder that looked like cocaine; a pair of handcuffs, possibly the very handcuffs I'd worn for our photographic session the previous day; and a Stanley knife. I pocketed the lot and hauled Brian to his feet.

'Right, walk,' I said, and with my arm round his shoulder, I coaxed him along like a friend helping a drunk back home. A couple of people passed as we made our slow progress, but both walked on by as though it were nothing unusual to see a man with a bad limp and a bloody mess on his jeans being escorted under the Thames at ten in the evening.

Half-way up the circular staircase, Brian suddenly stopped and began gasping with panic. 'I can't go any further, I can't go any further. They're all over the floor and the walls. I can't step on them, they're so full of slime and pus.'

'Brian,' I said, 'you've got to keep walking, they're all in your mind. It's the LSD, remember. You can control it if you try. There's nothing there.' I gave him a push and he staggered forward a few paces and threw up violently, retching again and again long after he'd voided the contents of his stomach. Too late for Brian, I thought. Most of the acid would have been absorbed by now.

'Oh Jesus God,' he moaned. 'They're inside me now, I'm throwing the fuckers up, oh let it stop, let it stop, let it stop.' I pulled him roughly by the arm and we made it up the stairs and into the humid night. The Cutty Sark was moored in front of us and you could see the brightly lit streets of Greenwich. I needed somewhere dark and out of the way. I dragged Brian away from the lights, towards the river, and soon discovered a rusty iron staircase leading down to a small, shingled beach in the shadow of a warehouse. I ordered Brian to go down first, saying he'd get the knife in the back of the neck if he tried anything on. Once we'd reached the bottom, I looked up and realized that no one could see us unless they came right to the edge of the embankment. In the middle of the beach, which was obviously covered by water at high tide, there was a post, seven foot high and holding a lifebuoy. I showed Brian the blade of my knife and he flinched. 'I'm not going to hurt you if you co-operate,' I promised. 'Hold out your right arm.' He did as requested. I managed to place one of the cuffs round his wrist and snapped it shut, though it was awkward with the penknife in my hand. 'Now stand with your back to the post,' I said. This was the crunch. I'd have to go behind him to put the other cuff on. If he suddenly ran forward there was little I could do to stop him. 'Remember I've still got the knife, Brian,' I said. It was actually on the ground between my feet because I needed both hands for this procedure. 'In the neck, remember. And, after that, in the eye.' But all the fight had gone out of him. His left arm was limp and I quickly snapped the other metal ring into place. There was a key which I removed and placed in my pocket.

I went back to look at him. Tears were streaming down his cheeks, snot was bubbling from his nose, and his mouth was smeared with sick. 'You're a fucking psycho,' he said softly, almost as if in recognition.

'No, Brian,' I said calmly. 'You're the psycho.'

'My leg hurts,' he said, perhaps aware of the pain for the first time. 'The blood will attract the slugs,' he added with sudden horror. 'Oh Christ, they'll come and gorge on me,'

'Calm down, it's only the chemicals. Hang on to that. All this is going to stop, very soon, if you talk.'

'I'll tell you anything, anything,' he said. 'Just don't stab me again.'

'Gradely,' I replied. 'Why did you cut out Sophie's tongue?'

'Because she laughed at me.'

'Is that the only reason?'

'Wintour wanted rid of you. He told me to keep an eye on you, find out what you were up to, come up with a reason to give you the push that wouldn't arouse any suspicion.'

'But why did he want rid of me?'

'He was worried that Harry Meadows was on to us. Harry made some kind of threat when he suggested you should be offered the job.'

'Harry Meadows?' I said. 'The comedian Joe Johnson's manager?'

'Yeah.'

'But what threat?'

'I don't know.'

'But what was Wintour so worried about?'

'The other stuff,' said Brian. 'Oh Christ, they're coming again. They're bigger now and juicier. I can taste them in my mouth.'

'No you can't,' I said, cupping his face firmly in my hands. 'Just look at me. What's the other stuff?'

'The kid's stuff. The torture stuff. Linda and her girl-friend bring it in from Europe. It's easy now with so few border restrictions and those two looking so respectable. I help Wintour with the copying and distribution.'

'Who else knows about it? Everyone at Botticelli Publications?'

'No. Just Wintour, Linda and me. And Linda's headmistress.'

Sweet funny little Linda, I thought. And her prim, grey-haired headmistress. Jesus wept.

'But why should Wintour think I'd find out anything when no one else on Botticelli Publications has guessed?'

'Because he thought Meadows had sent you specially to dig up the dirt. He said it was like having a spy in the camp.'

An unwitting spy, I thought. But perhaps they were the most effective. I'd succeeded in panicking Wintour and Brian into action. Perhaps Meadows had guessed that I would.

'Back to Sophie,' I said. Brian was snivelling again, and I slapped him round the face a bit. Perhaps harder than was strictly necessary.

'I knew you'd been up to something that morning when you went to the clinic and phoned from the pub. You sounded so excited. So I went through your wallet and found the card and went there myself. And she laughed at me.'

'Yeah, I know all that. It's the second time I'm interested in.'

'I just had a hunch when you left that afternoon that you were going back to Sophie's. I didn't have any definite plan, but I was determined to get back at her and if I could drag you into it as well, so much the better. So I fetched the mask, gloves and truncheon plus a change of clothes from home, and got a taxi. There wasn't much traffic and I realized that if you were going by Tube there was a good chance I'd have got there before you. So I hung about near the station, pretending to read the *Standard*, and saw you come out and make straight for the pub. Which gave me a few minutes to do what I did. There was a hell of a struggle and she banged her head badly on the chest of drawers, but I got her tied up in the end and taught her a lesson in manners she wouldn't fucking forget. No more laughter from her. And then I untied her, because I didn't want her to bleed to death. Except the silly bitch went into a coma and died anyway.'

I thought of Sophie's terror, as she struggled desperately with the man in the Elvis mask and the rubber gloves, before finally being overcome, trussed up, and seeing the Stanley knife for the first time. I felt like kicking the shit out of Brian, but there was no knowing how long this burst of coherence was going to last.

'And then what?'

'I took off the gloves, changed into fresh clothes, made sure the maid was immobile and went to the café across the road for a coffee. And then I realized I could screw you too. At first I was just pleased you were going to find that lovely little tart you liked so much with her tongue missing and bleeding all over the bed. But then I thought I could put you in the frame. I assumed you'd take one look and run. All I'd have to do was go back and make sure the maid couldn't talk for a bit either, phone the police anonymously and give them your name. But instead of doing a runner, you did your fucking Sir Galahad act. And as Wintour said, he could hardly sack a man the police evidently trusted and who had acted with honour. That would just make you even more suspicious. I thought Wintour would be really pleased with what I'd done but the ungrateful bastard was furious,' added Brian petulantly.

'Right. And tonight's plan?'

'That was Linda's idea. She'd brought this liquid solution of LSD back from one of her trips to Amsterdam. It's the neat stuff they put on the bits of blotting paper. I was going to get you to take the acid and then, when you were completely out of your skull, dump you in some public place where the police were sure to pick you up with the cocaine stuffed down your underpants.'

'What about the handcuffs and the Stanley knife?'

213

'I thought I might have a bit of fun first,' said Brian. 'Anything you said about what I'd done could be explained away as the ravings of a man on a bum trip.'

'But you're not having fun, are you, Brian?'

He began to shiver. God knows how he'd managed to keep control during the few minutes of our conversation. Perhaps after he'd thrown up he'd persuaded himself that he'd got rid of most of the LSD. But the acid was biting into his brain again now.

'I'm dead,' he screamed. 'I'm dead and this is hell. And hell is a constant fresh awareness of just what eternity means. Every second. For ever.'

I shook him hard again.

'Just a few more questions, Brian. You wouldn't want me to start doodling on your face with the Stanley knife, would you? And I've got some slugs in my pocket,' I said. 'They're hungry.'

Brian was shivering uncontrollably; his brow was exuding what seemed like pints of sweat. I exchanged my penknife for Brian's sharper Stanley knife and, partly to wipe him down and partly to scare him, cut off part of his shirt. He was very hairy indeed. Disgustingly hairy.

'Where does Wintour live, Brian? Where can I find him now? And where's the hard-core stuff kept?'

Brian gave the address of Botticelli Publications. 'Don't be silly, Brian,' I said. 'That's the office.'

'He lives there in the week. There's a bedroom and a kitchenette on the second floor. And all the hard-core stuff is kept in a lock-up round the corner in Pilgrimage Street. Needless to say, none of us ever go near the place during office hours.'

'And what about the people he supplies, the names and addresses?'

Brian obviously wanted to hold out on this one. 'I've told you enough. Wintour will kill me.'

The thought of Wintour, mild-mannered, be-cardiganned Mr Wintour killing anyone seemed remote, but then so did the idea of him being a hard-core pornographer. Brian was seriously alarmed by the thought of what Wintour would do to him. I had to make him even more alarmed about what I might do.

I showed him the Stanley knife again, and then, tantalizingly slowly, as we used to say in *Luv Bytes*, I undid Brian's belt, the top button of his trousers, and tugged at his zip. I slid it down an inch, and then another.

'What's it to be, Brian? Nice thin slices or all at once?'

He screamed so loudly I feared half of Greenwich must have heard him.

'Give, Brian.'

'The contacts are all on my computer,' he said in a rush. 'There's also quite a lot of hard-core material. It's easier to distribute by computer and more and more of our clients are getting on-line.' There was something in his manner that made me think he was still keeping something back. I yanked down his trousers and his pants, and spat on the blade of the Stanley knife. Sophie was right, I thought as he screamed again. He was very small.

I told him to shut up and slowly brought the blade to within half an inch of his prick. 'What weren't you going to tell me?' I asked. Brian began to talk very fast. 'You need to know the password. If you get it wrong three times, everything on the hard disk is programed to erase.'

'And what's the password?' I said. It was the question he seemed to like least of all. 'Come on, Brian,' I said gently, actually touching his cock now with the side of the blade. 'Stanley doesn't like being kept waiting.'

'It's Mammy,' he said.

I'd got all I needed to know, much more than I wanted to know. I threw the Stanley knife into the Thames and, with infinite regret, emptied the sizeable sachet of cocaine into the dark waters too. I couldn't take it from such a source and Brian was in quite enough shit as it was. Mammy. Christ.

'I'm off now, Brian,' I said, pulling up his trousers. 'I

could leave you here all night with only the slugs for company, but I'll try and get a police car here as soon as possible.'

He moaned, and began a mantra-like muttering. 'Oh, Mammy, make it stop, please, Mammy make it stop, oh, Mammy, Mammy, Mammy...' By the time I reached the top of the steps he was shouting for his dead mam at the top of his voice. I ran. Someone would surely hear him soon.

There was a pub not far from the Cutty Sark and I rushed into it and ordered a double Scotch and found the phone. It was still only 10.30 p.m. but I felt as though I hadn't slept for a week. I found the number I needed at the back of my *Theatre World* diary and dialled. Please let him be in, I muttered, over and over as the phone rang at the other end. I was sounding, I suddenly realized, a lot like Brian. Unlike him, I wasn't sure with whom I was pleading. Whoever it was didn't seem to be listening but then I noticed I had a mobile number for Harry Meadows too. He answered that on the second ring.

'Harry, it's Will Benson. Things have come to a head at Botticelli Publications and I need your help now,' I babbled. I suddenly realized he could be anywhere in the country. 'Where the fuck are you?'

'The Dorchester,' he said. 'Variety Club do. Bloody awful. Where do we meet?'

At that moment, I loved Harry Meadows.

'There's a pub in Tabard Street, SE1, called the Pride of the Borough,' I said. 'You haven't got your tame thug with you, I suppose?'

'No, only Joe and he's got to go on and do a spot.'

'We should be OK. I think your friend Mr Wintour will be on his own. I should be at the pub within twenty minutes or so, just in time for last orders.'

'See you then,' he said.

I tried Belgravia nick but Darbyshire wasn't there so I dialled 999 and asked for the police.

216

'I'm only going to say this once so get it down right,' I said. 'There's a man handcuffed to a post by the river at Greenwich, about one hundred yards from the foot tunnel. He's having a lousy LSD trip and he's wounded in the leg. He's wanted for the murder of a Pimlico prostitute. Sergeant Darbyshire at Belgravia police station is investigating the case but he's not there at present. The incident room will be able to confirm the details. This isn't a hoax, OK?'

'What's your name?' said the voice at the other end.

'Never you mind. But get someone to Greenwich fast.' I rang off. Time to move before the police arrived. There was a busy junction along from the pub and I picked up a cab without trouble. By the time I got to the Pride of the Borough it was ten to eleven, but Meadows had done the business and was sitting smugly at a table in his best bib and tucker with two double malts for each of us.

'My God, it's good to see you,' I said. 'But if you had any idea what you were letting me in for when you got me that job I'll bloody kill you.'

'Take a drink, and tell me calmly what's been happening.' His eyes were as disconcertingly dead as ever.

So I told the tale, or a compressed version of it.

'I guessed there was something going on,' said Meadows. 'You know about Joe and his predilections. That was, after all, how we first met,' added the manager with one of his wintry smiles. 'Joe's packed in the rent boys now but he still enjoys the gay porn and it's not doing anyone any harm, so why not? Anyway, someone offered him a video with boys in it, and Joe said yes, he'd like to have a look. Only it wasn't eighteen-year-olds stripping off and flexing their muscles, it was kids. Six- and seven-year-olds and adults doing terrible things to them. Joe said he almost threw up. Anyway, I got hold of the man who offered it to Joe, and twisted his arm a bit, and got the name Wintour and Botticelli Publications. And at about the same time you said you were looking for more lucrative work. So I phoned Wintour up and said I thought it would be a very good idea if he gave you a job, at a salary specified by me, and if he didn't a certain video might be sent to the police with a sticker with his name and address on it. He'd heard of me by then, which helped. I gave the bloke who gave Joe the tape a fairly torrid time and he must have reported back.'

Torrid times with Harry Meadows were not easily forgotten.

'Why not just send the tape to the police like you said?'

'Because I'd no proof at all that the tape came from Wintour and he must be excellent at covering his tracks. Besides, you needed the ackers and I remembered you had a knack for stumbling on the truth.'

'Stumbling's about right,' I said.

'So what now? You've got all the facts. Now would be the time to turn him over to the police.'

'Oh, I'm going to. But I want him to know Brian's talked because then he won't try to protect him from the murder charge. Once Brian's back in his right mind again it will only be my word against his, with possible tentative corroboration from Janice Cockett. And my actions against him tonight were criminal, well beyond necessary self-defence. At some point I'm going to have a lot of explaining to do myself. But Wintour knows exactly what happened to Sophie because Brian told him. And I have every hope that when each learns he's been betrayed by the other, they'll dish up all the dirt, out of spite and perhaps with the forlorn hope of getting some kind of deal with the police for co-operation.'

'Right. So what's the plan?'

'We finish these drinks, ring the bell and jump him. Wintour seems vague and urbane, but he must be hard as nails. He might have a gun up there somewhere.'

'He might bring the gun to the door.'

'But you're ready to chance that, aren't you, Harry?'

He nodded and we supped up, and walked across the

street to Botticelli Publications. The warehouse shutters were down, but there was a green side door that presumably gave access to Wintour's private flat. There was an entryphone, which was bad news as Wintour wouldn't come to the door himself and we could easily lose our element of surprise. I rang the bell and Wintour's voice crackled out of the speaker.

'Who's there?'

'It's Brian with some gradely news,' I said. I didn't have a chance of imitating Brian's real voice but his awful Yorkshire was easy. I just hoped he sometimes used it with the boss. The buzzer sounded and we crept up the stairs to an open door on the landing of the first floor. Perhaps Wintour was used to late-night visits from Brian, perhaps he just wanted to show how unconcerned he was about any news that Brian could possibly bring, but he wasn't at the door to greet us. He was sitting with his back to us at his desk, in the office where I'd twice been interviewed by him. I'd never noticed this second door before.

'Do come in and sit down,' he said, without turning his head. 'Shan't be a moment.' Wintour obviously took a real delight in patronizing his vulpine lieutenant. Harry and I nodded at each other. We rushed across the room, grabbed the arms of his fancy leather-covered captain's chair and pulled it violently backwards so Wintour ended in a heap on his carpet. Harry got his head in an arm lock, I pulled off my belt and bound his wrists behind his back. He didn't put up any kind of fight. His arms, I noticed for the first time, were thin to the point of anorexia. Hence the chunky cardigans, presumably. To hide the skin and bone. That night he was wearing pyjamas, a thick tartan dressing gown and his beloved slippers. We hauled him to his feet and threw him on to the sofa.

'Brian,' I said, 'has been singing like the proverbial canary.' What a pleasure it was to deliver that line. 'At the moment he's tethered to a post in Greenwich, out of his mind on LSD. That is, if the police haven't picked him up

219

yet. He's admitted to killing Sophie, and he's told me all about what he calls the "other stuff". And this, in case you're wondering, is Harry Meadows.' Wintour, for the first time since I'd met him, had lost his smug urbanity. He looked ill with anxiety.

'Brian says all the tapes are stored in a lock-up in Pilgrimage Street. Where are the keys?'

'Top drawer of the desk, right-hand side,' said Wintour. He'd recovered himself and his voice betrayed no sign of emotion.

Harry went to the desk and found a bunch of keys. 'Where exactly do I find the lock-up?' he asked. Wintour told him.

'Right, I'll go and have a shufti. Keep an eye on this cunt, Will.'

'I'll do just that,' I said.

Harry left the room. I went and inspected the fireplace. Real ash in the grate, real logs in the basket. But the evening was too warm for even the skeletal Wintour to indulge himself with a log fire. The bottle of grappa was standing by the espresso machine as always. I helped myself to a large shot and rolled myself an Old Disgusting. I looked at the splendid collection of books above the leather-bound Botticelli Publications. None of your Reader's Digest Condensed, but an extensive library of English literature, as well as translations of Greek, Latin, French, German and Russian classics.

'You read this, don't you?' I said. 'It's not just there for show.'

'When I have the leisure,' said Wintour.

'But how can a man who appreciates great literature make a living out of even the Botticelli crap, never mind what other filth you peddle?'

'It's a living, Mr Benson, a business. A demand exists, I supply it. But the evenings and the weekends are my own. I happen to choose to read good books.'

Harry returned after a few minutes. 'It's more like a

small warehouse than a lock-up,' he said. 'There's a fully equipped editing suite and a terrific capacity for copying videos. Most of the tapes are unlabelled, in cardboard boxes. But this was lying around on the editing desk.' He waved a cassette box, with the words PROMO VIDEO on the cover. In smaller letters it read, *A small sample of our biggest turn-ons.*

'Oh dear,' said Mr Wintour. 'I rather wish you hadn't found that. It's edited highlights of all our strongest stuff. What I'd like you to understand is that it's a trailer. This is what we show prospective, and I may add, carefully selected, bulk purchasers, in the hope of persuading them to buy full-length videos which are for the most part very tame.'

'Why don't you shut the fuck up,' said Harry. 'Where's the video?'

'In that cupboard,' said Wintour, pointing to a moulded, dove-grey door. I went over and yanked out the TV with its integral video and slammed in the tape. I'll never forget what we watched. A woman having one of her nipples burnt with a cigarette, another having her vagina sewn up with a needle and thread, a third having a pistol, a light bulb and finally a shard of broken pottery rammed up her. And then came the kids. A child of ten gagging on the penis in his mouth, a six-year-old girl being whipped, an eight-year-old hung upside down and molested. You knew the ages of the children because a caption helpfully supplied them, together with their Christian names. During one of the sequences you could hear the theme from *The Snowman* in the background. After about fifteen minutes, Harry stood up and turned off the TV.

I looked at the photograph of Wintour's two cheeky-looking sons on the desk. 'Not them too?' I asked, and Wintour had the gall to look outraged.

'This is a business, Mr Benson, not a hobby,' he replied icily.

We sat in silence for a couple of minutes, and then Harry

advanced on Wintour. He punched him in the stomach first and then flattened his nose. I cried out to Harry to stop, because he looked ready to kill, and Harry shuddered and went and sat down again. 'I'm sorry,' he said, to me not to Wintour. 'You're right.'

I went and poured Harry a glass of grappa, and recharged my own. Wintour sat with the blood streaming from his nose and began to bluster that he never set up any of the films, that most of them had been made abroad anyway, and he just dealt in a product for which there was a large existing market. So I got up, and punched him hard on the side of his face, and then he shut up.

We drank, and I smoked a roll-up, and then we had another drink. And still those terrible pictures kept appearing in my head.

'I'd better phone the police,' I said at last, and dialled the number.

Darbyshire was there this time. 'What's going on, Mr Benson? Greenwich police have picked up a madman screaming about slugs. An anonymous caller rang earlier and claimed the nutter was guilty of Sophie Brignall's murder and told the 999 operator to get in touch with me.'

'It was me that phoned,' I said. 'I couldn't get through to you. He's called Brian Waynefleet, he's taken a lot of LSD and he's admitted to attacking Sophie. I don't think he meant to kill her.'

'I think you'd better come straight here while we sort this out.'

'There's more,' I said. 'I'm at Botticelli Publications with the proprietor and a large amount of extremely hard-core porn that will interest the obscene publications squad. The addresses of all the subscribers are on a computer in a flat on the Kipling Estate, where Waynefleet lives, but the computer needs to be handled with caution. I'll explain when I see you. Oh, and there are two others involved. Linda Belling, who works at Botticelli, and her girlfriend, who's a headmistress. I'll just find out their address. It would be worth picking them up before they get wind of what's going on.'

I turned to Wintour and he gave the address and I passed it on to Darbyshire. 'I'll be with you in half an hour,' I told the sergeant. 'There's someone here to keep an eye on Wintour.'

'Right,' said the sergeant. 'I've got more bad news, I'm afraid. We found Henrietta's gun all right, and took it from her. And she seemed OK when the WPC left her with a neighbour this morning. Unfortunately this afternoon she got hold of a bottle of bleach. I've just come back from the hospital. She's dead.'

'Oh Jesus, sweet Jesus,' I said, and rang off.

'What's happened?' asked Harry. I told him about Henrietta.

'The poor cow,' he said. 'You'd better get on your way. I'll look after this one until the police arrive.'

I looked at him questioningly.

'I won't touch him,' promised Harry. 'We'll just have a little chat about how the other prisoners are likely to treat a child pornographer.'

'Thanks for all your help,' I said, and embraced him. 'You were there just when you were most needed.'

He told me not to be soft and to give his love to Kim. I left Wintour's office without a backward glance at my former boss and finally found a taxi to take me home. Where did the depravity start, I wondered, where did it come from? How could anyone take pleasure in the suffering of children? But that wasn't the really hard question. Those pictures had revolted and outraged, and I pitied those unknown women, unknown kids. But it was a detached compassion accompanied by a kind of relief. I hadn't sunk that low. But there were other disturbing images in my head and I couldn't get rid of them. They were mine and they had to be acknowledged. My doomed violent fantasy about Cathy as I struggled to produce a sperm sample. My instant excitement with Sophie, a

223

stranger who provoked a livelier sexual response than the woman I loved. The satisfaction of humiliating Adamson. And then, of course, there was Brian. As I'd manacled him to that post, and heard him scream when I produced the Stanley knife, I'd experienced a thrill of intense pleasure. Control, revenge, the ability to inflict pain – I had found them all damnably enjoyable. You started by masturbating over pictures of bimbos in magazines and, if you were mad, or bad, or perhaps just plain unlucky, you ended up feasting your eyes on images of raped and tortured children. Not me. Not ever. But after tonight I had no illusions about the purity of my own heart. It was dark, stained, corrupt.

The taxi drew up outside Rita Road and I asked the driver to wait for a few minutes before taking me on to Belgravia police station. I let myself in and found Kim in the kitchen, sitting opposite a bottle of malt whisky and listening to the ghetto blaster. She was playing the Tym Church song on Sophie's tape. She was a bit slurry, but not totally out of it yet, and I poured a large drink for myself, and hugged her and kissed her forehead.

'How was it?' she asked.

'Far out,' I said. 'You've no idea just how far out.'

I brought her up to date and she shuddered in all the right places, but I knew she was only half listening.

'There's just one other thing,' she said. 'My fucking period's started.'

A few days later I turned on the radio and heard that Jerry Garcia had died. It was that kind of summer. A bummer.